Too Many Hats

ALSO BY WILLIAM O'NEILL CURATOLO

Campanilismo: Crime and Intrigue

in International Biotech

Too Many Hats

William O'Neill Curatolo

Bayberry Institute Press

Connecticut, U.S.A.

Published by the Bayberry Institute Press in the United States of America.

The author may be contacted at
williamcuratolo@bayberryinstitute.com

ISBN 978-0-9896566-2-7

Cover: The flower depicted is St. John's Wort. Cover by Karen Brown Markley at karen@handtomouse.net

"The past is never dead. It's not even past."

— William Faulkner, *Requiem for a Nun*

Chapter 1

High above the Delaware Water Gap on the eastbound side of I-80, a New Jersey State Trooper and an Emergency Medical Technician stood by the sheared guardrail and looked over the edge. About 100 feet below sat a mangled car, probably black but otherwise beyond identifiable from their vantage point.

The EMT said, "How can I get down there?"

"Turn around and take the first Pennsylvania exit. In about a hundred feet you'll see a dirt road on the left. That'll take you down. I just called the PA troopers so they'll have someone down there soon too. I have to stay up here to secure the accident scene."

The trooper walked over to talk to the driver who called in the accident. The witness told him that an expensive-looking black car with New Jersey plates, maybe a Lexus, passed him in the left-hand lane at maybe 75 mph, then "punched it" and may have gotten up to about 90 then turned right directly into the guardrail and went flying over.

"Did you see how many people were in the car?"

"Looked like just the driver to me, but I wasn't paying much attention until he really hit the gas."

"Were there other cars or trucks around? Did he get cut off or forced off the road?"

"Nope, he had the road to himself. It looked intentional, like he just turned intentionally into the guardrail."

"Then what did you do, sir?"

"I pulled over where he went over the side, where I'm parked right now, and called 911. Then I got out and looked over the side. There's no way anybody survived that. It's terrible, why would a guy do that?"

The trooper took the witness's driver's license to his cruiser and typed the information into his laptop. When no alerts came up he got out and returned the license to the witness and said, "Thank you, sir. And thanks for calling in the accident. Please be careful pulling back out onto the road." He then waited for the highway guys to arrive to put out neon-red traffic barrels and yellow tape across the area of the broken guardrail. When they were finished, he took one last look 100 feet down at the rocky Delaware River bed where the Pennsylvania troopers and EMTs were removing a body from the wreckage. He was glad he wasn't down there dealing with that mess.

It wasn't an easy afternoon for the Medical Examiner at Stroudsberg Hospital on the Pennsylvania side. The I-80 crash victim was a torn-up mess. If that wasn't bad enough, the ME also had to deal with the body of a male found in a car with New Jersey plates in the Pocono Rest Stop off I-80 in Pennsylvania. This victim had been shot in the chest and head at close range. The Pennsylvania ME thought *Why can't these Jersey people make their messes in Jersey?*

Three Years Earlier

Chapter 2

Jimmy Delvecchio put down his coffee on the kitchen counter and picked up the phone. It was Jimmy's Uncle Carmine, his mother's youngest brother.

"*Zio* Carmine, good to hear from you. How's *Zia* Emerlinda?"

"Good. She's good. She's all excited; we're heading to Florida next week to see all the relatives. We miss everybody, but we like it too much here to move down. We should probably rent something for a few months in the winter down there, and go back and forth. So Jimmy, the reason I called is that I need to see you about something. Are you free sometime today or tonight?"

"Sure, actually I can come over now. Or you want to meet somewhere for lunch?"

"Good. You know the little park on 506 in Kearney by the river?"

"Sure."

"How about we meet there at 10:00? Then maybe we can go somewhere for coffee or lunch."

"Great. I'll be there."

Jimmy sighed as he hung up. Meeting in a park meant secrets.

* * *

Jimmy rose from a bench by the parking area as his uncle Carmine Casamento approached, and the two men shook hands.

Jimmy said, "*Zio*, good to see you. For some reason we haven't gotten together much lately. We have to fix that."

"We will. It's good to see you too, Jimmy. You know, I really miss your father. He was my brother-in-law, but he was also my closest friend." Carmine groaned as he sat down. "Don't get old, Jimmy."

"I'll try, but I don't think there's much I can do."

They both laughed.

"So *Zio*, what's up?"

"Jimmy, I've got a problem, and I thought you might be the only person I know who can help."

Oh, shit, thought Jimmy.

"We've still got all the trucking stuff going on, and two days ago we ended up with a tractor-trailer full of drugs, you know, medicines. A whole tractor-trailer. I don't know how to fence this stuff. It's not like TVs that you can sell anywhere."

"Why don't you just take it on 95 and leave it at a rest stop, and write it off as a mistake?"

"You-know-who doesn't want to. He thinks this is the most valuable truck we've ever jacked. It's stuffed to the gills, and with the price of drugs, *marone!*"

"*Zio*, who are these jerks? Don't tell me. You taught me the first rule of truck hijacking – Don't jack anything you don't know how to fence. And the second rule – Don't jack anything you don't know how to fence fast."

"And you remember the third rule?"

"Yeah, don't kill anybody."

"Good boy. You remember your *Zio* Carmine's lessons."

"*Zio*, I don't know what to do with that stuff. You know I have a legit drug discovery and development company now. We don't distribute drugs. My people are all scientists. We don't have warehouses and trucks and contracts with pharmacies."

"I know. But you know everybody in the pharmaceutical business in Jersey. You can tell us who to talk to."

Jimmy put his hand on Carmine's shoulder. "*Zio*, my contacts are all legit, not former wiseguys. I don't know if you appreciate this, but drug distribution is a highly regulated business; the government is all over it."

"I know. I know. I have no doubt that this is true, and I probably have no appreciation for how complicated this is. But he figures this truck could be worth a couple million, and that cannot be ignored. We're not just gonna leave it by the side of the road and walk away."

"Yeah, but fencing this stuff without getting caught is impossible. Pharmacies and distributers have logs for everything that comes in and out, and nowadays computer logs that get backed up automatically every night. You can't hide this stuff."

"Impossible, we've all heard impossible. That's what bribes are for, that's what muscle's for."

Jimmy thought, *Shit, I have to get out of this.* He said, "Look, you know I'd help if I could, but I can't. First of all, I don't know how to get rid of this stuff. But second, if I helped and word got out, everything I've built over the last ten years would go down the drain. I don't do this kind of stuff anymore. You know this."

"Jimmy, do you think I'd be here asking you this if I had a choice? Do you think you have a choice? We let you go to do your internet pharmacy idea ten years ago and then you sold it and got into this biotech stuff. We let you go, and we fronted you some cash."

Jimmy laughed. "Yeah, but when I sold the internet pharmacy business to the Israelis, you and your *capi* got about 50 million bucks. That was probably a one thousand-fold profit, one hundred thousand percent! Who ever got you anything like that before or since? I'm out. Tell them to just leave me alone. Where did all that money go anyway?"

"It went up the line. What do you think? You think I saw any of it? Just a little bonus."

"Tell them no."

"There's no such thing as no." Carmine patted Jimmy's leg. "Look, maybe all you gotta do is give us the right names. You know how this can be done. We look into these guys, get pictures with whores or plant child porn on their computers, and then they all of a sudden become very cooperative. You don't have to be directly involved in any way."

"*Zio*, you want me to give you names so you can fuck up their lives? I can't do this."

"Jimmy, please. I'm your blood. I have to do something about this."

Jimmy sighed and paused, then said, "OK, *Zio*, let me think about it."

"Well, think fast. This stuff has expiration dates, right? They're impatient at the main office."

"Do you guys know just what exactly was in this truck?"

"Somebody's got a list, but nobody understands what the stuff is. One of the guys had his kid google the names of the drugs on the computer to find out what they are and what they might be worth. Not that I know exactly what google means. A way to look stuff up on the computer, I guess."

"Idiots. Involving a kid with a computer. You guys are in the wrong century for this. OK. Let's forget about lunch today. How about if I come by the house tonight to talk some more? And maybe you can get me this list?"

"No, for now I don't think we should be seen alone together if this is gonna happen. Only at family gatherings. Nobody's watching this place, so how about here tomorrow at 10:00 again?"

"OK."

"I love you, kid."

"And I love you, *Zio*. But please tell your guys to stick to cigarette trucks, huh? Much easier to fence."

Chapter 3

On his way home from the lab, Dr. Frank Serono stopped at Farmer's Harvest Grocery to pick up some takeout food for his dinner. His wife Maria was working late at the hospital, and he didn't feel like cooking. As he walked through the store, a woman in a white labcoat standing behind a folding table asked him if he had trouble sleeping at night or if he ever experienced heartburn. She appeared to be about 40 years old, and he realized right away that she was probably a sales rep for an herbal remedy of some type. He said "No," and walked on. Then he turned around and walked back, wondering what she actually had to say.

"I'm sorry I was somewhat impolite. I do have occasional heartburn. Why did you ask?"

"Oh, I'm glad you came back. My name is Kara, and I'm here representing a new supernutraceutical that's helping lots of people with their medical problems. What's your name, if you don't mind my asking?"

Frank hesitated, then said, "Jim."

"Well it's nice to meet you, Jim. You know, heartburn is a terrible problem for many people." She smiled and said "Lord knows I've had problems sometimes. Most of us have. If you don't mind my asking, do you take drugs for your heartburn?"

"No, I don't mind, and the only thing I use is Tums." He was lying, and never had any heartburn problems except for a couple of times after eating a late-night Indian dinner after drinking a little too much wine with friends.

"I'm so glad to hear that. Some people take synthetic drugs that have horrible side effects because they're basically poisons. The big pharmaceutical companies don't want us to know this, and they bribe the doctors to prescribe their expensive drugs that in the end really harm people. You know, at best these drugs treat symptoms. They don't treat the real problem, and the pharmaceutical companies don't want the real problem cured because then they wouldn't be able to sell you more drugs."

Frank thought *What a bizarre spiel,* but he acted interested because he was genuinely curious about what she was peddling.

She continued, "I'm here because Dr. Samuel Roskamp decided to put an end to this, well this robbery and poisoning of patients really, and formulated a special all-natural supernutraceutical that attacks the cause of the heartburn problem." Holding up a bottle for him to see, she said, "It's called Equibalance, and it really works."

"How does it attack the cause of heartburn?"

"Well, the problem with heartburn is reflux of acid from the stomach into the esophagus, and the pharmaceutical companies think they can solve the problem by getting rid of the acid, but you need the acid to digest food. Dr. Roskamp researched the problem for years, and came up with a new approach. His superformula doesn't get rid of the acid. Instead, it's formulated to move the acid down the intestinal tract, in the direction it's supposed to go. Heartburn happens because the acid goes in the wrong direction, and Dr. Roskamp's formula makes the acid move in the right direction."

"How does it do that?"

The saleslady was starting to get a little nervous, uncomfortable with Frank's probing. "Well, Dr. Roskamp and his team studied the problem for years, and then based on their research, formulated a specific combination of natural herbs to reverse the problem."

"Do you know how it works?"

"Well, no. I'm not a scientist or a doctor, but I have complete faith in Dr. Roskamp. He's a highly regarded researcher and expert. A wonderful man who really cares about patients and their needs."

Frank started reading the label on the bottle. "I notice it says here that this also helps for sleep problems. Is Dr. Roskamp an expert in sleep too?"

"Oh, yes. He's a holistic doctor. His formulas treat the whole patient."

Frank said, "Is this approved by the FDA?"

"Well, I'm no expert on the government, but Equibalance isn't a drug, it's natural."

"But you told me it cures heartburn. That sounds like a drug, and I thought its safety and efficacy have to be determined in a large number of patients, and the FDA has to approve it."

"Oh, no sir, it's not a drug. It's all natural."

Frank looked at the bottle again. "It says here that this formula helps support healthy sleep and digestion and blood sugar homeostasis. Is there one formula for all three?"

"Oh, yes, it's holistic."

"How does that work?"

"Well, sir, there are technical details that I don't know because it's a proprietary formula. My focus is on patient interaction, not on the complicated medical science. I can tell you that a whole team of naturopathic scientists has been involved in the formulation. And there are lots of patient testimonials that show that it works."

Frank realized that he was wasting his time and nothing was to be gained by pushing this poor lady who was probably earning minimum wage and certainly wasn't profiting from this pseudoscience nonsense. He asked for a brochure, thanked her, and then as an afterthought said, "Do you know how I can get in touch with Dr. Roskamp? Where are his research labs?"

"I believe his main lab is in Europe. If you have questions, you can enter them on our website, and they'll be answered by a naturopathic specialist from Dr. Roskamp's labs."

Frank thanked her again and moved on.

*   *   *

After dinner, Frank went down to his basement office, which consisted of two tables, one with a computer and another with piles of paper. The large unfinished room was basically a storage area for beat-up athletic equipment, and not an organized one at that. But it was Frank's lair, and nobody bothered him there. He turned on his computer and went to the MetaboloGreens website, which described a variety of products "specially formulated" by Dr. Samuel Roskamp. It was the kind of crap he expected. The product claims were clearly written with a lawyer's help, going right up to the line of claiming to cure disease, but not quite saying it. Equibalance "helps support digestive health", and SereneGreens "provides calming support for anxious days". With a little googling, he found that "SereneGreens" contained St. John's Wort, a plant that contains a chemical that acts similarly to the antidepressants Prozac and Paxil. The capsules also contained what appeared to be a variety of freeze-dried vegetables.

Frank engaged the "Chat" function on the MetaboloGreens website, and typed, "Will SereneGreens ameliorate my depression, and if I take it, can I stop taking Paxil?" In about three minutes he received a reply from someone named Arthur. "SereneGreens is formulated to provide support for your mental health, especially on down days. Paxil is a non-natural chemical that has severe side effects in many individuals. SereneGreens is completely natural, and is made up of plant extracts chosen to alleviate your down feelings in a natural holistic fashion. Some of our MetaboloGreens clients find that when they take an appropriate course of SereneGreens, they can cease taking their synthetic drugs and avoid disturbing side effects. However, it is always best to consult a physician, preferably a naturopathic physician, when making any change to your therapeutic regimen."

Frank asked, "Will SereneGreens cure my depression?" Arthur replied, "Depression is a complicated multifactorial disease that may have both biochemical and situational aspects. SereneGreens will help you in your search for happiness in a mild holistic way, and treats your whole body and mind, unlike the harsh synthetic drugs that interfere with the chemistry of your brain in ways that are poorly understood. Synthetic drugs from pharmaceutical companies do not cure depression. SereneGreens helps you in your quest for mental peace, and works best when combined with healthy eating habits, exercise, and calming activities such as yoga and meditation."

Huh? thought Frank. *So does it cure depression or not? I guess only if you meditate, think good thoughts, exercise, eat right, and lead a good life. Pretty funny runaround to a direct question. But not funny, really.*

What really got Frank's goat, though, was the interview with the great Dr. Samuel Roskamp transcribed on the website. Dr. Roskamp apparently had a vision when his father had a heart attack. He realized that his life's work was to help others any way he could, and the way he chose was "to do everything in my power to help as many people as possible lead healthy satisfying lives". He said, "I know some people won't believe me, but I'm not doing this for money. It's my life ministry."

Frank googled Dr.Samuel Roskamp, and got more of the same, but did stumble on information about his education. Dr. Roskamp had an Associate's degree in Communications from Southwestern Louisiana Community College, and a Ph.D. from the Caribbean University of Naturopathic Medicine. The CUNM website, after careful digging through multiple levels, indicated that the school was "virtual", and had no campus. All courses were on-line, and there were no exams. Students had to check a box at the end of each course verifying that they had read the material. A thesis was required, and links to three examples were provided. Frank looked at these, and laughed when he saw that they were about five double-spaced pages in length, and each presented the student's personal beliefs about the superiority of naturopathic healing and the value of herbs for health.

Frank thought of himself as a somewhat cynical son of the Bronx. Regardless, he was flabbergasted by the audacity of the nonsense he read. He turned off his laptop, went back upstairs, and turned on a college basketball game.

Chapter 4

Jimmy pulled into the Delvono Inc. lot in Clifton, New Jersey, and into the spot marked "Mr. Delvecchio". The only other assigned spot was marked "Dr. Serono". Jimmy was CEO of a successful drug discovery company, but it had been a long hard road. In his younger days, Jimmy ran a trucking distribution center in western New Jersey that was a legal cover for a hijacking and fencing operation. In his early 40s, he got permission from his bosses to leave the trucking industry, and he started an internet pharmacy company that illegally sold medicines still under patent, but eventually morphed into a completely legal and phenomenally successful business. He made almost $400 million selling his internet pharmacy business to Haifatech Ltd. of Israel, and was a little surprised when he had to pay "juice" to his old superiors from his truck-thieving days. These mid-level crime bosses were absolutely shocked when they found themselves in possession of $50 million, $45 million of which they passed up the line to their superiors in New York City. Back then, Jimmy was treated like a king, and he was invited to meet with the *Capo di Capi* at the Shooting Range in Greenwich Village. The *Capo* was bowled over by Jimmy's success, and extremely pleased with the money, which seemed to be so simple for Jimmy to get, compared to all the people and work that would be involved in gathering that kind of payoff the usual way they did business. *La Famiglia* had invested minimal cash in Jimmy's internet pharmacy business and, by virtually any analysis possible, they had no right to that $50 million. But of course, the assumptions in their analysis were different.

Jimmy took the remainder of his $400 million and founded the biotech company Delvono Inc. with Dr. Frank Serono. Frank was 44 years old, ten years younger than Jimmy, and played the idealist to Jimmy's realist. He was raised in the Belmont section of the Bronx, studied Biology at Manhattan College while living at home, then on to graduate school and a postdoctoral fellowship in Boston, a faculty position at Columbia Medical School, and years in the R&D Division of a large drug company (Annexin Inc.) in New Jersey. Frank had the patience of a researcher, but when it came to practical things like raising money or eliminating roadblocks, patience was not part of his repertoire.

Dr. Frank Serono had pioneered the field of personalized medicine by using DNA sequencing to identify cancer patients who would benefit from particular drugs. This resulted in wildly unexpected cure rates for some tough cancers – breast and pancreatic cancers particularly. And it resulted in wild financial success for Delvono Inc.

As one might suspect, the big guns, that is, the big pharmaceutical companies, jumped on the bandwagon created by Frank and Jimmy, and ultimately blew right by them. This was a little disappointing, but the fact remained that they had sold their first three oncology drug candidates to large drug companies for a total of 1.1 billion dollars. Although they were swimming in money, they could no longer really compete with the big guns in the cancer area, and moved away from it. Jimmy was the money man, and he generally deferred to Frank on strategic scientific issues. Frank had pressed for getting into discovery of antibacterial agents for tough infections like hospital-acquired methicillin-resistant *Staphylococcus aureus*, known as MRSA. They sank a boatload of money into discovering drugs for MRSA and a variety of other antibiotic-resistant infections. In addition, Jimmy had insisted that they plow some money into childhood genetic diseases, particularly Tay-Sachs disease and Neimann-Pick disease. Jimmy had seen some of the devastation of these diseases through his work on various charitable boards, and was moved by what he saw.

Delvono had 284 employees in New Jersey, and outsourced as little as possible. While Frank was an idealist with a burning desire to cure disease (and get public credit for it), Jimmy was more measured. He wanted to employ fellow Jerseyites and to make a good life for his extended family. While Frank professed to be interested in the broader world, Jimmy unabashedly prioritized all his endeavors according to the Italian concept of *campanilismo* – the idea that everything important in life occurs in the area from which you can see the belltower of your town. Jimmy was wealthy and Frank made a comfortable salary, but they really did not have time to spend the money they made because they busily pressed forward with their work.

Jimmy bellowed "Hiya Josie" as he entered the lobby, and leaned over the receptionist podium and kissed Josie on the cheek. "It's a beautiful day in New Jersey!"

"Yes, Mr. Delvecchio, it certainly is."

"Is Frank in?"

"Yes, he's here. I'll call back and tell him you want to see him."

"No thanks, not necessary. I hope we haven't reached the point where we need appointments to speak to each other."

"I don't think that'll happen as long as you're here, Jimmy."

Jimmy walked down to Frank's office, stuck his head in the doorway, and said "What's up, *dottore*?"

"Hey, Jimmy, come on in. Anything specific, or are you just avoiding work?"

Jimmy sat down on the couch, leaned back, and clasped his hands behind his head. "Hey, work is my middle name. And speaking of work, the contract for licensing out the mTOR compound is all signed, and the money should be in the bank next week. It never ceases to amaze me how much the Big Pharma guys are willing to pay for these Phase II candidates. Twenty million here, fifty million there."

"Well, we de-risked the Phase III studies with all the genetic selection work we did. That's priceless for a Big Pharma company that's gonna lay out a hundred million dollars for a Phase III study. We've taken the probability of success from the usual 30% region to about 80%. We should charge them even more."

Jimmy leaned forward. "What are we gonna do with all this new money? I suppose we could hire 50 more scientists. Do you know what you would do with them?"

"It's a nice problem to have, but I'm coming around to your idea that it's time to get more organized. I've been sort of winging it up to now. I'm starting to think, how big do we really want to get? And the orphan drug projects, are they really worth the effort?"

Jimmy said, "The funny thing about the orphan drug projects is that they're worth real money if they succeed. The Big Pharma guys are interested now. I realize that the science is your call, but I'd really like to go all in now on the Tay-Sachs stuff. Go after a prenatal drug. Go after a bunch of these genetic diseases, really help some people. We could go after Alzheimer's like the big guys, but our effort would be a small drop in a big bucket. As usual my practical side says go easy on hiring, we may not always be so flush with cash. I don't want to fire people five years from now."

"Yeah Jimmy, but I guess my take is that we're not here to build some giant nest egg or to promise people lifetime employment. I do like the idea of going after what the big guys ignore, but it sure would be nice to be the ones to cure Alzheimer's."

The wheels were turning in Jimmy's head. "Here's what I'm thinking. I didn't want to do it before because I thought I could handle it myself, but maybe it's time to sign a contract with a big-time investment advisory firm. Instead of just burning through the mountain of cash we have and tossing the dice for the future, we admit we were in the right place at the right time with the cancer stuff and got lucky. Invest the cash like a university endowment and operate off the proceeds. I'm not looking to become Merck here."

Frank said, "Well, what kind of steady-state size are you talking about?"

"Realistically, we have about a billion." He laughed. "How the fuck did we get all that cash? Alright, so safe investments would spin off, say 7%. We'd need to have it grow somewhat to keep up with inflation, so maybe we could take out 5% per year. That's 50 million. At our current fully loaded burn of 250K per scientist, that funds around 200 scientists and all the associated support staff and supplies. Back of the envelope. Forever. How does that sound?"

"That's about where we are now. I was hoping to get bigger."

"Hey, then go back to Big Pharma and all the politics. Bigger destroys the fun. How many programs can you run with 200 scientists?"

"Well, it's really not that many, Jimmy. That's the size of a major academic biology or medicine department if you include the grad students and post-docs. But say six projects with about 30 people per project, that's decent manning. Say four Ph.D.s, twenty-six lab scientists per project. Depends a little on what kind of core facilities and resources we supply across projects. I guess we could still compete for other money. If we had more people, I'd probably put them on the same six projects rather than spreading them too thin."

Jimmy said, "OK, let's do this. We're not gonna figure this out sitting here. I'll talk to some people about a real analysis of our financial position. And you do some serious thinking about the right mix of projects going forward and the right resourcing. My two cents on this is if we have six projects, two should have the potential to return big revenue if they hit, say something like our antibiotic-resistant bacteria project. The other four can be orphan drug projects. If one of them hits, it could pay back the money spent on that project, which would be just fine. Also, maybe you could get together a few of the senior scientists and come up with some kind of logic for which orphan diseases we want to continue to go after. Up to now it's been pretty much just what I happen to be interested in."

"This is good. OK. Maybe more realistic than the way I've been thinking about it. A little more discipline. I'll take care of my part. Put it all together in a few weeks?"

"That sounds good to me."

Frank laughed. "That ten minute meeting would have taken 20 people and two months in Big Pharma. Not to mention the money for consultants."

Jimmy smiled. "Well, we know what we don't want to be. We have to decide what we do want to be. Wanna get a drink after work and talk some more?"

"Sure, but just a quick one. I want to be home for supper."

"Me too."

Jimmy was very satisfied. He walked back to his office, turned on his computer, and started to read his email. As usual, this primarily consisted of deleting 80% of the emails without opening them – various newsletters and alerts related to the professional organizations he belonged to and the technical and purchasing magazines he subscribed to. He read a couple of emails, put his digital signature on another containing an invoice for supplies, and then stopped. He felt his heart flutter. He couldn't ignore the request, the demand really, that had been made via his Uncle Carmine. His $50 million contribution to the *capi* four years ago when he sold his internet pharmacy company was now forgotten. They wouldn't leave him alone. They would never leave him alone. He had never requested or agreed to be a "member for life" of *La Famiglia*, but there he was. What a waste of his time.

Chapter 5

Frank liked to sit informally with young scientists to talk science and projects, and made a point to try to do it every day. It was always a little awkward because Frank was Director of Research and a company founder, and some of the young people were inhibited around him. Even more so, some were inhibited by Frank's fame in the drug industry, based on his pioneering work in using DNA sequencing to identify cancer patients who would be helped by specific drugs. In the early days at Delvono, when there were only about fifteen scientists total, they used to shoot hoops out back for fun, including one of the women. Now that there were about two hundred scientists, things were more formal even though Frank and Jimmy did everything they could think of to prevent it.

Frank got a root beer out of the free soda machine, took his sandwich and drink out back behind the building and sat at one of the picnic tables with Christina Lindbergh, who was sitting by herself. Christina was a young MIT biochemistry Ph.D. hired at Delvono after a two-year post-doctoral fellowship at Rockefeller University in New York City. She grew up in Montana and for a while stayed near home, majoring in chemical engineering at

Montana State. In her years in Boston, New York, and now New Jersey, Christina sometimes seemed like she was from outer space. She liked NASCAR, hunting, and fishing, and went to a pistol range for fun. She was off-the-charts smart.

Frank broke the ice. "Nice day, huh? I thought it was gonna rain, but this sun feels good."

"It sure does. I was thinking of spending the rest of the day out here."

"OK with me, as long as you're thinking about work."

They laughed, then Frank said, "If you don't mind me asking over lunch, how are things going on the MRSA project?"

"Don't mind at all. I love to talk about it. With all due respect to the people who set up the current plan, I think we're at a dead end. I realize I'm speaking with hindsight, but I think the traditional approach of looking for drugs to inhibit critical functions in the metabolism of the staph bacterium is a losing battle."

"Why so?"

"Again, I'm benefitting from hindsight, but it seems that every time you try to kill a staph culture by inhibiting a critical function, the low level mutation rate results in some mutated organisms that are resistant to whatever you dosed. It's random of course, but if you set up a thousand cultures on 96-well plates, you get one that's resistant to the treatment. Of course, that resistant strain may be weak and not capable of living in the wild or in a host, but it'll eventually mutate further in other ways to make it stronger and ultimately able to survive."

"So you're saying that the bug will always fight back as hard as possible if you go after a critical function."

"Yep. And maybe we can get around this by abandoning the usual approach of going after critical functions. I know it's counter-intuitive, and seems almost stupid in a way, but it's starting to grow on me. A colleague and I have been batting around the idea of going after changing the bug's DNA, maybe using a virus, and that might work, but I think using a virus as a drug is a non-starter for government regulatory reasons, at least in this century."

Frank paused and thought before commenting. "Yeah, well, it's hard to believe the FDA would let you get away with that, and maybe rightfully so. Viruses mutate too, and who knows what the unexpected consequences might be. Any other ideas?"

"Yeah, I have one, but it's a little wacky."

"Wacky is good. This is research. What are you thinking?"

"Well part of the problem is that unsuccessful antibacterial treatment in the real world isn't just about individual free-floating bacteria inside a person, but is also about biofilms that bacteria form when they aggregate and deposit themselves on some tissue, you know, in a way like plaque on your teeth. An approach may be to try to interfere with binding of bacteria to tissues and to each other."

Frank was getting interested. This wasn't turning out to be just a casual superficial lunchtime conversation.

Christina continued, "This is really relatively simple. Recalcitrant infections really depend on two things. First, the bacterium undergoes a random DNA mutation that makes it resistant to a particular drug. Now people tend to think of resistance as an all-or-none thing, but often the bug isn't totally resistant to the drug, but has developed a mechanism to be less sensitive to it. We know the mechanisms for the most part. That's a well-trodden road. If that were the whole story, then you should be able to just increase the drug dose or maybe dose two drugs, but that doesn't seem to work.

The second part of the picture in the real world is that the bug needs a protective home to hide out in. People used to call these infective foci, and for a century I don't think they thought much about it. They were just concentrated points of bug growth, say like spots on the lung. The bug never really coats the whole lung or whatever tissue we want to talk about. Today we call these foci biofilms but they're the same thing. I've been thinking a lot about this lately. I think the biofilm idea first came from research into fouling of ship hulls. Algae or barnacles end up in this encrusted slippery goo on the hull surface. That's why they make "antifouling" paints now. It's the same thing basically in people. A family of bacteria secretes some polysaccharide glue so they can stick to the host tissue and form an almost impenetrable mass. As the colony gets larger, drug molecules can't diffuse into the center of the colony so some of the bugs are protected."

She continued, "To be clear, I'm thinking that we dose a two-drug combo. One is a new or even a well-known old antibiotic that's effective, but not necessarily a real knock-out. With it we also dose something that prevents bacterial aggregation or the formation of a biofilm. Here's where I'm not certain how to proceed strategically. Maybe it's just a marketing decision problem. Do we want an oral product that can be swallowed, or are we willing to have a more expensive and complex injectable product? What do you think?"

"Well, when I worked in a big company, to answer that question we would've assembled a project team of people from across the company – research, marketing, sales, etc. We would have hired the Brookline Consulting Group to set up a decision process, for about three hundred thousand dollars. And we would have taken at least three months to have the final reports done and sanitized." Frank laughed. "Delvono is different. I say work on both. If we succeed with an oral product, great. If it has to be injectable, well that's technically tougher in some ways and more expensive, but that's OK too. We're talking about serious infections here, and most of the patients will already be in the hospital, so injectable is fine."

Christina thought for a few seconds then said, "If an injectable product is OK, this really gets interesting and maybe more achievable. I want to figure out the structure of the polysaccharide glue that binds the biofilm together and to the host tissue surface. Or maybe it's already known for some of the types of bacteria of interest. We look for enzymes that can chop that glue up, but not chew human polysaccharides up. Maybe we have to design this enzyme. Then we have to figure out how to make that enzyme non-immunogenic when injected into a human, again codosed with a new or traditional antibiotic. That's not gonna be easy."

Frank said, "Easy, who cares about easy? If it were easy, it would already be on the hospital shelf. As you were speaking, I realized that it definitely makes sense to go after an injectable first. We can work out all the science and come up with a solution without worrying about having a drug combo that can be orally absorbed. If we succeed with an injectable product, the world will beat a path to our door."

"Do you think we could get some funds for this, and maybe put a couple of people on it?"

Frank smiled and said, "Yep. We can put more than a couple on it."

He was excited, really excited. "I have to go, but I want to make sure I say something very important to you. I know you just came from academia where young people generally talk freely about their ideas, although older faculty are generally more circumspect because they realize they're in competition for grant money. Don't talk to anyone outside the company about this. I'm really serious about this. Make an appointment to talk to Bert Rosen, our patent attorney, about your ideas and nascent plans, and please make an appointment, say for two hours, with me later this week to continue this discussion and bring along your ideas for what resources you need. I like where you're going. Prevent biofilms or destabilize them if they've already formed, and then whack the free floating unprotected bacteria with a traditional or new antibiotic. The one-two punch." He laughed. "This is fantastic, Christina. Later in the week, right? And don't be cheap about your resource estimate. And I don't need a fancy formal report; handwritten estimates are fine at this stage. And listen, ten new people is not outside the realm of possibility."

"Sure. When you say don't talk to people, it's OK to talk to people here, right?"

"Definitely, but when you do, tell them in no uncertain terms that this can't be discussed outside the company. And take some time to write out your ideas in your bound lab-notebook and get someone to cosign it."

"OK."

"OK, then. Spend the afternoon sunbathing and thinking if you want. I'm glad somebody's thinking around here."

Frank got up and headed back to his office. *This is why we hire smart young inexperienced people in addition to the experienced ones.* He got a big kick out of telling a young scientist that she could have resources on the fly. Back in Big Pharma, a scientist would have to wait until the right time of the fiscal year and write a formal Project Operating Plan, and then move the Plan through multiple layers of management where unspoken ulterior motives could sewer the idea at each level of review, and almost certainly would kill it without a powerful champion. *Small is better.* Frank was the King-With-The-Big-Checkbook, and he loved it.

Chapter 6

Jimmy dialed the phone.

"Hello, Bill O'Hara."

"Hi Bill, this is Jimmy Delvecchio. How are ya?"

"Good, really good. Hey Jimmy, I haven't seen you in years, not since the internet pharmacy days. It's nice to hear from you. It really is. How's the drug discovery business going?"

"Fantastic. We've got some leads on new antibiotics, and I'm having a great time. Day to day of course, it's the same old business stuff, but it feels good. It's a long hard road."

"So what's up?"

"I'd like to get together to talk, you know, about old times. Any chance we could meet for lunch today?"

"OK, I understand. I'm available. Where do you want to meet?"

"How about the Wendy's on Bloomfield Avenue in Nutley?"

"We can eat someplace better than that."

"No, that's really my preference. I'll explain. How about noon?"

"Noon it is."

Delvecchio and O'Hara pulled into the Wendy's parking lot at the same time, and Jimmy waited until O'Hara walked into the restaurant before leaving his car. It was an old rule that he still followed – avoid being seen in public with a collaborator whenever possible.

In the lobby, O'Hara smiled, and joked, "You like the food at Wendy's now?"

"It's OK. I really don't like to meet in my favorite restaurants because they're probably being watched. I guess it's residual paranoia from the old days."

O'Hara laughed and said, "It never changes for you, huh, after all this time. These days the friggin' government probably has satellites taking pictures of everybody, and following their cell phone GPS signals. There's probably a drone looking in our bedroom windows at night."

"Hey, as long as there isn't a drone looking into our girlfriends' windows and taking our pictures." They both laughed. "Welcome to leftist world. The fucking communists are taking over."

They made small talk while they ate, then Delvecchio broached the subject on his mind.

"Listen, I need your advice on something. Can you swear confidentiality on what I'm gonna talk about?"

"Well, you know stuff about me that I don't ever want to see the light of day, so, yeah, I swear confidentiality, for what it's worth. If they put me on the rack or tie me up to be drawn and quartered, all bets are off."

"I see you still have your sense of humor, or maybe it's a sense of honesty. I'll give you a hypothetical situation. Some low level guys hijack trucks for a living. Always stuff like clothes, radios, TVs, stuff that can be fenced. Then one day they make a mistake and hijack a truck containing prescription medicine from a distributor. A big truck. A very valuable truck. They and their bosses have no idea how to fence this stuff."

"I'd tell them to drive it to a rest stop on the Jersey Turnpike and walk away."

"And what if their greedy bosses think it's too valuable to walk away from?"

"Well, there's no question it's valuable, probably more valuable by orders of magnitude than anything they've ever stolen. But Jimmy, why are you involved in this?"

"I'm not. This is a hypothetical situation."

"OK Jimmy, but I've gotta make it clear that I can't get involved in anything like this."

"I understand. I really do. And I wouldn't ask you to get involved in a hypothetical situation like this. Let's just have a little fun and talk about what somebody could do in this kind of situation."

"OK, I'll play. Look, this is a lot like money laundering, but worse. Every bottle of medicine and every box of bottles on this hypothetical truck has an ID number on it. If the stuff makes it to a pharmacy, it'll be identified because of stolen drug alerts that all pharmacies get. It'll get traced back to everyone who ever touched it, and finally to the hijackers. This *Omerta* stuff might work back near the hijacker level, but once you get to bona fide drug distributors and pharmacies, there's no way of assuring confidentiality. Unless, of course, some intermediary is scared shitless and is willing to take the rap with his mouth shut if things go wrong."

"Look, in this hypothetical situation, you can always solve the problem by blackmailing people or worse, but for now, let's try to be a little more creative."

O'Hara continued, "OK. Let's have a little fun. Look, it's like changing the VIN on a stolen car, but much worse. If you have the right facility, you can repackage all the drugs in new phony bottles and boxes. They're no longer traceable, but they're identifiable as phony because the new ID numbers don't correspond to anything the drug companies would have used. But that's a hell of a lot of work and expense."

Jimmy smiled and said, "Let's follow this line of thought. You could just use numbers that follow from the numbers initially on the bottles, and you could also put on later expiry dates, but of course you wouldn't know what expiry dates would be appropriate for those ID numbers. But this also gives you more time to get rid of the stuff because you now have later expiry dates."

"But Jimmy, you're still screwed. You still have a trail of people involved in distributing the repackaged stuff, and you have to keep their mouths shut."

"Yeah, but maybe the stuff is all in patients' hands in a couple of months, and nobody ever has any reason to suspect that anything was wrong." Then Jimmy thought quietly for a few seconds. "OK. Let's start with the pharmacy. Let's say it's a CVS or something like that. It would be a lot easier to do this with a Mom and Pop pharmacy, but there are hardly any of those left around, and the remaining ones aren't big enough. The distributor delivers the repackaged medicines to a variety of pharmacies, the way he always does. Would the pharmacist suspect anything? I don't think so, right?"

"I don't know, Jimmy. Initially, the pharmacy might not see anything wrong, but eventually there'll be abnormalities that turn up with respect to duplicate ID numbers, but maybe not until an audit, which could occur almost a year later."

"OK. Now back to the distributor. Where does he get his stuff from? Sometimes a bigger distributor, but more likely from the drug companies, right?"

"Right."

"So the distributor has to be in on it. Is there any way of fooling the distributor?"

"You could fool the distributor if all the drugs were from one company, and you could phony up all the paperwork. But you would have to know a lot about how this distributor operates, and how that drug company operates, what all their paperwork looks like, who calls who, etcetera. You'd need somebody on the inside at the distributor. I don't see how you fool people here in a one-off operation. What was in this hypothetical truck?"

"For the sake of argument, let's say it was from a major pharmaceutical company. About ten drugs."

"How much of each."

"About five pallets of each drug. Each pallet is hypothetically about three feet by three feet by three feet. The drugs are in cartons containing boxes of say twenty bottles, maybe twenty boxes per carton, maybe 250 pills per bottle. These are pharmacy bottles that the pharmacist breaks down to provide smaller bottles for patients."

Bill O'Hara raised his eyebrows. "Holy shit. 250 Pills per bottle times 20 bottles per box times 20 boxes per carton times maybe 20 cartons per pallet times five pallets. Let me think. That's 20 cubed, which is, what, 8000? Times five pallets is 40,000. Times 250 pills. I'm gonna need a calculator. He pulled out his i-phone and called up the calculator app. Jimmy, that's ten million doses. And you said ten different drugs? That's about 100 million doses. Even if my calculations are off by 100%, that's still 50 million doses. At retail, that's well over 100 million dollars, depending on what the drugs are. That's some hypothetical truck. They should have had a car full of hypothetical guards in front and behind with hypothetical AK-47s."

"Yeah, but you know the reality is just like when they quote street value of confiscated heroin shipments. That 100 million is at the pharmacist-to-patient level. The pharmacy markup is 100%, so right away we're down to more like 50 million at the distributor level."

"OK. So this is a lot of stuff. Basically, you have to get a large distributor to take it. A CVS or Walgreen warehouse, or a guy who distributes to CVS or Walgreen. Where is this discussion going? What do you want from me?"

"Just this hypothetical discussion we're having. This is good. I still don't think we've come up with a solution to the problem that minimizes risk and maximizes profit."

O'Hara said, "You know of course that the cops, and probably the feds, would already be looking all over for this stuff. If I were these hypothetical hijackers, I'd load these pallets ASAP on a ship, and figure out how to sell the stuff in Yemen or Turkey or somewhere."

Jimmy smiled. "That's a good thought. It sure would be nice, hypothetically, to just sell the whole shipment to someone who can take care of it. You're right. There are too many complications here, and too many ways to get caught, no matter how many people are bribed or blackmailed. Just out of curiosity, would you hypothetically be interested in getting involved with this hypothetical problem?"

"I wouldn't touch it with a ten-foot pole. They make it hard for a guy to make a living these days, huh?"

They both laughed.

"Yeah, you're right. I wouldn't touch it either. Anyway, this discussion has been fun. I really miss working with you in the old internet pharmacy days. Let's get together once in a while to shoot the breeze, not about this sort of hypothetical stuff."

O'Hara laughed. "Absolutely, but let's eat at a better place."

Chapter 7

The following Sunday, Jimmy and his wife Gina pulled into the driveway of Uncle Carmine and Aunt Emerlinda's house, one of the 1950s-style attached houses in Lodi that looked just like the old Brooklyn neighborhood from which Jimmy's parents' generation had moved to New Jersey. Why that generation made that move always seemed like a mystery to Jimmy. They had not actually "moved up", but instead moved to an architecturally similar neighborhood, where neighbors were again all Italian and Italian-American, and where whole blocks of stores seemed to have moved en-masse. The reality was that they had moved because of fear of changes they couldn't control. As they saw other ethnic groups start to expand in Brooklyn, they became increasingly uncomfortable.

Jimmy was born in Brooklyn and grew up in Lodi, and it was an idyllic childhood. His aunts and uncles and grandparents lived nearby, and as a kid he could walk to his cousins' houses. Every Sunday around 1 PM, some subset of the family gathered at one house or another for a feast. As a child, Jimmy's mouth watered each Sunday morning just thinking about the macaroni and sauce and the incredible desserts. The elders of course had a more refined taste for the other foods being served, and there was always enough variety to satisfy everyone. Sunday dinner was the stake in the ground to which they were all happily tied. No matter what happened at work or in school, no matter who was born or was sick or died, no matter the weather, Sunday dinner bound everyone together. The importance of family did not require intellectualization; it was as natural as hand-eye coordination.

Jimmy lived nearby in Verona now, and on this particular Sunday, as he and his wife Gina arrived at the Casamento house in Lodi just before 1 PM, the house was already crowding with a group of around twelve people. Jimmy walked into the kitchen and bellowed, *"Buona sera, Z'Emerline!* How's my favorite aunt?" He gave his Aunt Emerlinda a hug and a kiss on the cheek.

"I love you, little Jimmy," she replied in her thick accent. *"Come stai?"*

"I'm good. Work is good. Gina's in the living room, catching up. I'll send her in to say hello and learn some of your cooking tips."

"Managia! You chooch. Gina doesn't need any cooking tips. She's the best. That's your wife you're talkin' about."

Jimmy tore a piece of semolina bread off one of the loaves sitting on the counter, dipped it into the pot of sauce, and took a bite out of the steaming bread. "Ohhh," he moaned. "I'm in heaven, *Z'Emerline,* and you are an angel."

"Get outta here! You're gonna eat all my food! Show a little patience. *Managia!"*

Jimmy kissed his aunt on the cheek again, finished his piece of bread, and walked into the living room. Uncle Carmine, younger brother of Jimmy's deceased mother, called out to him, and Jimmy joined the men sitting at one end of the room.

"Your wife looks beautiful today. You're a lucky man," said Uncle Carmine.

"Yes, I am. How's everybody doin' here?"

The men talked about sports and home repairs, and Jimmy joined in, showing respect for the knowledge of his elders and his cousins. Of course, things had really changed over the last ten years. Jimmy, now 54 years old, was a multimillionaire many times over. He never ever talked openly about money with his relatives, and they religiously avoided the subject. In the extended Italian family, age was the currency of status. A younger person who boasted or tried to act important was seen as a backwoods boor, a *cafone*, and 54 years was not quite enough currency to achieve exalted status. In private, his cousins and even his uncles would ask Jimmy for investment advice, but in public, even at close family gatherings, Jimmy was exquisitely deferential.

By around 1:30, the crowd swelled to about sixteen, the adults sat down in the dining room, and the children sat at the "children's table" in the foyer. The food was fantastic and the conversation fun, ranging from politics to food and back and forth. Discussion of bread quality was engaged in as seriously as discussion of property taxes. When the meal was over, and everyone had finished their second helping of pastry and coffee and Sambuca and Amaretto, the group thinned. Carmine asked Jimmy and Gina to stay for a while because he wanted to talk to Jimmy. Gina joined a couple of the remaining women and older girls to play tombola in the kitchen.

Jimmy and Carmine sat at the cleared dining room table with a bowl of nuts and a plate of sliced apples and small glasses of port. They cracked open nuts as they talked.

"That was a good meal, huh Jimmy? This is what life is all about."

"I couldn't agree with you more, *Zio*."

"So how are the kids? Linda still down south?"

"They're good. Yeah, she and her husband are still in Houston. He's finishing up his residency at the big cancer center there. She's still working as a computer programmer, and seems a little lost, doesn't seem to know what she wants to do next. No kids on the way as far as I know. Anthony's still up in Boston, getting his Ph.D. He seems like he's doing good. Gina and I, we really miss them. It's hard, you know, when you realize they're really gone."

"So are things good at the company?"

"Fantastic."

"Jimmy, I have a little favor to ask, and then maybe we can talk about that thing we discussed before."

"Sure. What can I do?"

"Do you remember Angela's little girl, Anna Lisa?"

"Sure," Jimmy nodded.

"Well, she's all grown up now, and she just finished her masters at Rutgers in some kind of science. She's looking for a job, and it's tough, and she started looking up in Boston and down in D.C., and her parents are worried that she'll move away and never come back."

"*Zio*, lots of people move away and then come back these days. Sure, some don't, but it's a different world. You go where the opportunities are. Boston is an exciting place for a young scientist."

"Yeah, but New Jersey isn't so bad either. And the PATH train takes you to the center of the universe. Whatever you want is in Manhattan. So anyway, could you look at her resume and see what you can do?"

"Sure. No problem. As long as there's nothing really screwy, we'll bring her in for an interview. But I'll be honest,

I'm gonna talk to her about her aspirations and what's best for her."

"OK. Whatever you think. Thank you. Now about the other thing."

"You wearing a wire?" asked Jimmy.

"No. You wearing a wire?" responded Carmine. They both laughed, and Carmine got up and turned on the radio, tuned it to a classical station, and raised the volume to a level a little loud for conversation. "Can't be too careful. You never know if some *faccia di merda* has placed a bug."

"I hope not. Not in your own house. OK, *Zio*. I've talked to a few people without revealing anything significant. Just asking questions about how things are done. It's all computers now in the U.S., and it's virtually impossible to distribute this stuff here and make good numbers. You have to believe me on this. You would have to take extreme measures, you know what I mean, and even then the probability is high that someone goes to jail. And for a long time."

"Jimmy, I told you we don't have a choice. *Marone*, this is not an acceptable answer."

"*Aspetta*, I'm not done. Look there are lots of countries where you could move this stuff, and the close ones are Canada and Mexico. Canada's got the same computer controls as here, and Mexico has low prices and you'd have to bribe so many distributers and politicians and *federales* that the return isn't worth the risk. And forget the third world, like some place in Africa. And China, no way; they already have cheap drugs, cheap crappy drugs."

"Are you gonna tell me anything I want to hear?"

"*Si*. Look, you have to pick a place where there's lots of money, and where there are people who are willing and able to pay top dollar for the brand name drugs because they don't trust the local generics. Here's what I come up with. You want to unload this stuff someplace like Saudi Arabia or Abu Dhabi. I know a guy, a retired drug company scientist who's a pharmacist. He has a brother-in-law in Abu Dhabi who keeps bugging him about starting some kind of pharmaceutical business. His brother-in-law has lots of connections. *Zio*, you know guys who know how to move stuff onto ships. You put this stuff in a container going to Abu Dhabi. I know you guys know how to get it unloaded there. I give you the name of a guy who'll pick the stuff up. So far, so good?"

"Yeah, I'm beginning to feel a little better."

"I'm not gonna get my pharmacist friend or his brother-in-law in trouble. I treat my friend like he's family, *capisci?*"

"Of course. I understand."

"Your business friends take all the risk in the US, but I don't see much risk here because you guys control the docks in Elizabeth. On the other end, maybe we set it up so the guy picking up the stuff doesn't know what it is or any names. After that, it's the responsibility of my friend's brother-in-law to distribute the stuff. As I understand it, he'll have no problem."

"This seems like a lot of trouble to fence a truckload of stuff."

"I gave you my first round of advice a couple of days ago, when I said take the truck to a rest stop on 95 and walk away from it. That's still my top level advice."

"OK. We can get everything you described done. How does the money work?"

"I don't know much about laundering cash. You guys have a department that handles that, right?" Jimmy laughed. "But with regard to the amount, here's how I see the numbers. For starters, the numbers are very big, bigger than I'm sure the guys usually deal with, so there's risk that someone may want to go independent and really screw things up. Anyway, from what you've told me, we're talking about $100 million street value, meaning sales price to the patient in an American pharmacy. Let's just say that pharmacy value in Abu Dhabi is half that, let's just say $50 million in round numbers. From what I've been told, the pharmacy markup there is just like here, 100%. So the pharmacies would normally pay the distributor $25 million, but in this case they'd pay less because it's stolen stuff."

"So we got what, maybe a 15 or 20 million dollar load? That's lots of millions disappearing somewhere."

"*Zio*, this is all standard markups just like the US. No skimming yet. The guy in Abu Dhabi will probably be willing to pay your guys 5 million. He's taking almost all the risk, and he's the one doing the distributing. Your guys just have to get the stuff on a boat to the right port, and you should probably pay off the shipping people a relatively low amount so they don't suspect they're moving something incredibly valuable and get ideas of their own. I never had anything to do with any of that kind of stuff, but I bet you can get it done for twenty large."

Uncle Carmine looked pissed. "You're telling me we make 5 million, and this Arab makes what, 10 or 15 million? No way."

"No, the Arab has to sell it at a discount, so he may only get, say, 15 million total, and *Zio*, all you're doing is putting the stuff on a ship and going to the bank. When do you guys ever see 5 million dollars for putting one container on a ship? If you didn't have me and my contacts, what would you have? I'll tell you what you would have – *niente*. "

"Jimmy, you tell your friend to tell his brother-in-law 7.5 million. What's in this for you and your pharmacist friend?"

"What my friend gets is between him and his brother-in-law. I made it clear that I don't want anything. I don't want to have anything traceable to me. I've got my company and more money than a Rockefeller grandchild. I'm helping you out here because we're family. You know I left the life ten years ago, and I don't want any part of it. I don't even like having this conversation. I have a lot to lose."

"OK. OK. You tell these guys our counteroffer. All we need from you is the name and number of someone in the Middle East. You're completely out of it. But Jimmy, you gotta realize that if something goes wrong and somebody gets greedy or pulls something on us, you become involved as far as the big guys are concerned. I don't like saying this, but you know it's true."

"Yeah, OK. I'll get you the name, and then after that I have nothing to do with anything. And please, no funny stuff on your end of this. I worry more about your guys than the Arabs."

"Jimmy, it bothers me that you say "your guys" instead of "our guys". You may be Mr. Big Shot Drug Company CEO, but you're still a member of the family. This never changes. And some advice here. If you ever talk to the guys at the main office, or anybody down or up the line for that matter, you say "our guys". When you say "your guys" it sounds like you're turning your back on us, and that means you could turn people in if there's pressure on you. You know who you are, Jimmy, and where you came from. This cannot be changed. OK. I think this'll all work out. That's enough".

Carmine got up and turned down the radio to a pleasant level and said, "Let's get the ladies back in here and have an espresso and some pleasant conversation."

"Good." Jimmy got up and said "I've gotta hit the can." As he walked out of the room, he thought *It never ends. It just never fuckin' ends.*

Chapter 8

Frank spent a lot of his time in his car these days, driving to academic medical centers to interview job candidates and to set up and monitor progress on Delvono clinical trials. He always listened to AM radio stations out of New York City, and the shows fell into two categories: right-wing talk shows and infomercials for so-called natural remedies. These infomercials were generally presented as interview shows with "doctors" who pushed products that "the big pharmaceutical companies hate", and Frank had reached the point where his blood boiled every time he listened. But he couldn't stop listening. A surprising observation was that the right-wing political talk shows often had these natural remedy companies as advertisers. The political talk shows even played prerecorded testimonials for the herbal products by the right-wing talk show hosts. This didn't make a lot of sense to Frank, but there it was.

He exited from the NY State Thruway at Exit 15 and merged onto the Garden State South, heading back to the lab after a meeting with an antibacterial specialist at Yale. He turned on the radio and hit the AM button.

DR. BOB ROLLAR: Our guest today is Dr. Francine Albertson, who is an arthritis expert and the inventor of a breakthrough approach for overcoming arthritis pain and reversing the arthritis process itself. It is indeed a pleasure to have her here with me today – a medical revolutionary who has been able to cut through all the misinformation of the past, and to clearly provide a path forward for patients who have suffered too long. Good afternoon, Dr. Albertson. It's a pleasure to be with you again, and I thank you for taking time out from your busy schedule to talk to our listeners.

DR. FRANCINE ALBERTSON: Well thanks, Bob, for inviting me. I've always been impressed with the information you provide for patients. I'm on the road in my car a lot, and I always tune in to you in the afternoon to hear the latest breakthroughs in medicine.

Frank had been distracted, thinking about problems with a clinical site where Delvono was testing a new antibiotic. But the discussion on the radio caught his ear, and though it was repetitive and unabashedly self-congratulatory, after a few minutes he started to listen intently.

The host continued in a voice and cadence typical of infomercials.

ROLLAR: So you mean to tell me that after all these years and hundreds of millions of tax dollars spent on research, the government and the academics have not even gotten close to understanding the cause of arthritis?

ALBERTSON: Well that's true. And part of it is because the so-called academic researchers are all in the pocket of the drug companies. The drug companies pay physicians to prescribe their drugs, and the companies also give grants to the medical school arthritis researchers basically to keep them quiet. The researchers can do whatever they want with this money, and I hate to say it, but it sure looks more like payoffs than grants.

ROLLAR: This is a story I hear over and over and over, and I have to say that it really disgusts me. The drug companies seem to have a lock on the doctors, and with the exception of some very brave revolutionaries like you, the doctors refuse to consider the proven powerful natural remedies that are already available, and not at the ridiculous prices people pay for drugs. I see Jeannie in the control room signaling me that it is time for a commercial. We'll be back in five minutes.

The prerecorded commercial began, presented by the host Dr. Bob Rollar. It went on and on about the value of natural remedies and "megapowered nutraceutical supplements" for a variety of ailments. Frank started muttering, "Those are drug claims. You can't make drug claims without running clinical trials, submitting a New Drug Application, and getting FDA approval. I have to spend 80 million dollars to do this, and you don't have to spend anything." He was annoyed and yelled "Fuck!" as he banged his hands on the steering wheel.

The commercial ended with:

This is Dr. Bob Rollar, and I care about your health. Every Rollar's Medicine Shoppe is a full-service pharmacy with a degreed nutritional consultant ready to evaluate your medical needs. Your search is over. We're here to help. We have our original two locations in Manhattan, one by Grand Central on

Third Avenue at 45th St., and the other on the West Side on Broadway at 78th. We also have stores in Bayside, Queens, and in Park Slope in Brooklyn. We just opened a store in Commack out on the Island, and next month we'll open our first store in the Bronx on Fordham Road. And don't worry, those of you in New Jersey. We're planning stores in Hoboken and Montclair, and we're all excited about bringing our exclusive health help to you in New Jersey. So come in and see us, it's worth the trip. You won't regret it.

The broadcast interview continued, and Dr. Francine Albertson discussed the basis for the efficacy of her "power-supplement" called "ArthrAloe".

ALBERTSON: Bob, I know that you read the professional medical literature and the alternative medicine literature deeply and often. There's no way that people should refer to what I do as alternative medicine. It's real medicine, and it's done without poisonous chemicals. My 'ArthrAloe' is all natural, and contains a variety of specially formulated naturopathic extracts in conjunction with glucosamine and chondroitin. Now you know that glucosamine and chondroitin have been around and sold in health food stores and pharmacies for years for arthritis pain. But what people don't know is that these earlier products, while they may have helped some people a little, they left a lot to be desired. My colleagues and I have spent years researching why these products performed poorly, and the result of all our work is a new naturopathically-formulated glucosamine/chondroitin, combined with a special formulation of sixteen proprietary natural extracts that are present in specific ratios that result from our research. And I'll make no secret of the incredible almost magical additive we've used, which is aloe extract, and I'm sure your listeners are well aware of the incredible healing power of aloe.

ROLLAR (sounding like he's reading from a script): And I understand from what you told me during the commercial break that you've carried out clinical trials that prove the efficacy of your formula.

ALBERTSON: That's right, Bob. Ours is the only naturopathic arthritis supplement that has been tested in clinical trials and shown to be efficacious. There is no other glucosamine-chondroitin formulation on the market that can make this claim. As a matter of fact, our clinical results were so striking that we put them in a patent application and the United States Patent Office issued a patent to us based on these striking results.

This was the straw that broke the camel's back for Frank. Frank started mumbling to himself in his head, *Bullshit. Anybody can get a patent for a 16-component formulation with specific ratios, as long as it's novel and non-obvious and has a use. Any 16-component combination of anything is novel and non-obvious. And you just have to say that it's useful for arthritis; you don't have to prove it. Shit, it's got glucosamine and chondroitin in it, so almost anyone would buy the argument that it has use in arthritis, whether it really works or not.* He was pissed off. *Clinical trials have nothing to do with patents. This is not FDA approval or approval by anybody.* He made a mental note to check out this patent although he certainly had more important things to do.

Frank turned off the radio.

* * *

After dinner, Frank poured a glass of Balvenie single-malt scotch with one ice cube, and went down to his basement office. He turned on his computer and googled Dr. Francine Albertson, and after adding some further keyword constraints found a Wikipedia page that gushed with praise about her scientific background, dedication to medicine, and practical accomplishments in the fight against arthritis. He was curious about her D.N. degree from Chalmar University of the Naturopathic Medical Sciences. *What the fuck is a D.N. degree?* he thought. He googled the University, and after reading a lot of repetitive mystical-sounding stuff about naturopathic remedies and Ayervedic medicine, he realized that it was another on-line school. On further reading, it became clear that 50% of the credits toward the D.N. (Doctor of Naturopathy) degree could be covered by life experience. There were no exams or thesis requirement, or bachelor's degree entry requirement. The student paid for each course, which was to be downloaded and studied. Each course was considered completed when the student checked a box indicating that the materials had been read and the associated questions answered and compared with the provided answer key. Frank laughed and thought *I could have saved myself a lot of work and anxiety if I had gotten my degree here.*

He was even more surprised when he did a patent search on Albertson's name. She said on the radio that they had done a clinical study of their "ArthrAloe" formulation, and that the results were so convincing that the US Patent Office had awarded them a patent. Frank was suspicious because he knew that you did not need human clinical data to get a patent, and in fact, you could have no data at all as long as you provided logic for the utility of your invention. The gold standard for government approval of a novel therapy was FDA approval of a

New Drug Application, which would require study in thousands of patients for an arthritis drug. A patent turned up in the search, titled "Arthritis Medicine", with Francine Albertson as inventor, so she wasn't lying about that.

As Frank read the patent, he began to laugh. There was a clinical study alright, but it was a clinical study in horses. Furthermore, the design was ridiculous. Apparently, the so-called inventors had subjectively measured the gait of four old horses by eye. Then they gave the horses "ArthrAloe" every day for five days, and subjectively measured gait again. In two of the four horses, they determined that gait improved. There was not even a nod to standard scientific procedure. Obviously not statistically significant. Obviously subjective evaluation. Obviously not double-blinded. Obviously not randomized. Obviously not a human clinical trial. Obviously garbage.

When Frank stopped chuckling, he thought about the fraud perpetrated on the naive desperate arthritis sufferers listening to the radio ads. Not so funny. He decided that it was time to do something about this crap.

When he arrived at Delvono the next morning, he stopped in at the IT room where the computer geeks worked, and asked if anyone had any experience with blogging. Margaret McGarry, a recent Rutgers computer science graduate, volunteered that she knew a lot about it and in fact had her own weekly blog on which she discussed her favorite TV shows. He sat with her for 15 minutes and discussed how to get set up, which were the best services, etc. She offered to help but Frank said that it really was not directly work-related, so he probably would need some outside help. Margaret said that she had a friend who did freelance website design who also had a site on which she hosted a variety of bloggers who discussed everything from science fiction to gender politics. She gave Frank her friend's phone number and said she would tell her friend that Frank would call.

Within two weeks, Frank was all set with the technical issues related to publishing a blog. The young woman who set it up did a first-rate job, and Frank gave her $200 more than she had asked. He decided to call the blog "NATURAL ENOUGH FOR YA?", and got right to work on his first post.

Chapter 9

NATURAL ENOUGH FOR YA? #1

from the desk of Frank Serono, PhD.

<u>Another Maligned Miracle Cure</u>

Have you ever heard of *Sophora flavescens*? It's an herb that comes to us from Chinese Medicine, where it is called "ku shen". It has been purported to "fight cancer". That's not "cure cancer" or "increase the lifespan of cancer patients". What does "fight cancer" mean? Nothing, of course.

S. flavescens also has other uses, and has been purported to be active against asthma, atherosclerosis, eczema, hepatitis, high cholesterol, and kidney disease. Amazing, huh? Why don't our doctors tell us about this miracle? I guess the big drug companies have paid them off.

No, what I actually believe is that our doctors have not told us about this miracle herb because they're not idiots. In a recent radio broadcast featuring host Dr. Bart Johnson, who owns a chain of "Dr. Bart's Natural Medicine Stores" in the New York area, we were regaled with descriptions of human clinical trials that have demonstrated the myriad therapeutic activities of this amazing herb. These trials were described as if they demonstrated therapeutic activity with the same certainty as trials of drugs carried out to obtain FDA approval. For example, Dr. Bart said, "These are not laboratory studies in cells or animals. These are the real deal, controlled clinical studies conducted by nutritionally-aware doctors in the same way that the FDA demands for drugs." Well, I looked at the actual publications describing these trials, and they tell a somewhat different story. These human trials were published in third- and fourth-tier journals, some of which do not involve anonymous peer review. "Picky, picky," you may say. OK then, let's look at the published clinical trials themselves.

Unlike Dr. Bart Johnson, the authors of these clinical studies were somewhat circumspect about the results. In a 16 patient study of hepatitis, the study leader said that *S.flavescens* "may help in the treatment of hepatitis C." This is a far cry from Dr. Bart's misleading statement that "In a controlled clinical trial, *S.flavescens* knocked down the hep C virus." It would take at least a 20-fold larger number of patients to demonstrate believable therapeutic activity in hep C patients, and the study in question showed no significant results. I suspect that Dr. Bart knows this, but why get bogged down in details when you have herbs to sell?

Dr. Bart Johnson also talked about studies that demonstrate that *S.flavescens* treats high cholesterol, and railed against the "chemically poisonous statins sold by the big drug companies". Well, again the studies he mentioned were in a very small number of subjects, and the authors only said that *S.flavescens* "may help treat high cholesterol", which is code for "inconclusive results" or "no significant effect". By the way, Dr. Bart was so excited that he forgot to mention that these studies were carried out in rats.

Throughout his whole presentation, he repeatedly talked about "gold-standard human clinical studies carried out by highly regarded researchers". He even managed to get in the names Harvard, Yale, and NYU multiple times, although he was careful not to directly say that any of the studies he discussed were carried out at these institutions, which would be untrue.

Dr. Bart Johnson's hour-long radio infomercials are carefully scripted to fool the listener into thinking that there is an enormous body of highly-regarded work supporting his claims. He does get sloppy and actually makes illegal therapeutic activity claims on the radio, but it appears that the FDA is not listening. I have read what it says on the bottles of herbs he sells, and the manufacturers are much more careful to avoid breaking FDA drug law. They say things like "helps support heart health." Sure, and so does a candy bar.

I will say this for Dr. Bart Johnson. Unlike many in his business, he actually has a bona fide degree, a Pharm.D. from an approved pharmacy school. He should know better. He also has an MBA, which seems to have gotten the better of him.

Chapter 10

Jimmy pulled into the west parking lot of Washington Park in Lambertville, New Jersey, on the Pennsylvania line. This was certainly a strange place for Uncle Carmine to want to meet him – a pain-in-the-butt drive. Jimmy got out of his car, and after walking about fifty yards down a dirt path, came to a clearing with a view of a pond. A beautiful place with full growth trees, and today in late summer the sweltering heat had passed. Jimmy thought *I'd love to just sit here by myself and have some peace. Why am I meeting with these guys? This cannot be good if Uncle Carmine suggested that we park in separate parking lots.*

His Uncle Carmine and a man Jimmy did not know were sitting on a bench. Jimmy walked up and said, "Good Morning, fellas."

Carmine rose and shook Jimmy's hand and said "Jimmy, thanks for coming. I'd like to introduce Alfonso Gentilella. This is my nephew Jimmy."

Gentilella did not stand up, but offered his hand to Jimmy and Jimmy shook it. He said, "Please, take a seat, and please call me Funzi."

Jimmy was shocked and wondered what the heck was going on. This was not going to be a typical morning, not by a long shot. Alfonso Gentilella was a ghost rarely if ever seen, a legend and possibly a myth who Jimmy was not sure really existed until today. While Alberto Graziano, the *capo di capi*, sat daily in a private club in the Little Italy section of Manhattan and formally lorded over the remaining so-called Italian Crime Families of New York, the mythical Funzi Gentilella was rumored to truly be in charge, living a quiet protected life somewhere in Bucks County, Pennsylvania. *Holy shit*, thought Jimmy. *Am I supposed to kiss this guy's ring?*

Gentilella was about 75 years old, dressed in preppy clothes: khaki pants, brown belt, an unbuttoned pullover pink Izod shirt, and slip-on sneakers. He was a fit man, with a full head of grey hair, and certainly did not look like a guy who spent his days sitting in a club eating pasta and pastry, drinking wine and espresso. He actually looked like an aging corporate CEO with a personal trainer.

Gentilella broke the ice and said, "I'm really pleased to finally meet you. I've known your uncle for a long time, and he's always spoken very highly of your abilities and dedication. I've been involved in the administration of our businesses for a long time, and I have to say that nothing ever impressed me as much as the amount of money you made for us with your internet pharmacy work. Clean money. And then your counsel recently on getting rid of that truck full of medicine – that was right on the money. You know, our organization has a long history, and some of it isn't pretty, but now we have a very large stable of legitimate businesses, and we're quite successful. The old ways are dying out. Or maybe a better way to put it is that the old ways are dying out for us. The Russians and the South Americans – maybe it's their turn now to pull themselves up by their bootstraps and get a foothold in America. Maybe the Chinese too, but they don't seem as organized. I'm rambling a little so I'll cut to the chase. It's time now for us to be like Joe Kennedy and pass the ill-gotten gains on to a clean generation. We've been working hard at this, and I'm here to ask you to join our main office."

Gentilella paused after dropping that bombshell, and Jimmy remained quiet for a few seconds until it was obvious that he had to say something. He very carefully began, slightly baffled, and aware that there could be consequences for saying the wrong thing. Jimmy smiled and said, "Well, if you wanted to catch me by surprise, you've certainly done that. My first reaction is that I'm honored. I'll certainly give this opportunity serious consideration. I have lots of balls in the air right now, and it'll take a lot of thought for me to move on to something new. Just like any job, I'll have to know what you're looking for and whether I'm the right person for you."

Gentilella smiled and nodded. "To be a little more clear, I'm inviting you to take over as CEO of the group that oversees our many legitimate businesses. It's quite a diverse stable, and it needs oversight by someone with experience, common sense, and in my estimation an appreciation for our history. I know this is a big surprise. And I know you're quite unaware of the size and workings of our organization. Why don't we leave it at this. We'll arrange for you to come in to talk to some of our people at Liberty Holdings in Stamford, Connecticut. I think it'll be good for you to see the office, and we'll be able to give you an overview of the businesses we have. We'll arrange a small lunch group so you can get a feel for the kind of people we have. How does that sound?"

Jimmy realized that only one answer was possible. "That sounds great. I'm very interested."

Gentilella nodded. "Good. I'm happy. Carmine, thank you for introducing us. This worked out nicely. I have to get going."

He stood up and offered his hand to Jimmy. Jimmy rose, and they shook hands. Carmine said to Jimmy, "Good, very good. Let's talk later. Maybe you and Gina can come over for coffee and cake after dinner tonight, huh?"

Jimmy replied, "Sure *Zio* Carmine. Sounds good." Gentilella and Uncle Carmine headed off to the east parking lot, and Jimmy headed to the west.

*   *   *

The following Monday, Jimmy found himself sitting in a conference room at Liberty Holdings in Stamford, Connecticut, drinking coffee and eating a bagel with cream cheese while listening to a series of presentations on the various businesses managed by the staff there. The oddity of the situation was immediately obvious to him. The presenters were not behaving like they were interviewing him for a job; they were behaving like he was a high-powered consultant who they were trying to impress. He realized that they may have been told that he was likely their future boss. Jimmy realized that Gentilella was probably not in the middle of a long process of identifying and interviewing CEO candidates; Jimmy was his choice and that was that.

Liberty Holdings consisted of 32 employees on one floor of a modern four story building in a heavily wooded white collar industrial park. The surroundings were landscaped to give a rural atmosphere, while the Liberty offices were sleek and modern. The office environment and the people who worked there were about as far as you could get from anything you might associate with the Jersey or New York Mob. Jimmy had lunch with three of the senior people, two men and a woman, each of whom oversaw groups managing Liberty's 20-odd businesses. He was surprised to learn that they had MBAs from Harvard, Northwestern, and Penn, and he joked with them about having gone to Rutgers, the "Jewel of the Ivy League". They were clearly driven people, but polite and deferential, and he liked them.

After lunch, he met with Jeanette O'Reilly, the Chief Financial Officer, an MIT Sloan Business School graduate and an alumnus of Goldman-Sachs. She ran through a somewhat detailed overview of the financials of each of the Liberty companies, a diverse group including two software houses, a business service company, an airline seat factory, three herbal medicine companies, a furniture distributor, and about fifteen others. The aggregate value of these companies was in the vicinity of 1.5 billion dollars. Later in the afternoon, he met with Paul Kispert, who managed Liberty's more liquid investments. Paul gave him the rundown on the approximately $200 million held in stocks and bonds and funds of various sorts.

Finally he met with Drew Carrier, who with his administrative assistant comprised the HR Department. They talked about the benefits available for employees at various levels of the company and where Liberty stood as a desirable employer relative to similar companies. When their discussion was finished, Jimmy was deposited with Melanie Pellett, whose office door identified her as "Executive Secretary". Her office opened into another office with a closed door marked "Chief Executive Officer". This finally gave Jimmy the entrée to ask what he had been wondering about all day. "I haven't asked anyone this before, but who is or was the CEO here at Liberty?"

"As strange as it may seem for a firm this big, we don't really have one. Mr. Gentilella is Chairman of the Board, and they meet four times per year for two days, during which all the companies and investments are reviewed. The people who you met here today all work quite independently. Occasionally, Mr. Gentilella comes in and uses this office, but generally it's up to me to assess when he should be sent documents to review or sign. I set up phone conferences whenever one of the senior people here think he should be consulted."

"Does the firm have an in-house attorney?"

"Oh yes, that's Mr. Whitfield. He's basically Mr. Gentilella's right-hand man, and he has a para and an admin working with him. He handles all the contracts and other legal issues related to oversight of the companies."

"How about a tax accountant? Things here look like they must be very complex."

"Mr. Whitfield oversees our taxes, and uses an outside firm for all accounting. It's a big expense here."

"I bet it is. It seems like you must be a busy person, given the decentralized nature of how things are organized here."

"I certainly am, and I've been telling Mr. Gentilella for the last two years that he really needs to put someone in daily charge of the whole operation."

Jimmy smiled and said, "Well, maybe that should be you."

Ms. Pellet smiled and blushed and said, "No, that's the last thing I want. I'm not a referee by nature, and I don't want the anxiety associated with being responsible for such a big operation. I'm a logistics and execution person."

"Well, knowing yourself and what you want and don't want is one of the most important things in life. At least that's how I see it. I have to say though that I sure get the sense that you're critical around here."

"Well that's nice of you to say. I agree with you on the know-thyself thing. So, Mr. Delvecchio, my last responsibility related to your visit today is to tell you that Mr. Gentilella would like you to call him at four o'clock to discuss your visit." She handed him a piece of paper with a phone number on it. "You can sit in the inner office to make your call. It's 3:40 now and I'll be here till 5:00, so if there's anything you need before you leave, just let me know. I'll be out here."

Jimmy thanked her and walked into the CEO office, which looked like it had been put together for a Hollywood movie – dark wood cabinets, beautiful rug and paintings, the works. Ms. Pellett closed the door behind him. He sat at the desk and at 4 PM called Gentilella.

"Well Jimmy, what's your impression?"

"My impression is that I'm impressed. The people here are great - very smart and apparently very collaborative. I had no idea you had all these businesses. I really just got a flavor for things today; I can't really express any opinion about any particular business."

"Well Jimmy, the reality is that the business is Liberty Holdings itself. The component businesses have to take care of themselves. We watch the balance sheets and step in when there's a problem. Aside from that, each business has its own CEO who provides the goals for that business and is responsible for reaching those goals."

"I can see that it would be difficult to micromanage so many businesses. I have a question that I hope you won't think inappropriate."

"Any question is fine, Jimmy."

"Who owns Liberty Holdings?"

"Basically, the Gentilella family owns it. It's not owned by one of the underworld *famiglie* if that's what you're wondering about. And it's not owned by a consortium or anything like that."

"So who calls the shots here? The place seems leaderless, although it seems like everybody knows what to do."

"That's the problem I have to fix, Jimmy. On paper, Liberty is run by a Board, but in reality I'm in charge. It's way too much for me to do a good job, I have too much else to worry about. If I didn't have Melanie Pellett there, I probably couldn't make it work. She's worth her weight in gold."

"I could tell that in the brief time I've been here."

"So Jimmy, will you help me out and take over as CEO?"

"I have to ask why you're not looking at a more seasoned senior business person."

"Jimmy, you are a seasoned senior business person. For a job like this, I need a person with smarts and common sense who can deal with people, someone who has some finesse and perspective. I've decided that you fit the bill. Are you on board?"

Without hesitation Jimmy said, "OK, I'm on board. This'll be very stimulating, lots of interesting stuff to learn, and you've already put together a team that seems to be humming. I'm in."

"Good, Jimmy. You won't regret this. I'll talk to our attorney Bob Whitfield about putting together an offer package. I know you haven't asked about money and I haven't thought too much about it. How about $500K and maybe some stock as a bonus at the end of each year if things are going well? And we'll pay for an apartment in Stamford and expenses. Does that sound OK? I know you're already wealthy so I don't know what'll motivate you to keep the job."

"Mr. Gentilella, don't worry about it. $500K is fine, and I can work the stock thing out with Mr. Whitfield and then see what you say. I'm anticipating really enjoying this challenge, and hope that all these smart MBAs will accept me being in charge."

"Don't worry about that either. You're gonna be the adult in the room, and they'll welcome having someone there steering the ship. So start next week?"

"OK, I start next week."

After they hung up, Jimmy sat for a few minutes almost paralyzed by the decision he had just made. He wondered *What makes Gentilella think I have the depth to run this complicated thing?* And then he wondered *How the hell did he get all this money? Alfonso Gentilella must be one smart guy, and maybe one ruthless guy. I guess you have to be smart and ruthless to get where he's gotten.*

Chapter 11

NATURAL ENOUGH FOR YA? #4

from the desk of Frank Serono, Ph.D

<u>A Plant or Herb Must Be Better Than a Drug, Right?</u>

In previous blog contributions, I have focused on unsupported medical claims, and on bogus credentials of "doctors" who have "formulated amazing natural supernutraceuticals". Today I would like to address the issue of ingesting plants or herbs for their therapeutic effect, instead of a similarly-acting FDA-approved drug. Many drugs are chemical modifications of bioactive chemicals found in nature, and proponents of alternative medicine often proffer the opinion that it is better and safer to obtain these therapeutic benefits by taking the bioactive compound in its natural state, along with all the other materials found in the original plant or herb in which it is found. I am not aware of any evidence in support of this, and today I report on a case where this is definitely untrue.

Dr. Evgenyi Bobrov of Queens College of Medicine was researching the ability of chemicals from plants to precipitate cholesterol, thus making dietary cholesterol unavailable for absorption from the GI tract, in the hope of lowering blood cholesterol levels. It has been known for many years that plant compounds called saponins have the property of precipitating cholesterol in test tubes and, in fact, some saponins have been used for over 50 years in this way in a method for the purification of cholesterol. Dr. Bobrov discovered that a saponin from alfalfa sprouts is particularly effective at precipitating cholesterol, and that the purified saponin, also called a steroid glycoside, lowered the serum cholesterol concentration in animals who were dosed with this material. A pure chemically-synthesized version of this glycoside is currently being tested by a large pharmaceutical company for its ability to lower cholesterol in humans, and for potential toxicity, using standard approaches approved by the FDA.

Something else very interesting was learned along the way in the early development of this alfalfa sprout glycoside saponin. Early on, before this saponin was identified and isolated by a chemist collaborator, Dr. Bobrov explored the idea of studying and developing a "natural" cholesterol-lowering therapy utilizing alfalfa sprouts themselves. In the spirit of pioneering 19th and early 20th century physician researchers, Dr. Bobrov experimented on himself. For months, he ate about four ounces of dried alfalfa sprouts daily, equivalent to about two pounds of undried sprouts.

His cholesterol level went down, but he got very sick with an unusual serious autoimmune disease similar to lupus. It turns out that alfalfa sprouts contain an unusual amino acid called L-canavanine. It turns out that Dr. Bobrov's body used L-canavanine in the synthesis of bodily proteins (which are long polymeric chains of amino acids) instead of the usual chemically-similar amino acid arginine. His immune system recognized the non-native canavanine-containing proteins as "foreign" and attacked them, resulting in lupus-like autoimmune symptoms. Luckily for him, when he ceased eating large amounts of dried sprouts, his symptoms ameliorated.

Dr. Bobrov could have marketed a formulation of ground dried alfalfa sprouts for cholesterol lowering without doing a single efficacy or toxicity study, and people would have been harmed. As I have argued in the past, it is time for the US Congress to legislate that the FDA have oversight over "natural" herbal products in the same way that the FDA protects the American public with its oversight of therapeutic drugs.

ONE YEAR LATER

Chapter 12

Jimmy was just putting his breakfast dish and coffee cup in the sink when the phone rang.

"Hi Jimmy, it's Carmine."

"*Zio* Carmine, hello! We haven't talked in a while. How is Z'Emerlinda?"

"*Mezze mezze.* That's actually what I want to talk to you about."

"Is she OK?"

"Yeah, but I want to talk to you about her health, and she's home, so I don't want to talk on the phone. You think you could meet me today by the lake in the park like we did before?"

"Sure. I'm in Jersey today, going in to Delvono to see what's going on. My schedule is open for you, so you name the time. You want to have lunch?"

"No, just sit in the park. How about ten o'clock at the park in Lambertville?"

"That's way over by Pennsylvania. Can't we meet closer?"

"No, let's do that same park in Lambertville. And park in the west lot, OK?"

That's strange, Jimmy thought. "OK. Whatever you say, *Zio.* I'll be there at ten. Give Z'Emerlinda a kiss for me."

Jimmy thought *All this old world mob secrecy is almost comical. I'm obviously not going to meet with Zio Carmine. I'm almost certainly meeting with Gentilella, but who knows? I can call Gentilella anytime I want, so obviously he wants to talk about something that he doesn't want overheard.*

At about 8:45, Jimmy powered down his cellphone and drove to the park in Lambertville. At a couple of minutes before ten, he walked down the wooded path to the lake, and saw a man sitting on the bench where his Uncle Carmine was supposedly meeting him. There was a boom box underneath the bench playing an AM radio talk show relatively loudly. As he got closer he recognized the man on the bench.

"Mr. Gentilella, this is a surprise! Hello."

"Hello, Jimmy. You know I want you to call me Funzi."

"Yeah, I know. I just have this tendency to naturally show respect. I don't know where I got it from."

They both laughed.

"Please. Sit down, Jimmy."

"OK." Referring to the radio, Jimmy said, "You a Rush Limbaugh fan?"

"Not really, but I like to hear both sides. Today I have the radio to just make a little noise while we have a conversation. Are you wearing a wire, Jimmy?"

"No, I'm not. With all due respect, are you wearing a wire?"

Gentilella smiled. "No, I'm not. Never have, never will. You know, except for Board meetings I haven't talked to you in person since we met over a year ago right in this spot with your Uncle Carmine. How is he?"

"He's good, he's good. When he asked me to meet him here today, I suspected I might be meeting you. It's good to see you after mostly interacting on the phone for a year."

Gentilella smiled. "Your uncle's a good man. Sensible, not a hot head like a lot of others. I've always liked him and of course trusted him."

Jimmy gathered his courage. "So what's on the agenda today? How can I help you?"

"We can get to that in a few minutes. First, how are things going in Stamford? I hear good things about you."

"Well, that's nice. Thanks. Things are going well. I think I have a good handle on the breadth of the holdings we have, and I think we have them under good control. A couple of the software businesses are struggling, but I think we know what to do. It's a lot to oversee. I'll tell you one thing though, I wonder about all these MBAs from Harvard and Yale and Northwestern – I wonder what they think of me being their boss."

"I'm sure you and they have mutual respect. So Jimmy, when we meet like this I want complete openness from you. The only way I can make good decisions is if everyone tells me the truth. Don't ever cover up problems. Unresolved problems are not a sign of weakness. Hidden problems are a sign of weakness. Understood?"

"Understood."

"So Jimmy, I asked to meet you in person today so we can have an open talk about some sensitive subjects. For all normal Liberty Holdings business you can still just phone me."

"OK. However you want to communicate is fine with me."

"So Jimmy, are there any problems with keeping a wall between Liberty and the old dogs down in New York? I worry about that."

"Yes and no. You know, the newer businesses – computers, financial services, the airplane seat plant – those are all good. The problem is with the older businesses like the bars in the city and the laundry services, things like that. You know, when I signed on, I didn't realize that these businesses were also included, and they're a whole other kettle of fish. The older guys in these shops are still trying to hold onto the old style. I'm telling you what you already know of course, but these old habits die hard. The old way was that you took over a business by getting the owner into loan trouble, and then you used it as a way to launder money from other activities. But, you know, these guys also took advantage and robbed some of these businesses blind, maybe without the approval of the central office in New York, but then again maybe it was permitted to keep the footsoldiers happy. We've been consolidating some of these businesses into larger ones, so they can be flipped into legit businesses and be kept or sold. Unfortunately, when our auditors go in, they find all sorts of crap. And then somebody shows up and tells the auditors to take a hike. And they don't tell them in what I would call a professional way. This is a big problem."

"I'm glad we got together today. I know it's asking a lot, but I'd like you to act like you have two separate jobs. One is cleaning up and consolidating the old businesses and the other is overseeing the legit Liberty Holdings businesses. Let's make sure there's no misunderstanding here. I want a cement wall ten feet thick between Liberty Holdings in Stamford and the old world in New York and elsewhere. You're gonna have to figure out how to do that and I don't want you involved in any way with pushing these old and not-so-old crude guys out of the old businesses or negotiating with them. I can probably figure out ways of doing that, and I'll probably have to lay down the law with these people. I realize this is messy, so let's talk about this a little, and come up with a way of dealing with it."

Jimmy said, "You know, it's complicated because in the case of a bar for example it's not necessarily the formal owner who's the problem. It could be the employees who are part of a crew that's shaking him down. Actually, it's a given that our guys have filled these businesses with friends and relatives, so it's really inbred. The private carting, the bars, the restaurants, the commercial laundries, it's all the same. And I don't know if you've considered this, but when we start to run these businesses in a legit way, the new Russians and South Americans will just start to put the arm on them and shake them down the way we used to. And it's not just in New York. It's out on the Island, in Jersey, probably Pennsylvania and up in Providence too."

"Well, you know what Jimmy? It's a new day. We're done with all that crap. We can't fix everything everywhere. We just deal with our own family's holdings. These small businesses will always be vulnerable to shakedowns and maybe we should just get out of all of them."

"Well how do I get some help? The fact is we're not exactly trying to get out of them yet. We're consolidating and cleaning them up."

"It's true that I didn't think this all the way through, but we're both learning here. Maybe we should just sell them all at fifty cents on the dollar. We've already made a lot of money from them."

"Well, obviously I don't have the big picture, and to be honest I may not want to have the big picture. But common sense says that a clean break is a clean break. Instead of trying to consolidate all the small shops, maybe we just sell them off one by one to whoever wants them, using lawyers and doing it clean."

"Yeah, well Jimmy, I've thought about that, and some of our own guys will want to buy them. They're all relatives and relatives of wives' relatives, and they'll run the businesses the same and they'll want muscle to solve problems. And they'll want our organization to front them the money to buy them. We end up in essentially the same place."

Jimmy hesitated, then spoke. "I have trouble getting myself to call you Funzi, but I will. Funzi, the question here is when you say we're getting out of these businesses, who are you talking about? If it's just you and a few senior guys, then we can do this. If it's everybody's extended family, it's a mess. And to be frank, I'm a little confused about who owns what. What belongs to *La Famiglia* and what belongs to the Gentilella family? And who am I really working for here?"

"It's very simple. The old businesses are owned by *La Famiglia*. The legit businesses are owned by me. You work for me and unfortunately for the time being it's my job to deal with the old businesses so I'm asking your help. I also want to say something a little personal here. I have a son who ended up in the business, a daughter who married someone in the business, and two sons who have legit jobs and never got involved. My grandchildren are all in college or headed for college someday. The story is the same for my grand-nieces and grand-nephews. When you and I are finished with this work no Gentilella will be in the old businesses, thank God."

"I don't presume to be your *consigliere*, but you have to figure out how to make sure they're not dragged back in. Where are your brothers and cousins on all this?"

"Same place as me, mostly."

"With all due respect, you can call a sit down with the other families and tell them that the old businesses are for sale and they have first dibs, or you can just place ads in the newspapers or wherever and sell to the highest bidders. Greeks, Russians, Chinese, Irish, WASPs, whoever."

"I have to be practical here. There are still people around who operate in the old ways, and they'll be unhappy if, for example, I sell our carting businesses to the Chinese. There may be a bullet in it for me, or worse a kidnapping of someone in my family. And it's even more complicated. Each business, each bar, each carting company, each laundry has a different owner, as you know. The money came from us, but each business has a different owner or it's a family or whatever. A mess."

"Funzi, do you owe anybody any money? Are these businesses heavily leveraged?"

"I don't think I should get into that with you. But the basic situation is that I don't personally owe anybody money, and the same is true for my brothers and my children. When you talk about the individual businesses, then it's complicated."

"Are you rich? Could your grandchildren and your brothers' and sister's grandchildren live without working for the rest of their lives? I'm not saying they should. I'm just trying to get a sense of your financial position without directly asking how much you have."

"We're as wealthy as the big Jewish New York real estate families. Maybe as rich as the Kennedys in the 40s. A lot is in assets, the businesses, but the cash and stocks alone are enough for generations as long as people don't go crazy with it. And you know all about the legit businesses that are completely clean."

"So here's an idea. Why don't you just give all the old businesses to the people who run them? Or maybe set it up so the employees get them?"

"Jimmy, think for a second. Many of these businesses are not formally mine to give. They have individual owners."

"Then what is it that you really own here?"

"*La Famiglia* fronted the money to start or buy these old businesses, for the most part without any written contracts. Sometimes we bought them in ways that were not very nice. Old times. We take money out of these businesses on a regular or irregular basis. Call it juice, call it dividends, call it profits, call it whatever you want. But it's all informal; nothing really on paper. Enforced by muscle. I'm now telling you more than I intended to, but you've been around, you know what goes on."

"With all due respect, you have a lot of your personal pride and identity invested here. You like being in charge of all this stuff. Do you really want out?"

"Jimmy, I'm 76 years old. My parents brought me here as a baby. I have grandchildren. It's time for the Gentilellas to be respected Americans. Not respected hoods."

"If you mean what you say, then I think it's pretty straightforward, and it's gonna cost you and *La Famiglia* a lot of lost money, whoever or whatever *La Famiglia* really is. Just go to each business owner, and tell him that the unwritten covenant is torn up. Nobody owes anybody anything going forward. In cases where you're a formal part owner, I can get our business people to figure out how to transfer your ownership to the other owners. Does that make any sense as a strategy?"

"Jimmy, you're very helpful to me. I'm afraid you're right. I have to let go of the greed; I have enough money."

"This isn't my area, but I want to ask about something else. You have a lot of muscle guys who enforce these so-called covenants and help the business owners, let's say, convince their customers to use their services. What about all those guys? Could you give them cash and send them on their way?"

"You're right. This is not your area, and shouldn't be. But I think it'll be relatively easy. I can give each a little bonus, but the reality is I don't use them much to enforce my covenants with the formal business owners. The existence of the muscle guys is enough enforcement without them having to do anything. We have them more to deal with customers of the businesses." He shrugged. "The old ways. The business owners will have to run their businesses however they decide to run them. If they employ the muscle guys, so be it. They would be better off if they gave up the old ways, but I guess that wouldn't be my problem anymore."

"You could give them the businesses, and also give each of them, say, fifty grand to hire consultants to teach them how to run a legit business."

"That's a little naive, Jimmy. They'll take the fifty and spend it on a Mercedes or a few trips to Florida and Vegas."

Jimmy laughed. "Yeah, you got me there. OK. I still have two questions. First, will your brothers and cousins be on board with this?"

"My brothers and I have talked about this till we're blue in the face. They want out. My cousins, look I care about them, but they'll have to figure out their own lives. What's your other question?"

"Who'll be angry about all this?"

"I don't know. I'll have to think about it. That's not your problem."

Gentilella stood up, indicating that the meeting was ending. "This was good. Please look into the small businesses where I'm part owner and set up papers to transfer ownership. No auditors. If I have to sell, sell for a dollar. And don't get any of this mixed up with the Liberty Holdings businesses. Use consultants if you have to. Keep everything separate. Don't worry about cost."

"There may be tax consequences for you or for people you transfer ownership to."

"Render unto Caesar. Again, you've been very helpful to me, Jimmy. You're doing a great job."

"Thank you, Mr. Gentilella. I'm enjoying my work."

"Please give your Uncle Carmine my regards."

"I will, I will."

Funzi Gentilella bent over, turned off the boombox, and picked it up. The two men headed off in opposite directions to different parking lots. Jimmy thought *What a fucking mess.*

Chapter 13

After leaving the park, Jimmy decided to swing over to Lodi to see his old school friend Nick Kares at the Acropolis Diner. If there was anyone on earth who came close to understanding Jimmy, it was Nick. Shared childhood and teenage experiences can only occur once in a lifetime, and Nick and Jimmy had shared them. Nick had worked in his family's diner since he was about seven years old. He bought out his sister Kristina's share about ten years ago, and was the owner and manager, and by dint of his personality, unofficial mayor of Lodi. He was a 53 year old widower, a guy who had life figured out then had to refind his way.

As Jimmy came through the door, Nick spotted him and smiled. "Hey, Jimmy. How are ya?"

"Hey, you still serve coffee here?"

"Yeah, I think we can manage that. You're staying for lunch, right?"

"That's the plan."

"OK, grab a booth in the back. I'll be right there."

It was the tail end of the lunch hour and the place was still crowded, but Jimmy found an open booth in the back of the diner and slid in. Nick joined him carrying two cups of coffee.

Nick said, "It's good to see you. Always good. What's it been, almost a year? How did we let that happen? So how are Gina and the kids?"

"Good, good. You want the short story or the long story?"

"I'm not going anywhere. I live here. The long story is fine if you want to tell me the long story."

"I'll tell you the short story. Gina's really good. Still loves being principal of the elementary school over in Montclair. When we hit it big, she could have quit but she's what they call a grounded person, she knows who she is and what she wants. The kids, they're not kids anymore. Anthony's finishing his Ph.D. in biochemistry up in Boston. The news I guess is he's got a girlfriend who does the same thing. She's really nice, we like her a lot. But Linda's the one with the real news. She just told us she's gonna have a baby. Her husband Will is finishing up his oncology residency and looking for a permanent doctor job, so hopefully they'll be moving back here from Houston. We have our fingers crossed."

"Linda's working as a scientist, right?"

"Yeah, she studied Physics, but she's working as a computer programmer down in Houston."

"Hey, fantastic. Grandpa. You're gonna be a grandpa. Lunch for you is free today."

"OK. Now you. How are the kids?"

"Kids? You mean the Kares grown-ups. Actually nothing really new since I saw you here last year. George still works for American Express and helps out here on the weekends. I'm thinking and hoping he might be reaching the point where he sees the family business as an opportunity and not a trap."

"That seems to happen at about 30 or so, when they come to their senses. More likely if they find themselves in a job they don't have a passion for."

"Yeah, well that's what I'm hoping. I'm not saying I don't want him to have a passion for something. I'm just saying I don't see that with his American Express job. But you never know. Anyway, Nina graduated last year, and finally got a teaching job right here in Lodi at the middle school. She loves it, and she's still living at home with me and George. It makes you feel good when your kid loves what she's doing."

"And how's your sister?"

"Kristina's great. She and Andreus have been really good to George and Nina since their mother died. The kids are close to their cousins. Kristina comes in here for a few hours occasionally and takes over for me so I can have some time off. You gotta take a shower once a week, you know."

They laughed.

"So Nick, how are you doing? It's been a couple of years now."

"I'm getting used to it, I guess. We've talked about this before and it's pretty much the same. I miss Sophia. It's still like there's a ghost in the house. An absence. My Lodi High School sweetheart. A lotta years."

"Any dates?"

"No, I'm not interested in that. Maybe someday. The ladies down at the Greek church are always piling me up with food containers when I leave every Sunday. Hey, what kind of host am I? Whaddya wanna eat?" He laughed.

"How about a heart attack special? A bacon cheeseburger deluxe medium and a refill on the coffee."

Nick went off to put in their orders, and in ten minutes the waitress delivered the food. Jimmy dug in with gusto. "I love this stuff. You try to watch what you eat, but there's nothing like a cheeseburger with bacon and lettuce and tomato, smothered in catsup. And I've always loved the coffee here. Since we were kids."

"So Jimmy, what's up with you? I still don't understand why you left the biotech place you founded with that guy Frank. You loved that job."

"Yeah, well, this is a problem. You know me better than anyone. Probably the job I liked the most was getting the internet pharmacy up and running. That was thrilling. But Delvono, the biotech place, that was really just as good for other reasons, and that's where I'd rather be now."

"So why aren't you there?"

"Same as I told you the last time we met, nothing's changed. I'm like Michael Corleone. 'Just when I thought I was out, they pull me back in.' Whattaya gonna do, huh? It's like the Acropolis Diner and your son George. You can't get away." Jimmy laughed.

"Alright wiseguy, alright." Nick laughed. "So what are you doing out there in Connecticut?"

"You wearin' a wire?"

"No, and I'm not working with the cops. And to my knowledge, the diner isn't bugged. You wearin' a wire?"

"No, Nickie, I'm not wearin' a wire." Jimmy laughed. "Look, you know the score. They needed me, and I stepped up. I'm running the entire legitimate business portfolio for the boss's family. Nothing dirty or even remotely dirty. Computer repair shops, dotcoms, factories that service various industries. We're making all the metal poles and seats for the New York and Boston and D.C. subway systems. We're doing computer programming for a payroll company. We have a software company that makes big programs for expense report tracking and finance and stuff like that for large multinationals. It's about twenty separate businesses, and an investment company that invests in stocks and bonds and real estate."

"You majored in Italian History. How do you know how to do this stuff?"

"You got me there. Some of the people who report to me are ivy league MBAs. They can run rings around me, and a couple of them could actually do my job, but not all of them. I've learned that once you move above a certain level, it all becomes common sense and asking the questions that a smart high school student would ask. And human nature, understanding human nature. You can't get into all the details, too many separate businesses."

"So nothing is dirty. That's hard to believe. I know who your so-called family is."

Jimmy decided not to tell Nick about the aggravating old businesses. "Look, they put me in charge basically because of the old ways. Someone with a *La Famiglia* background has to be on top of the operation, even though it's completely legit. The difference here is that there's no funny stuff with these businesses. No funny books, no coercion, no nothing."

"Jimmy, you know who you're talkin' to. Sooner or later, it'll get ugly. Maybe in a way you can't imagine today."

"You're probably right, but you're the only person on earth I can admit it to. For now, I can put it out of my mind because the work is intense and interesting. But I'm not stupid. There's eventually gonna be people who feel they have a right to get involved, and that means that right now they're trying to figure out how they can personally profit from these legit businesses. Also, I'm sure there are people who think the money my boss used to buy these businesses wasn't really his money. Maybe they're right. For now he has it under control. But when he retires or worse, I don't know what happens. Maybe nothing. It's all legit, but the problem is that there are all these oldtimers and newtimers quietly looking at what we have and thinking how to grab it. Like the Goths and the eastern Roman Empire. And time is on their side."

"Tell them you want out."

"I was out before, and technically I'm still out. I just run a two billion dollar business that has unconventional investors."

"C'mon, there's gotta be a way. Did you have the option of turning down the job in the beginning?"

"I didn't explore that. I suppose if I'd been insistent, I might have been able to stay out. You know how it is. I felt a little flattered, like I was being recognized by my family."

"Some family."

"Yeah, but you know my Uncle Carmine was involved, and I could tell he was proud. He's like my father now. But I also had that twenty years in the business inside me, everything I'd seen. That said you never say no."

"But you were out already."

"Nicky, it's like a Greek Diner. You're never out. You're away for awhile. You're never out."

"OK. I'm no MBA, but I have some common sense. Like you. Why don't you groom some Harvard MBA to take over for you in one to two years. Find a guy with an Italian last name if you have to. Makes it totally legit if the Feds or anybody decide to look at it."

"But the family will still want someone to be watching it."

"So you have a board of directors, like a board for a big family-owned company or a family-funded charity. The board is all legit appropriate people, and there's one family member on the board."

"This isn't a normal family, Nicky. The family member on the board would have to have veto power."

"Sorry then, Jimmy. You're legit business is all bullshit. You can have a mob-guy as chairman of the board, but in a legit business he can be voted out."

"Voted out by the stockholders. And who are the stockholders in this situation?"

"Then just tell them you want out, and that you think the CEO should be a business guy with no ties to the family. You go back to your biotech company, but sit on the board of the Stamford company. Better if they find a different guy to sit on the board, then you'd be totally out. You helped them out when they had a need, and now it's time for you to go back to your other life."

Jimmy sighed. "Your logic is sound with one exception. I don't work with people who play by the same rules as everyone else."

"No Jimmy. I think you're the problem here. Maybe you like your new job. Or maybe you're too afraid of people who really have no effective way of putting the arm on these legit businesses anyway. Screw 'em. If these really are legit businesses, then if somebody tries to strong-arm them, call the cops. That's what it means to be a legit business. If a business is legit, then nobody has any basis for blackmailing and robbing it. You're just not thinking like a really legit businessman."

"It's complicated."

"No, it isn't. It's just complicated in your head. Where's the old Jimmy? When did you become chickenshit?"

"Hey, Nick."

"OK. OK. Look, you know what I'm sayin'. I don't have to repeat it twelve ways to Sunday."

"OK. I got it. I appreciate it. You're my psychologist and business consultant. Let's have another cup of coffee and talk about the Giants and Jets."

"Good. Good. But remember, the food is free but my consulting fee is still $1000 an hour."

"Send me an invoice and I'll have my people cut a check."

The two old friends laughed.

Chapter 14

NATURAL ENOUGH FOR YA? # 16

from the desk of Frank Serono, Ph.D

If It's the Right Food, It Will Cure You! Listen To These Testimonials!

Yesterday, I was driving in my car listening to the radio, and I had the pleasure of hearing a 1 hour medical information show (aka infomercial) in which the guest expert was Dr. Robert Jameson, inventor of the natural superformula "HomeoVerdure". This incredible medical miracle formulation is composed of 26 fruits and vegetables, that's right, 26 fruits and vegetables packed in a small capsule. Dr. Jameson, a chiropractor from Utah, said that he studied the composition of various fruits and vegetables for over ten years, and his scientific research work resulted in the choice of these specific 26 plants and the unique ratios of each what would give optimum health.

He said that over the last 15 years we've heard testimonials about the superfood of the month, lots of hype about acai berries, red beets, and such. He knew that it was nonsense, and that kept him searching for the right combination of real foods, not fad foods, that would change people's lives. As a God-loving man (his description, not mine), he has dedicated himself to improving the lives of his fellow man.

Dr. Jameson spewed the usual mumbo-jumbo about supporting heart health, balancing the body's blood sugars, helping prostate function, contributing to healthy sexual performance, and providing an all around state of wellbeing (whatever that means). He said that HomeoVerdure "cleans the whole cell, nucleus and all". This is just fruits and vegetables, mind you. And by the way, how much fruits and vegetables do you think can fit in two gelatin capsules?

In a special one-day offer, a bottle of 120 capsules was offered for just $10.99 plus shipping and handling. I don't know how much the shipping and handling charge is, but $10.99 didn't sound too bad for a month's supply of anything. Until he expanded on his dose recommenda-tions. If you're in reasonably good health, but find yourself dragging sometimes during the day (like everyone else on earth), he recommends 2 capsules in the morning and 2 at night, covered by the one month supply of 120 capsules. If you have some general medical issue like obesity, he recommends 4 capsules in the morning and 4 at night. If you have a more serious issue like diabetes, he recommends 6 capsules in the morning and 6 at night (now up to 360 capsules needed per month). And if you have a serious problem like cancer, he recommends 12 capsules in the morning and 12 at night. What is the basis for his recommendations? Who knows? There are no clinical trials. Trust him – he's a God-loving man.

I guess that one could take the approach that no harm has been done. After all, people are just eating fruits and vegetables. That's good for everyone, whether healthy or sick. But Dr. Jameson's infomercial proceeded to go down a road I had not seen before. For about ten minutes, we heard brief testimonials from clients who used the product, taken over the phone. Many of the testimonials were from people with working class New York/New Jersey accents, still common with New York area senior citizens. Some examples:

"I started to take the product, and by the third day I was getting up early in the morning full of energy."
"After two weeks on the product, my blood pressure was normal and I was able to stop my blood pressure pills."
"My blood pressure was down after just three days on the pills."
"Thank God. I don't get sick anymore. Nothin."
"After two months on the HomeoVerdure, I went for my teeth cleaning appointment and the hygienist said 'Your teeth are beautiful. I feel funny taking your money because your teeth are perfect.' No tartar, nothing."
"My cholesterol went from 270 to 215 after I started on the HomeoVerdure."
"I have bladder cancer. My numbers are down with the HomeoVerdure. I'm so thankful."

"After starting the HomeoVerdure, I was off all my prescription medications in the first 30 days."
"I have hepatitis C, and my liver enzyme numbers went way down after starting HomeoVerdure. It cleanses the liver. I didn't want to be a guinea pig for doctors and their drugs."
"I had a bad headache, and it went away one minute after taking the capsules."
"My tremors are better."
"All my numbers are dramatically better."
"The HomeoVerdure took care of my asthma and allergies."
"No flu, no colds this year."
"I cut my blood pressure meds in half after starting the HomeoVerdure."
"I threw away my other supplements."
"Two weeks after starting the HomeoVerdure, a hemorrhoid went away."

And on and on, for ten minutes. Pretty ingenious. The makers of HomeoVerdure have made no illegal efficacy claims. They have just provided a space on the radio for clients to make unsupported anecdotal statements. I wish the clients had identified themselves. I'd love to talk to them about this miracle cure for hemorrhoids, hypertension, flu, high cholesterol, diabetes, asthma, allergies, tremors, headaches, bladder cancer, hepatitis C, and tooth decay. I'd love to know what motivated them to make these public, but anonymous, statements.

Chapter 15

Todd Singleton sat in his office at the nutraceutical company Phoebus Herbals, on the 21st floor of a gleaming glass office building in downtown Salt Lake City. His intercom buzzed. "Mr. Singleton, I've got Mr. Ling Li from Malaysia."

"Thanks, Hannah. I'll pick up."

"Hello Ling. Please accept my apology for arranging a late night call. We have a problem, and I want to deal with it at our level to make sure something happens."

"Hello Mr. Todd. This is no problem. The time zones dictate that phone calls with American customers can be at any time, day or night. How can I help you?"

"Ling, I'm calling about our big St. John's Wort order. We've been waiting for over a month, and our supplies here are getting low. We have to formulate and distribute product to our buyers, and if we don't have product, we lose business. We're in the same position with our order for black cohosh root. If you don't fix this fast, we're going to have to go to a different supplier."

"Yes, I understand. There is much demand for the plants, so many businesses now. We are having difficulty getting the leaves and roots. In any case, as usual we can supply whatever you need."

"Yes, well we've been through this sort of problem before, and you know the potential solutions."

"Of course. We can use a different plant for the wort, and add some mild sedative or perhaps Zoloft."

"Please make sure that the plant powder looks the same as St. John's Wort this time. We had a color problem before. And no Zoloft, too expensive and too risky. Maybe use something cheap that will give a sedative effect. A very mild effect. And do the same for the black cohosh root. As long as the patients feel some sort of effect, we keep selling."

"Very good. We know what to do, and we are always here to help you with our 'special sauce' as you like to say. We have found with our other customers that this is the best way because the real herbs do not work very well. Are you sure you do not want us to use the Zoloft or perhaps Prozac or Paxil? The generic drugs are very cheap and we have large supplies."

"Ling, we've been through this with you before. Your synthetic drugs are garbage. You know that. I would rather get caught here with the wrong herb and a little aspirin or something like that. I don't want to get caught with product containing a highly impure batch of the exact drug we say we're replacing with our all-natural product. You may not realize what happened with the diabetes drug you spiked into our pancreas extract. We had to change the name of our company and rotate the senior management and make big political donations. Anyway, you understand what to do. Use your 'special sauce'. No notes from this conversation. The labels say St. John's Wort and Black Cohosh Root, as usual. And make the analytical data look good."

"Certainly, Mr. Todd. We will be careful, and you will be very happy with the material we send."

"And I shouldn't have to say this, Ling, but I will. No lead or pesticides or anything else like that. Clean up the materials. Things are starting to get messy here in the States. If we get caught with the wrong herb here, we're still OK. But poisonous stuff in the product doesn't fly anymore. Too many people out there doing analyses."

"Is the FDA now doing analyses?"

"No, we've got the FDA under control through politics, but some pharmacy professors and the damn drug companies are starting to analyze our stuff. So far we've had no big problems. So Ling, are we good?"

"Mr. Todd, we are good, as you say. It is always a pleasure to work with you."

"Yes, OK, Ling. My best wishes to your brother, and I hope that your family is doing well. Bye-bye."

"Good-bye, Mr. Todd. My best wishes to your family."

Singleton pressed the intercom button. "Hannah, I'm going to be leaving for the Natural Remedies Luncheon in about an hour. Could you please bring my slides in on a thumb-drive? I have to go over them quickly, and I want some time if I have to make changes. Thanks." Singleton was President of the Natural Remedies Manufacturers of America, and a big man in Salt Lake.

Chapter 16

Frank picked up the ringing phone at Delvono, and his assistant Marge said, "There's a Mr. Harbon on line two, who says he's an attorney for a medical professional organization. Do you want to take it?"

"Sure, thanks." Frank pushed the line two button. "Hello this is Frank Serono."

"Hello Dr. Serono, this is John Harbon. I'm an attorney at Burnham and Jones in Salt Lake City, and we represent a non-profit professional organization call the Natural Remedies Manufacturers of America, or NRMA. Do you have a few minutes to talk?"

"Sure, I can talk, but I'd appreciate it if we can get to the meat of the issue quickly."

"Not a problem. Dr. Serono, are you familiar with the NRMA?"

"No, I'm not."

"Well, the NRMA is the public voice of a large proportion of the alternative medicine establishment in the U.S. The organization runs conferences and provides information for patients who are looking for alternatives to Big Medicine and

Big Pharma. The NRMA is primarily funded by companies that provide alternative treatments for medical conditions."

"By alternative treatments, do you mean untested ineffective impure non-FDA-approved herbal remedies?"

"Herbal remedies, yes, but of course I wouldn't put it the way you just did. In addition to lots of other things, including mixtures of vitamins and nutrients formulated to help with various ailments."

"I'm really interested in these sorts of products. Since you're a lawyer who's involved in this industry, maybe you can explain to me how these products can make drug claims without running any trials in humans to demonstrate efficacy."

"Well, you probably know that our members never make drug claims, they don't claim to cure disease."

For no particular reason, Frank was in an argumentative mood. "Hey, you yourself just made a drug claim a few seconds ago when you said 'alternative treatments for medical conditions'. Cut the crap. Your clients say things like 'may help control cholesterol' or 'helps support vascular health' on the label, but when they get on the radio or on TV they say things like 'lowers your cholesterol' or 'lowers blood pressure' or 'controls diabetes'. And of course, it's untrue."

"With all due respect, Dr. Serono, you don't know that it's untrue; you haven't tested these products."

"And neither has anyone else."

Harbon calmly continued. "Dr. Serono, we don't need to have a debate here. I'm sure both you and I are well versed in all the arguments. The reason I'm calling is that many of the members of the NRMA are quite worked up over statements you've been making in your blog, and I've been asked to speak with you about tempering some of this stuff. I know everybody tends to exaggerate to make points, just like you said about our representatives on radio shows. And you tend to exaggerate to make your points. Members of our organization are worried that your blog will have a negative effect on their businesses, and worse, encourage the government to interfere in the right of Americans to choose whatever treatment they want for their medical problems."

"I'm in favor of Americans having a right to choose their medical treatments, but you talk out of both sides of your mouth. Your public position is that your clients are not selling medical treatments. They're selling botanical supplements. Of course everyone else calls them herbal medicines, which sounds a lot like medical treatments to me. I just think it's the place of the FDA to inform patients and doctors about which treatments have been shown to be efficacious, and in a realistic way to the degree possible, what proportion of patients will be improved by a treatment. And I think it should be the responsibility of the FDA to prevent unproven treatments from being misrepresented as efficacious. And to be complete, I think the FDA should demand data demonstrating lack of toxicity."

"Dr. Serono, you know as well as I that patients are individuals with different makeups, and that some so-called unproven treatments may work in some patients."

"That's your escape hatch, I know. Somewhere out there your capsules of spinach powder and eye of newt may cure someone's cancer. It's bullshit and you know it. This is all about lost opportunity cost for the patient. While a patient is taking a so-called natural remedy that's certain to fail, he isn't taking a drug that has a 50% chance of curing him or lengthening his life."

"OK, Dr. Serono, we're not going to get anywhere in a debate today. Here is what I have to say. The client companies in the organization I represent have a significant potential financial loss resulting from your blogging activities. In fact, some of them already claim to have a demonstrable real loss. What I want to know is what you have to gain in all this. You're a successful man. I freely admit that you've personally made incredible strides in anti-cancer medicine, and I have to say I personally really admire you for this and wish you continued success. But I don't understand why you're going after my clients. What do you gain?"

"Why do I have to tell you why I'm doing what I'm doing? Who are you to ask me?"

"Dr. Serono, my clients have asked me to engage you in a discussion to try to find common ground. For example, perhaps you could sit on a discussion panel at one of our scientific conferences. We'd like you to see our side. We may not agree, but we could move toward a situation where we coexist and try to move forward both traditional and alternative medical approaches. If I could understand what you really want, I could try to engage in some creative solutions for how to get you some of what you want while not hurting the business of my clients. If you were some low-paid college professor, maybe some grant money for your research would help, but I assume that you're a well-off man. What do you think of this discussion? What do you want, and how can I help you get it?"

"First of all, you just said 'alternative medical approaches'. You didn't say 'botanical supplements'. What I want is very simple. I want the FDA and the Justice Department to crack down on your clients' unsupported and illegal medical claims. Maybe that requires legislation from Congress. Whatever it takes. I want the FDA to record every radio infomercial that your clients put out there, and every time your clients step over the line and make an untested drug claim, I want the FDA to come down hard. I want the FDA to test the contents and purity of the concoctions your clients sell. I want the presidents of your companies arrested for fraud if warranted. I want patients who have been harmed by taking your clients' supplements instead of known effective drugs to sue your clients until they run out of money."

"You want my clients out of business."

"No, I want them to play fair. If they pay for large Phase III Clinical Studies of the efficacy of their concoctions and show that they really work, then all is well. And I want them to run toxicology studies to demonstrate safety. And I want them to follow the same rules for purity as drug manufacturers do. And if they do this, I wish your clients success."

"You want my clients out of business. They can't afford to do those studies."

"Why not? Look, here's an analogy. Some guy drives without insurance, and says he shouldn't have to pay for insurance because it's too expensive for him. So the cops and courts should say 'We understand, go ahead'? How's that different from what your clients are doing? Your clients want to make money without spending money and, to be blunt, don't give a shit about the health of their customers."

"Dr. Serono, do you have a deathwish? I mean that figuratively, of course. Do you realize that the supplement and nutraceutical industry is gigantic, with enormous resources? Do you know how many politicians are on our side, Democrat and Republican? Do you realize the media empire we have at our disposal? You can't be that naive. My clients will bury you if you decide not to be reasonable. Please cooperate. Nobody on our side wants to go to the next step."

"You can't hurt me. How can you hurt me?"

"You can become so publicly controversial that no academic medical center will want to run clinical trials for your company, out of fear of being dragged into a public circus. I want to be clear. I'll be blunt and honest. You know very well why my clients have been so successful in avoiding FDA oversight. They've poured enormous amounts of money into political campaigns at all levels. They basically own Utah. Congress won't touch legislation for oversight of supplements with a ten foot pole. And everybody from far left yoga nuts to right-wing survivalists wants freedom to choose their medicines. You can't win. You'll be crushed like a bug, and for what? For what, Dr. Serono? Please, come to your senses."

"Look I don't want to be unreasonable, I just want to be straightforward. I don't think there's common ground here. I'm planning to continue my blogging on this subject. Maybe you'll find that I become relatively ineffective at some point, and you'll stop worrying about me."

"We're worried about a groundswell."

"Well, as I said, I don't think we're going to find common ground."

Harbon regained his lawyerly calm. "OK, then. Please think about what I've said, and please call if you want to discuss this further. If you don't mind, I'd like to give you another call in about a week to see if you've come up with any creative idea for working with us and we'll try to do the same. Thanks for talking with me. Have a good afternoon."

"You too. Bye."

Frank wondered what that was all about. Was it a threat? It sure sounded like a threat. He had to admit that it felt good. His blogging was actually having an effect, although he could not be sure what effect. Somebody in the nutraceutical con-game was feeling some pressure from somewhere. Of course, it was also possible that he had just pissed off one influential businessman, and there really was no significant effect of his efforts. He wondered how to move his effort forward. He understood full well that the FDA doesn't make the rules, it only enforces them. He had to find a mechanism to force the politicians' hands to write new laws governing supplements and herbal remedies. The only thing that really forces politicians' hands, other than money, is some well-publicized tragedy. Frank thought *Maybe I should look for one.*

Chapter 17

After his lunch with Nick Kares, Jimmy pulled out of the Acropolis parking lot and headed to Delvono to say hi to everyone and see how things were going. His job in Connecticut was a logistical pain in the neck. As far as he was concerned, his home was in Verona with Gina, but he generally stayed at his apartment in Stamford during the week, driving home to New Jersey Friday afternoon and heading back to Connecticut on Monday morning after rush hour. It was starting to get to him. He tried occasionally to come home for a night in the middle of the week, but the traffic was awful. The George Washington Bridge was a nightmare. He made a mental note to look into getting a limo and driver.

On top of that, he had loved his work at Delvono, and hated giving it up. Running a drug discovery company was satisfying; he felt like he was providing something positive for the world. The bigger thing though was the personal interactions, and the fact that Delvono employed lots of Jerseyites, Jimmy's people. He was contributing to the wellbeing of his neighbors, providing jobs with benefits. The job at Liberty Holdings in Connecticut was becoming more and more aggravating. The people at Liberty were great, but the work had recently primarily defaulted to arguing with people at the older businesses who did not want to cooperate.

Jimmy walked into Delvono, and kissed the receptionist Josie on the cheek.

"Jimmy! To what do we owe this surprise?"

"I was in the neighborhood, and wanted to make sure that people were still showing up for work here. Especially you. With all your money, why do you work?"

"With all your money, why do you work?"

"You got me there. Is Doctor Frank in? Hey, I don't need a visitor pass, do I?"

"Nope, no visitor pass needed for you. Dr. Serono is in his office."

Jimmy stuck his head through the half-open doorway and knocked. "Is the doctor in?"

"Hey, Jimmy, you're a sight for sore eyes. Your daily phone calls have stopped, and I really miss you here. Come back, please come back."

"Believe me, I'd rather be here. With the Board running around in circles on replacing me, you've been stuck overseeing everything. How's it going?"

"Well, it's taking some of my attention away from the research side, which isn't a good thing. My relatives are impressed that I'm now President of a company, for what that's worth, but I really mean it Jimmy, we need you here. So to what do I owe the pleasure of your visit today?"

"Hey, I still like to check up on things, even though I'm technically not involved in decision-making here for the time being."

"For the time being? You have some kind of announcement to make?"

"No, no. But the reality is I'm looking to get out of my job in Stamford. I always thought of it as a temporary thing. People asked for help and I helped. I think I've got a lot of messes cleaned up."

"You want to come back here? Fantastic. Even though you've been out for almost two years, your spirit is still walking the halls. It'd be great."

"I'm working on it. So how's the Tay-Sach's stuff coming?"

"It's early days, but I think it's gonna be amenable to traditional drug treatment, prenatal of course. We've got inhibitors of a couple of logical enzyme targets, and we're just starting the animal work. I'm optimistic. I know you're hot on us doing this, and we've talked about it endlessly, but I have to repeat my two main objections, or maybe you can call them concerns. First, it'll make zero money."

"That's fine, you know I don't care."

"Second, you'll allow a baby to be born who'll pass the mutant gene to his or her baby some day. You're weakening the population, instead of letting the mutant gene die out through childhood death."

"Better to light one candle than to curse the darkness. I understand, and I guess I just assume that someone later in the 21st century will solve that problem. We're here, now, and we can fix the heartache of parents, and maybe bring a productive individual into the world."

"Who would ever have taken you to be such a softie?"

"I'm not a softie. I know who I am and what I think is important. As the psychobabble people say, I'm a grounded person." He laughed.

"OK. We're continuing the project as if it's the most important thing in the world. As you suggested, I had some of the scientists talk to some Tay-Sach's parents to get the scientists emotionally involved. It worked. And since you're in here asking for high level reports, I have to tell you that the MRSA project is going gangbusters. That young lady Christine was a fantastic hire, she's gonna solve it. And that'll make real money and help lots of people."

"Yeah, until the next drug-resistant bug appears. Just like the Tay-Sachs problem. Solve one problem, you've permitted the next to occur. But you fight the battle in front of you. That's why we're here. You help people who are in need now."

"We need you back, Jimmy."

"I'll be back, like Aaahnold! So Frank, I didn't just drop in to shoot the breeze, I have something specific I want to talk to you about."

"Shoot. Figuratively, of course."

"I got a couple of calls about your blogging. You've got a lot of people spooked, and the herb people are afraid of government hearings. They've managed to avoid the FDA, and that's the way they want to keep it."

"You know the story, Jimmy. They're a bunch of con-men. If people aren't hurt directly by their garbage products, they're hurt because they're not seeking competent medical treatment."

"I know, I know. But my concern is that they're gonna hurt Delvono. We have a good thing going here, and they know it. I know you're getting a kick out of being a widely followed muckraker, and I agree with your point of view, but you've gotta stop."

"Why? What can they really do to us? Did you get a call from some lawyer from Utah?"

"Yeah, I got a call from him. I wouldn't dismiss him. He made some threats about making you look like a buffoon, and he rattled off a variety of examples of deaths caused by prescription drugs. They're preparing their battle against you."

"Bring it on."

"I don't think you understand who you're dealing with. These people in Utah make the modern Mob look like small change. They've got everyone in their pocket, and they look on the surface like squeaky clean country club businessmen who go to church and care about the little guy. Look, I'm drifting here. They're gonna silence you by going after Delvono, screwing up our ability to get trials done at certain medical centers, whatever they can think of. And these are creative people with connections. They will viciously protect their property. They'll make you look like a nut."

"Jimmy, you know I'm right."

"Look, kid, you've got to decide. Are you a cop, or are you a drug discoverer? They're both admirable professions. If you want to be a cop, join an organization with clout that can back you up. Join the FDA. Fine with me. Maybe you could get away with this stuff if you were an academic, just maybe. But you can't be fuckin' Charles Bronson in 'Deathwish'. You'll end up dead or in hiding. Or more likely you'll fuck up what we've built here. You've got important work to do. You're a well-known respected scientist with years of great work in front of you. Wise up."

"OK, Jimmy. Duly noted. Can we change the topic now?"

"No, I have something very direct to say. You're a critical employee at Delvono, our resident smart guy. We need you to focus on understanding and curing disease, and we don't need you undermining our efforts. You're an employee and Delvono pays you lots of money. This is your job. Do it."

"Jimmy, continuing to argue isn't gonna be productive."

"I thought I understood you, but I don't. You're a fucking bug in search of a windshield. OK, I've said my piece. I've gotta get going."

"Have a good day."

"You too."

As Jimmy walked out to his car, he could feel his elevated blood pressure. What he didn't tell Frank was that Liberty Holdings, the company he was CEO of, had significant investments in supplement companies in Utah. Jimmy was surprised to learn the depth of it and the internecine connections. Their largest holding in Utah was a company called "BotaniBalance", which primarily sold vegetable powders in bottles and capsules. These were mixtures of desiccated and milled vegetables in various combinations that were said, without data of course, to benefit various human ailments from obesity to forgetfulness to erectile dysfunction. With the recent legalization of marijuana in Colorado, BotaniBalance had opened a factory there, and had commenced manufacture of a variety of creative powdered marijuana-based products for use in everything from baking to spiked coffees. Jimmy had also learned that earlier BotaniBalance products aimed at relief from pain, anxiety, and depression had already taken advantage of the natural powers of marijuana, and had done so surreptitiously for at least five years. They could not afford to have the government nosing around in their records. Liberty Holdings also owned two other herbal remedy companies in Utah, both much less creative than BotaniBalance, but Jimmy could only wonder what could be uncovered. One of them was "Phoebus Herbals", the company headed by Todd Singleton, which unbeknownst to Jimmy used Malaysian suppliers he knew from a past lifetime that he wanted to forget. The other was called "Cog Nutritionals". Jimmy had recently received phone calls about Frank from the CEOs of all three, and what was said was not pretty.

Chapter 18

NATURAL ENOUGH FOR YA? #18

from the desk of Frank Serono, Ph.D

Is What You See What You Get?

When a pharmaceutical company submits a New Drug Application (NDA) to the FDA, it must provide reams of data on clinical testing for efficacy, often in thousands of patients, in addition to a variety of short-term and long-term toxicology studies in multiple species. While the average layperson may not know much about these requirements, most know to some degree that such requirements exist. Less well-known is the section of an NDA called "Chemistry, Manufacturing, and Controls" or the "CMC Section". It contains detailed information about the synthesis and purity of the drug, the impurities present, the ingredients added to the formulation (e.g. the tablet) and their sources and purity, and stability studies that demonstrate the chemical degradation of the drug over time under various conditions of storage. These stability studies are the basis for the proposed shelf-life and expiry date for the product, and assure that the product will not degrade significantly under real-world conditions such as shipping, pharmacy storage, and storage in a patient's humid bathroom for months. An important component of the CMC Section is a detailed description of the laboratory methods used to measure the purity of the product and the levels of degradation products.

What CMC-type studies must be submitted to FDA for an herbal product? None. The manufacturer is on the honor system. So how honorable are these manufacturers?

Earlier this year, in the journal Medical Biotechnology, Professor Albert Sanford and colleagues at three medical schools and two chemistry departments reported on the use of a technique called DNA Fingerprinting to identify the herbs in a variety of herbal products. These researchers studied 36 bottles of herbal supplements sold by 10 companies, having purchased these in health food stores, pharmacies, and supermarkets. One-third of the supplements tested contained none of the "therapeutic" herb purported to be the active ingredient of the supplement. That's right, none. For example, of three bottles of St. John's Wort, which may be effective in mild depression in some individuals (but never proven in prescription drug-type FDA-approved trials), one bottle contained St. John's Wort. Of the other two, one appeared to contain rice flour and some other fillers, and one contained Alexandrian senna, a plant material known to have laxative effects. Bottles of echinacea supplements were found to contain bitter weed, *Parthenium hystorophorus*, instead. One bottle of another herbal supplement that contained the stated therapeutic herb also contained black walnut (not listed on label), a potential issue for patients with nut allergies.

Of course, two thirds of the products tested contained the herb that was stated to be the main active ingredient of the product. Do you know how to pick those particular products off the shelf? I don't.

It's time for the FDA to get involved, and they can only get involved if Congress passes legislation mandating it. If you care, contact your Representative and Senator.

Chapter 19

Frank was in a deep sleep when Maria shook his arm hard. "Frank, there's something going on outside."

He heard sirens approaching, and he ran to the front of the house to look out the window. In the driveway, the interior of Maria's Volvo wagon was engulfed in flames. Frank ran downstairs to the kitchen, picked up a fire extinguisher, and ran out the front door just as a police car pulled up in front of the house. A police officer jumped out of the car and yelled at Frank to get away from the burning car. Frank started spraying into the car through the broken driver side window, as the officer grabbed him by the arm and pulled him forcefully down toward the street. "Sir, I said get away from the car." Maria appeared in the open doorway in her bathrobe, and another policeman yelled, "Ma'am, get back in the house and close that door."

Within a minute, Maria appeared next to Frank out at the street, having exited around the back of the house. A fire engine arrived just as a burst of flame shot out of the broken car windows and rejoined itself in an explosive ball above the car. Frank and Maria felt the palpable heat down at their position at the street, like the blast when opening a hot oven. Neighbors were now out on their lawns, watching the spectacle like the Fourth of July. Two firemen sprayed fire extinguishers through the side windows, then retreated because of the explosion danger. Within another two minutes, a fireman commenced spraying water into the car with a hose from the truck. A great billow of smoke and steam arose and in about three minutes it was over.

A fireman said to Frank, "When was the last time this car was used?"

Frank looked at Maria and she answered, "Around four o'clock, when I drove home from my shift at the hospital. Not since."

The Chief came over and said to Frank and Maria, "Don't touch this car. It's a potential crime scene. We'll have an arson investigator swing by in the morning after everything has cooled off."

As Frank and Maria stood numb, a fireman touched Frank on the shoulder. "You have an enemy, pal. You might think about getting a gun if you don't have one."

Frank suspected that the car fire was not an accident. When interviewed by the police in the front yard after the fire trucks left, Frank acted mystified and said that he couldn't imagine who could possibly want to intimidate him or destroy his property. They probed a little about his work, and gingerly asked questions about whether he had any problematic personal relationships. One cop directly asked "You having an affair with somebody else's wife?" The police also interviewed Maria separately, and asked her similar questions, which she honestly answered similarly.

Back in the house after the police, firefighters, and neighbors had retreated, Frank and Maria sat together on the couch in the living room.

"What's going on Frank?"

"There's nothing going on. There must have been a short in the battery, or maybe some static charge built up and there was a leak in the gas tank. Maybe you didn't put the cap back on tight. A perfect storm of conditions that independently would be nothing."

"There's a dashboard light that comes on if the gas cap isn't on tight. The light wasn't on. Come on, what's going on? I could have been in that car."

"I don't know."

"You look like you know something."

"The only thing I can think of is that it's related to the blogging I've been doing about the herbal and supplement companies."

"It's all true, right? You haven't been making any of it up, libeling people, have you?"

"No, it's all true. They're a bunch of con men who forty years ago would have been selling swampland in Florida."

"But who would set our car on fire?"

"I got a call from a lawyer from Utah, telling me nicely that they want me to stop, and telling me they could make trouble for Delvono."

"Why didn't you tell me about this? You've got to stop. These people are nuts."

"I don't know that they did this. I really don't think they did. I'm not gonna stop."

"Yes, you are."

Chapter 20

The next morning, Frank sat at his desk at work, getting more and more perturbed with time. He knew the fire had to be related to his blogging, and thought *This is war*. He called Dr. George McCann, Head of Analytical Chemistry at Delvono, exchanged pleasantries, then asked him to assign one of his best chemists to a special project that Frank had in mind. After a few back-and-forths about the type of expertise needed, McCann said that Frank could have Jan Mullany for a few months, or for longer if he needed her. He recognized that Frank was the boss, and it made no sense to question or resist. Mullany's current projects could be covered some other way.

That afternoon, Frank met with Mullany, and asked her to extract and analyze a variety of herbal supplement products and search for chemicals that shouldn't be there. For example, they might look at an herbal product that's claimed to "help" depression, and search for the presence of any known antidepressant drug such as Prozac, Zoloft, or Paxil. Likewise, they might look at "natural" supplement products that were purported to "help high cholesterol", and see if they surreptitiously contained Lipitor or some other cholesterol-lowering drug. Mullany was very quick and sharp, and suggested that if she were trying to sneak drugs into herbal products, she would consider adding about five or ten active drugs at low levels so no one drug would stand out in an analysis. For example, ten different blood-pressure-lowering drugs could be added at low levels to an herbal preparation claimed to "help" blood pressure. Each individual drug might be present at a level difficult to detect, but the sum activity of all ten could result in real blood pressure-lowering activity if the drugs were chosen carefully. Frank pointed out that there were scientific arguments against this being an effective approach, but who knows?

As they talked, Mullany got more and more enthused. They agreed that she would obtain standard samples of approximately 50 common generic drugs with a variety of activities. They agreed initially on antihypertensives, antidepressants, sedatives, anti-heartburn drugs, and oral antidiabetics. It would take Jan about a month to set up the assays for all these drugs, and she would ultimately be able to set them up in 96-well format, which would permit fast analysis of a sample for the presence of a variety of drugs. She would also buy a few randomly selected herbal products, spike them with real drugs, and work on developing extraction procedures that would permit identification of those drugs if they were present in an herbal product. She would do the same for some non-herbal "special" vitamin supplements. Both Frank and Jan would search the supplement world and make lists of potential products to analyze for the presence of these drugs. They talked about doing weight lifter protein supplements, but decided to put that off until later. Jan was a proactive highly-experienced chemist, and she had her work cut out for her. They agreed to meet in one month to discuss progress.

Frank was pleased.

Chapter 21

Jimmy sat on the Amtrak Acela train heading to Washington, D.C. from New York City. Two days ago, he received a call from the Chief of Staff for Senator Sam Packard of Utah, requesting that he meet with Packard in Washington to discuss an important matter. For the last two days he had speculated about the subject of this meeting, but he really had been given no clues. Jimmy took it in stride, and read the NY Post sports pages and dozed as the train barreled down the northeast coast.

The train arrived at D.C. Union Station at 5:45, and Jimmy caught a cab to Georgetown, where he had a 6:30 dinner appointment with the Senator at Warburg's Steakhouse. He walked into the darkly lit restaurant at 6:15 and took a place at the half-filled bar. Except for the black-and-white tiled floor, every surface in the place was paneled in dark wood, from the walls covered in dark-framed black and white photographs to the table booths to the coffered ceiling. Every man at the bar was in a dark pin-stripe suit and every woman in a sharp lady's business suit – all black or dark blue with a slight touch of color in an accessory. Jimmy looked at the bar menu, and ordered a double Glenfiddich 12-year-old scotch with a single ice cube. He nursed his drink, listening to conversations that all sounded the same – petty discussions of government office politics. No discussions of policy, current events, not even sports – just what asshole said what to whom. Around seven o'clock, as sitting there was starting to feel a little old, a young man in a dark suit tapped Jimmy on the shoulder and asked if he was Mr. Delvecchio.

Jimmy followed him to a back room where there were four tables, three of which were empty. At the fourth sat a tall 70-ish man in a dark suit who Jimmy recognized from C-Span as Senator Packard, the undisputed powerbroker of the Senate for the last 15 years. Jimmy walked over and Packard got up.

"Hi! Mr. Delvecchio, I presume." The Senator offered his hand and they shook.

"Hello, Senator. Pleased to meet you."

"And I you. I'm gonna have a drink, it's been a long day. What are you drinking?"

Jimmy answered, "I guess I could go for another double Glenfiddich."

"A man after my own heart."

The waiter appeared and they ordered their drinks.

The Senator said, "I really am glad to meet you. I've heard a lot about you from your colleague Alfonso Gentilella, who I've known for years. We've had lots of mutually important things to work on together, although for obvious reasons that work has not been very public. The people you work for play an important role in American society, more than you may know. Anyway, you probably do know, or you wouldn't be where you are. You've quickly gained a reputation for an ability to herd cats, some dangerous cats. And a reputation for running an extremely complicated portfolio of businesses."

"Well, thank you. It's one of the most interesting things I've ever done. But we pay our taxes, we follow the rules, we cut no corners. Mr. Gentilella is a great man, but if you don't know, he has a hands-off approach to the businesses I run. He is of course our major investor. As far as the government goes, we make the maximum allowable contributions to both parties, no more, no less."

The Senator raised his glass in a faux toast to Jimmy. "And we appreciate your financial contributions! But don't worry, that's not what we're here to discuss."

"And what are we here to discuss?"

The Senator raised his hand to indicate a pause in the conversation, and suggested that they order some food. He said that he would not stay long, and would only have a salad, but Jimmy should sit and enjoy a good meal after his long trip down to D.C.

When their salads came, the Senator said, "I'm told that your Liberty Holdings group has some businesses in our state. I'm talking about the health food and medical supplements stuff. These businesses are very important for Utah, and are part of a whole ecosystem of health-related businesses. When people think of Utah, they usually think of the Mormon Church, not surprisingly. I'm actually a bishop, but I have to admit that I don't have much time for pastoring these days. We all contribute in the way we best can. People in the know realize that the herbal product and medical supplement and vitamin industry in the US is all centered in Utah. Heck, maybe 15% of the big buildings in downtown Salt Lake are headquarters for supplement companies."

"I know it. We're paying some New York prices for office space there." Jimmy laughed. "Somebody's getting rich in commercial real estate, maybe the Mormon Church."

"Well, there may be some truth to that. But before we continue, I have to get something out of the way."

"Shoot."

"Are you carrying a recording or transmitting device?"

Jimmy laughed. "Nope, no recording device. No transmitting device. No FBI. No cops. Just me. So Senator, you wearing a wire? Is this room bugged, any video recording? You called me here mysteriously. I'm the one who should fear entrapment."

"OK. OK. Let's not get our panties in a bunch. We have something very important to talk about, and I want to assure that we can both be very straightforward and honest. In my business, and I'm sure in yours, there are people waiting in the wings who would love to take statements out of context to knock me or you down a notch or out of commission. In order to do great things you have to stay in a position to do great things."

Jimmy thought *This asshole has been around so long that he believes his own bullshit. Do great things. Yeah, pocket lots of money.* Then Jimmy said, "Excuse me Senator, you didn't answer. Are you wearing a wire, are we being monitored, are you working with an investigative agency?"

"OK. No, no, and no." The senator smiled, then sighed. "Look, here's the deal. The herbal medicine industry is crucial to the economy of Utah. As a senator from the state of Utah, it's my responsibility to do everything I can to stimulate and maintain economic health. As I'm sure you know, one reason this industry is so profitable and stable is that it's not overburdened with government regulations. I've fought long and hard for this and will continue to fight for this. People should have the right to choose whatever form of medicine they want, and there's no reason why the FDA should apply its burdensome drug regulations to natural herbal products and supplements that have been around since the ancient Greeks."

"I think I know what's coming."

"I'm sure you do. Look, your herbal medicine companies are part of our ecosystem, and we're happy to have you. Your friend with the blog is causing real trouble. Trouble for you and trouble for some of my constituents. I understand that he sees himself as some purist who's discovering drugs to cure disease. But he's causing big trouble. There's a move starting in the Congress to expand the purview of the FDA Drug Division to the herbs and natural space. Staffers are reading your buddy's blog and putting excerpts in position papers. Some of the FDA people are finding religion and making noise."

"And what do you think I can do? I'll tell you this – I've already talked to him about it."

"It's not my job to tell you how to do your job. I just want to communicate a few things as clearly as I can. As Alfonso's friend, I'm just helping you understand how to remain successful. You and your blogger buddy have one of these high tech biotech outfits. I've been told that there are people who can make you guys pariahs in that field. As far as your herbal medicine companies with Alfonso, there are people in Customs who can quarantine every foreign delivery you get. There are people who would be happy to assure that you get no shelf space in national chain drug and health food stores. Your distribution centers can be inspected and shut down. I don't need to go on. The people who are upset say they'll give you two weeks to fix this. After that, I call Alfonso. To be clear, I'm just trying to help you because you're a businessman operating in Utah, and it's my responsibility to help you. What I'm going to say now, I really mean. I've heard a lot about you, and I have high respect for you. I want you and your companies to continue as successful Utah businesses."

Jimmy was in no position to say anything but "I'll get him to stop."

The Senator added, "At this point, stopping isn't enough. He has to move to a position of public support."

"I don't know if I can do that."

"Sure you can. You're a smart resourceful guy. Well, I have to go. Please stay and have a nice steak, it's on my tab. I'm sorry we had to meet this way. I'm sure we'll have a productive future together."

The two men stood and shook hands. The waiter came over, and Jimmy ordered a porterhouse medium, a baked potato, and grilled asparagus. Might as well have a good meal to salvage the day.

Chapter 22

Jimmy was between a proverbial rock and a hard place. On the train back from Washington, he sat with a beer and thought about a plan. He certainly did not have his ducks in a row, as he liked to say. His old friend Nick was right – he had to get out of the Stamford job and back to Delvono and New Jersey, but not back to *La Famiglia*. The Frank problem had nothing to do with Jimmy's early life commitments or his current job, and maybe could be solved completely independently. *But how?* Jimmy laughed. The easy way out would be to have Frank hit. At this point, there were probably multiple people who would support this approach and would be willing to fund it but of course would not want any connection to it. *So what else is new?* He did not seriously consider this, and told himself that it was a joke.

Jimmy's life was going well in almost every way. Gina and the kids were doing great. The Stamford job, despite its complexities and less-than-desirable connections, was truly interesting. And he owned essentially all of Delvono and could go back anytime he wanted. *Why was Frank such an asshole?* Jimmy thought about how Frank essentially blackmailed him into funding Delvono nine years ago, threatening to ruin Jimmy with information about his past business dealings. Maybe for the first time Jimmy faced the fact that his business partner really was unstable, smart with some undeniable good qualities, but in the end a loose gun on the table. Frank was a guy who couldn't play by the rules when they got in the way, no matter whose rules. As Jimmy had accused him of years before, Frank was really into gaining fame for himself. He was a successful famous scientist, but now he needed to be a famous muckraker. *Self-destructive asshole.*

When he got back from Washington, he called Frank and asked him to meet for lunch at the McDonald's on Route 7 in Belleville, where they had first agreed to work together almost a decade before. As they ate their meals, they talked generally about things at Delvono, and then Jimmy got to the point.

"You remember my lecture maybe eight years ago about *campanilismo?*"

"Yep, but as I recall we were eating in your friend Nick's Acropolis Diner. I remember it well, better food than here, and I've thought about it a lot over the years. That's the first time I learned about the Sicilian Vespers and that you were actually an educated guy, not just a street thug."

Jimmy laughed. "Thanks for the compliment." He paused and then said, "Frank, I'm worried about you."

"Here we go."

"I mean it. It's like you have some kind of death wish. You built a fantastic scientific career. You're one of the world's best-known biologists, shit, maybe even a Nobel prize some day for the cancer stuff. You have a couple hundred people funded to do basically whatever you want as long as it's aimed at new drugs. You don't have to write grants for money. What's the problem here?"

"The problem is that there's a world of charlatans out there promising phony cures, taking people's money and basically convincing them not to get the medical attention they need. Stopping these people is as important as discovering new drugs."

"I beg to differ."

"Do you read my blogs? It's true."

"Hey, I agree that there are charlatans out there. Always have been, probably always will be. I can't believe the crap I hear in their infomercials on AM radio. But I don't agree that stopping them is as important as discovering new drugs. And by the way, they're probably not all charlatans. You know what I think? I think you're steamed because of how these infomercial assholes insult you. Not you by name, but all the people who do good biology and chemistry and drug discovery, and the doctors who really help people with properly tested drugs. Their bullshit about how the pharmaceutical companies hate them because they have real cures and the pharmaceutical companies just want people to stay sick so they can keep selling them drugs that don't attack the real disease, yadda, yadda, yadda. You take their bullshit personally and want to hit back. Face it, you really can't hit back effectively. These people are playing to peoples' fears and they'll always find scared patients who wanna believe they've been dealt a bad hand by crooked doctors and by big bad drug companies. It's funny – it's an argument that resonates with both far-right and far-left people. And the less educated the better. But you can't stop it. You're wasting your energy and your talent."

"Hey, admit it, you really want me to stop because you have a dog in this race."

"You're damn straight I have a dog in this race, and so do you. You know, maybe that's a better way to get at this. Forget logical argument. I have a financial and personal interest in

Delvono Inc., and you're interfering with that. Maybe you have your reasons. My opinion is that you should see a psychiatrist, but maybe you have your reasons." Jimmy looked directly into Frank's eyes. "Stop. Is that clear enough? Stop."

"Come on Jimmy, you're making a mountain out of a molehill. I can continue to do this stuff, and nobody's gonna hurt Delvono. We have a triple-A reputation for quality and innovation. That doesn't just disappear."

"Did somebody blow up your car?"

"Yeah, what about it? It's true, the cops verified it. But whoever did that doesn't scare me. It scared Maria big-time, and I'm sorry about that. If they really wanted to hurt me, they could have. It's really just an indication that I'm having an effect. They're scared, not me."

"That was a warning, asshole."

"Look, even if they killed me, which I don't expect, there would be more to follow me now that I've broken through."

"You're delusional. Let's come back to earth here. Do you want out of Delvono?"

"Of course not. Are you nuts?"

"OK. I'm giving you an ultimatum. Stop or I'll push you out of the company."

"You can't do that."

As Jimmy got up from the table, he said, "Try me."

The two old friends walked to their cars without saying a word, both steaming.

Chapter 23

Over the course of about six weeks, Jan Mullany did a beautiful job of setting up assays for about 70 drugs. A creative perfectionist, she designed and assembled a robotically-controlled system that could analyze a single sample for the presence of seven anti-diabetic drugs at once. Likewise for drugs from other therapeutic areas. Her initial screen of a group of antidiabetic and antidepressant herbal supplement products was also complete. She now sat next to Frank Serono at a conference table as they looked at tables of data on Jan's laptop.

Jan said, "I think you may be a little disappointed. I've been through about ten supplements that claim to help blood sugar control, and I didn't find any drugs, no Januvia, no Glucotrol, no nothing. Pretty much the same for antidepressants and the St. John's Wort products, with the exception of one that actually had about 20 mg of Prozac in each capsule."

"Which one was that?"

"One of the Chinese products I picked up in Chinatown. Nothing in English on the label."

"We can't do much with that. The FDA's not going to care too much about some imported Chinese product that can only be bought in Chinatown by people who speak Chinese. How did you even find that one?"

"I went into the shop and asked for something that could help with my father's depressed mood. I brought it back here and had one of the Chinese guys translate the label for me."

Frank sighed. "You're right. This is disappointing. I thought there would be a lot of adulteration going on. Most herbal supplements in general don't show therapeutic activity in reasonably designed trials, but there sure is a lot of anecdotal evidence of efficacy sometimes. I could believe a placebo effect in depression, but not in glucose-lowering."

"Maybe in glucose-lowering too, who knows? We still have lots more supplements to test. I haven't even started on the sedatives or antihypertensives or cholesterol lowering ones. I guess I should say supposedly sedative and supposedly antihypertensive and supposedly cholesterol-lowering."

"Well, keep going. I'm looking at this like we're just starting out, and we have a long way to go."

"OK, will do. While we're here though, I want to show you something a little funny. I don't know if it means anything." Jan pulled up a chromatogram on her laptop and said, "This chromatogram is for one of the products that says it helps high blood sugar. See this peak? It's reproducible and absorbs in the uv, so it's like a drug or a vitamin or something. When I extract and analyze a variety of relatively pure herbs, not the formulated products in capsules, but just the plant stuff itself, I never see a peak like this."

"Do you have any idea what compound it might be?"

"Well, it absorbs in the uv, and I checked its spectrum and it's clearly a heterocyclic, which makes me think it could be a drug, but it's not one of the seven antidiabetic compounds I ran as standards. Maybe it's another drug we haven't set up an assay for yet."

"Or it could be rat poison or a pesticide. It could be anything. Have you seen anything else like this?"

"Yeah. I saw something like this in a couple of other so-called antidiabetic herbal products, and also in a few of the so-called antidepressive ones."

"Well, we can't just analyze for every known drug in each therapeutic area, but I guess as I'm speaking I have to say I don't really know why not. It's just a question of how much effort we want to put into this."

Jan smiled and said, "Why don't I talk to a couple of the other analytical people, and see if we can identify a couple of these compounds. I can do some prep HPLC and isolate enough material to get a mass spec and an NMR. Let's just see if we can identify one of these mystery substances."

* * *

Over the next few weeks, Jan Mullany worked out a method to extract about 50 mg of "Mystery Substance X" from one of the antidiabetic herbal products. She had an elemental analysis done, which gives the identity of the various atoms that make up the molecule and their relative ratios. She sent a sample to the mass spectroscopy lab and to the NMR lab, and then studied the data with the technical experts. They proposed a structure for Substance X with high confidence. It definitely was not one of the known marketed antidiabetic drugs, but it bore a passing resemblance to the drug glucofar. Jan had her computer convert the proposed chemical structure into a so-called "SMILES" sequence, which is a system for describing chemical compounds as a linear sequence of letters and numbers. She then did a computer search of the SMILES description of Substance X to see if it had been previously reported anywhere in the scientific literature.

She got a hit. The compound was described in a paper in the Journal of Medicinal Chemistry twenty-two years earlier. The paper described work from the Beerli Pharma company's R&D Division on discovery and testing of a series of potential antidiabetic drugs. As is typical, they reported the structures of approximately 60 structurally similar (but distinct) new chemical compounds that had been tested in various animal models of human diabetes. The 60 compounds varied in their glucose-lowering activity, and Jan noted immediately that one of the compounds (number XXVII in the paper) had eventually become the marketed drug glucophar. This was one of the drugs that Jan had screened for in her tests of herbal products. Mystery Substance X was compound number XXXIX in the J.Med.Chem. paper, and it was reported to be one of the three most active compounds, one of which was the compound eventually called glucophar. Jan had worked in drug R&D divisions for eighteen years, and knew that a drug discovery group often discovered a whole series of compounds that had a specific potential therapeutic activity, and one had to be chosen to move into expensive human clinical trials. Sometimes the choice was a guess, sometimes the choice was dictated by observations of toxicity for some of the compounds, sometimes only one of the active compounds was orally absorbed.

The importance of this identification of Substance X was immediately obvious to Jan. The herbal product supplier had spiked the product with an antidiabetic chemical that had never been studied in humans or presented to the FDA for approval as a safe and effective drug. Jan grabbed her laptop, walked down to Frank Serono's office, and knocked and opened the door.

"Frank, I think I have something you're gonna want to hear about right away."

Jan took Frank through the various analytical data supporting the structural proposal for Substance X, and with a little dramatic flair, the demonstration of glucose-lowering activity in the J.Med.Chem. paper.

Frank was shocked. "You know, we're dealing with very smart, very devious people here. More pedestrian crooks might secretly spike their herbal product with a marketed drug without telling anyone. They get efficacy and just have to hope that nobody analyzes their product. That's what we saw with the Chinese St. John's Wort product that contained some Prozac. A smarter more devious crook might try what you suggested once – spike the product with low levels of, say, seven antidiabetic drugs. You might actually achieve efficacy but with low levels of each drug that may be difficult to demonstrate in a chemical analysis of the product.

But these people are superbly devious. I have to tip my hat to them. Go to an old scientific publication and identify a compound that has antidiabetic activity in animals, but has never been dosed to humans and thus is unknown to the FDA and the general scientific community except for the small number of researchers who were following this area of medicinal chemistry 20 years ago. Spike your herbal product with that compound and you likely have glucose-lowering activity. An all-natural herbal product requires no human testing, no analytical chemistry testing, and no FDA approval. No one is wise to the spiking. If some obsessed psycho like me or you decides to analyze the product for the presence of antidiabetic drugs, none will be found because the spiked glucose-lowering compound is unknown at FDA and has never been a marketed product."

Jan said, "So what do we do now?"

"I don't know. I don't know. I guess one thing I'll do is get a technician assigned to work with you. Please continue to analyze all the herbal and natural products we have, and look for the presence of unusual HPLC peaks. Isolate the compounds and identify them and see if they're known to have therapeutic activity in some animal model. I'm thinking we're just seeing the tip of the iceberg."

Jan smiled. "Aye-aye, sir!"

Frank smiled back.

Chapter 24

Frank asked his admin Marge to schedule a call with Dean Tinney, a lawyer Delvono used regularly on issues of FDA regulations. Later that day, Frank rang Dean.

"Hey, Dean, how are you?"

"Good, very good. You got some business for me? If it's urgent, hang up and find somebody else. I'm going to the Yankee game tonight."

"No, nothing urgent, but it sounds like you may have more money than you need if you're automatically turning down potential work."

"Nope. Always need money. Two kids in college and a third still to go. What's up?"

"I'm looking for some general information about which kinds of products require FDA approval and which might be legal or illegal."

"OK. Shoot."

"OK. Let's say somebody has an herbal supplement or medicine that is purported to have an effect on, say, high blood pressure. In general, it's highly unlikely that the herb really has an effect, but there's some folklore out there that says it does.

Now say the manufacturer spikes the herbal product with a chemical that actually lowers blood pressure."

"You mean an antihypertensive drug?"

"Well, I'm avoiding the term drug because the blood pressure lowering compound has never been tested in humans and so has never been marketed as a drug."

"How do you know it lowers blood pressure?"

"Let's say that 20 years earlier, a Big Pharma company had an R&D program aimed at evaluating a particular mechanism for blood pressure lowering, let's say for the sake of argument they were looking for angiotensin AII antagonists. They synthesize and test a few hundred compounds in some animal model of hypertension and they identify ten compounds active enough to potentially be a human drug. Of course, only one of the ten will go on into expensive human clinical trials, and it may go all the way and become a marketed drug. Along the way, the company publishes its data on all the compounds tested, either in a patent application or in a scientific publication. So the structures of nine undeveloped compounds that were active in an animal hypertension model are then publicly known. The herbal supplement company synthesizes one of these compounds, and uses it to spike its herbal product to give it antihypertensive activity."

"But that compound could be toxic. It's never been through tox studies, right? And it might not work in humans because of absorption or metabolism or some other reason, right?"

"Correct."

"Well I hope you're not thinking of doing this, but it's interesting. OK, they're not using an approved drug, so they haven't run afoul of any FDA regulations about demonstrating bioequivalence, purity, stability, etcetera. Do they make medical claims?"

"No, they say their product works with your body to maintain a healthy heart and circulatory system."

"That's a good one. Means nothing. Anyway, they've been careful not to make a medical claim, so they're technically not obligated to run clinical trials or file a New Drug Application at FDA. I'd say they're free and clear."

"Free and clear, how can they be free and clear?"

"Well, free and clear with respect to drug law. Now, they may be afoul of food law, and I'm not up on that subject. It seems that there must be regulations that control placing chemicals in food. You've got me curious, so I'll ask around."

"One more thing. What if the seller imports the herbal product from, say, India or China, and doesn't know that it's spiked?"

"Well, a good lawyer could probably get him off, but he'd have to convincingly demonstrate his ignorance. He'd be fine as long as discovery doesn't turn up some written document like an email that says he knew of the adulteration. I find this whole thing quite disturbing because I'm having a hard time imagining how such an adulteration would ever be caught. Why are you asking about this?"

"It may be going on, and it may be going on a lot. If I had data demonstrating that this was going on, would I have any legal obligation to report it to some authority?"

"Without running through all the details, I'd say probably not. I'd also say that you might have a moral obligation though. But I'd be very careful. You could open yourself up to an expensive lawsuit, even if you're ultimately demonstrated to be correct. There are lots of legal arguments that could be made against you, like poor chain of control for your samples, for example."

"Gotcha. Well, this has been very helpful. Thanks, Dean. Enjoy the Yankee game tonight."

Chapter 25

NATURAL ENOUGH FOR YA? #20

from the desk of Frank Serono, Ph.D

It's An Amazing Herbal Super-Nutraceutical, Really!

Twenty-two years ago, scientists at the research division of a major pharmaceutical company discovered a series of 17 novel chemical compounds that had therapeutic activity in an animal model of human Type II Diabetes. They applied for a patent, reported the discovery in the Journal of Medicinal Chemistry, ran toxicology studies on two of the compounds (one of which turned out to be toxic), and took the non-toxic compound into extensive human clinical trials, ultimately in about 5,000 patients. That compound became the very useful diabetes drug glucofar, which was marketed by the inventor company as Glucarin. This drug is now off-patent, and sold by a number of generic companies throughout the world. More about this below.

In our lab at Delvono Inc. in New Jersey, we have recently undertaken a study of a variety of marketed "Nutraceuticals" or "Herbal Medicine" products, in an attempt to uncover the basis for their purported therapeutic activity. As I have reported in previous blogs, purveyors of these products are careful to avoid directly saying that they can be used to treat disease because the products have never been tested in human clinical trials adequate for FDA approval as a drug. Rather, they are stated to do things like "help sugar control" or "help heart health" or "help you on your down days". Likewise, in almost all cases, the toxicity of these products has not been established in any systematic way. Of course, the products are "all natural", and thus are declared by the manufacturers to be intrinsically safe.

To date, we have studied about 30 herbal products purchased on the open market, and have collaborated with another company to use the new technique of DNA-Fingerprinting to identify the herbs in each product. So far, we have found that about one-third of the products tested contained none of the major "therapeutic" herb listed on the label, purported to "help" with various health problems. We are preparing a scientific paper in which we will publish these surprising results. This should be disturbing to "naturopathic" and traditional physicians both, and to patients who use these products.

Today, I would like to report an observation that was truly surprising (as if the absence of the "therapeutic" herb wasn't surprising enough). In our analytical study of a "sugar control" product called "FenuSeng UltraPlus" (from the company Phoebus Herbals), we observed the presence of the two active herbs listed on the label, fenugreek and ginseng. So far, so good. Whether they work or not, at least they were present. We also looked for the presence of seven known prescription antidiabetic drugs, and found none. Also good. However, we noted the presence of about 10 mg of a chemical that did not look like it belonged there. We identified the chemical and it turned out to be one of the 17 active compounds identified by the inventors of glucofar, and described in their patent and Journal of Medicinal Chemistry paper twenty-two years ago. It was not glucofar, and it was not the compound that failed toxicology studies. In fact, it was compound #39 in the Journal of Medicinal Chemistry paper.

So FenuSeng UltraPlus contains a synthetic chemical with some glucose-lowering activity in animals that has never gone through toxicity studies or human clinical trials. The devious folks at Phoebus Herbals have provided an "all natural" herbal product that "helps sugar control", spiked with an unapproved untested synthetic drug of unknown toxicity. The folks at Phoebus should be given a prize for their disingenuous cynical creativity.

FDA take notice.

Chapter 26

The shit hit the fan.

Jimmy quickly turned on his computer in his Stamford office and read Franks's blog #20 after receiving an angry call from Todd Singleton at Phoebus Herbals. Jimmy could not believe his eyes. *That fucking idiot is using Delvono resources to analyze other companies' products.* Of course, Frank did not know that Phoebus was owned by Jimmy's Liberty Holdings. If he had, maybe he would have thought twice about what he did, maybe not.

Other phone calls quickly followed. The CEOs of the other two natural product companies owned by Liberty Holdings wanted to know whether their products were under study at Delvono. Jimmy promised to find out and to do everything in his power to stop release of any harmful information. Like clockwork, a call came in from John Harbon, the attorney for the Natural Remedies Manufacturers of America.

"Mr. Harbon, I know what this is about, I saw the blogpost this morning, and I'm investigating."

"Well, Mr. Delvecchio, that's good of you, but your business colleague has already crossed the Rubicon. I'm calling to politely warn you that there better not be any more unsubstantiated revelations coming. Your company Delvono and your colleague Dr. Serono will receive notices of injunction this afternoon preventing release of any more libelous information. You've poked the wrong bear."

"Mr. Harbon, I'm sorry that this has occurred. However, even though I'm not a lawyer, I've been around the block a few times. I don't see how the organization you represent has any standing in this matter. You have not been directly harmed. Phoebus Herbals is obviously in a different situation, and we'll have to see how that company responds. So you can take your injunction and shove it. You know it's not enforceable. That being said, you and I do have mutual interests here, and I assure you that I'm going to do what I can to stop any additional release of information and get to the bottom of whether and how work was done at my company Delvono."

"Mr. Delvecchio, if a war is started here, you know we'll win. It may take a while, but you and Delvono Inc. will suffer one way or another."

"Calm down. At this point I don't know who you're really the mouthpiece for and I don't know what other products have been analyzed at Delvono. For the sake of argument, if Dr. Serono is removed from the company, would your clients go after him personally and not Delvono Inc.?"

"You know I can't answer that now, but I will point out that Delvono has deeper pockets than Dr. Serono. You're correct in saying that at this point only Phoebus has suffered potential harm, and I'm not counsel for Phoebus, but that company is a member of our trade association. How this proceeds will depend on what additional unsubstantiated or even substantiated attacks Dr. Serono makes on other natural remedy providers. My firm directly represents a number of them here in Utah. Stop him, Mr. Delvecchio, just stop him."

"Will you admit that what he has done to date, excluding yesterday's Phoebus Herbals stuff, is free speech? You may not like it, but it's free speech."

"You know I'm not going to answer that question."

"OK, Mr. Harbon, I'll do what I can. Thanks for the call."

It seemed pretty clear from the discussion with Harbon that he didn't know that Jimmy was CEO of the holding company that owned Phoebus, but that piece of information would probably come out sooner rather than later. Jimmy was screwed here, forced to be his own opponent.

Jimmy called Frank and told him in direct and vulgar terms that his blog party was over. Frank, of course, did not agree, and haughtily asserted that his right to freedom of speech was being abridged.

"You were using Delvono resources to analyze other companies' products. That's not the remit of Delvono. What the hell were you thinking? Now you've drawn us directly into the line of fire."

"I'm the President and Director of Research at Delvono, and have the freedom to pursue whatever I deem worth pursuing. And the last time I looked, Jimmy, you were not formally associated with Delvono except as Chair of the Board of Directors."

"Frank, I'm also the owner and I'm gonna to do whatever I have to do to protect Delvono."

Jimmy decided that dealing with Frank directly was useless and over the next couple of days he brought a motion before the Board of Delvono Inc. to have Frank removed as President and Director of Research. This was not made any easier by the fact that Frank, with Jimmy, was on the Board. Jimmy revealed to the

Board that there had been veiled and not-so-veiled threats against Delvono previously because of Frank's extracurricular activities. He did not go so far as to describe his meeting with the Utah senator. After two hastily called uncomfortable Board meetings, Frank was removed and, to state the obvious, he was angry. Jimmy was somewhat disingenuous, not notifying the Delvono Board that Liberty Holdings actually owned the company Phoebus Herbals that Frank attacked. However, he felt that he was on steady ground because the issue from the perspective of Delvono's Board was that the weight of the natural remedy world in general was going to come down on Frank and on Delvono.

Frank was given a one year consulting contract at half his generous current salary. He had to turn in his laptop and all paper records; all computer access to Delvono data was blocked. He was told that he could only visit Delvono with an appointment previously approved by Jimmy, and he was not to have phone contact with any Delvono employee unless two employees were on the line and the call was previously approved by Jimmy. If Frank broke these rules, his contract would be voided. The contract also said that Frank would cease his blogging efforts, which Frank balked at. Lawyers got involved, impassioned discussions about free speech occurred, and everyone settled on some wording that Frank would have to use in his blogs identifying himself as principal of his own consulting firm. Frank signed on, but had no intention of abandoning the battle.

Although Jimmy was not currently involved in the day-to-day activities of Delvono, the Board took his advice on a short-term reorganization that left Jimmy as the de facto part-time President and CEO. This was clearly not a sustainable solution. Christina Lindbergh would continue to head the Anti-Drug-Resistant-

Bacteria Group. In addition, the three Senior Scientist Heads of the other Therapeutic Discovery Groups would report to her. Christina was young and inexperienced, but Jimmy felt that she had the chops. She reported to Jimmy, as did the Heads of Accounting, Clinical Supply Procurement, Clinical Trials, and Regulatory Affairs. Luckily, these four groups were essentially self-running, and most of their work was outsourced. Jimmy was not an employee, which was a problem, so a one-year contract was arranged. His pay was one dollar. The Board was relieved but not happy, and committed to spend the next three months working on a long-term solution. Jimmy got Gentilella's permission to do this, but only short-term.

It took a very busy week to get all this done, and Jimmy had not shown his face even once at the Liberty Holdings office in Connecticut.

Jimmy was approaching the end of his rope.

Chapter 27

Frank and Maria Serono were sitting on an Amtrak train, returning from D.C. where they had spent the weekend visiting their daughter Anna at Georgetown University. They got to see their son Frank Jr. much more often because he was near home at Columbia. Anna was a different story - they missed her in a big way.

Maria was a skilled amateur violinist and classical music buff and she had passed that gene on to Anna and Frank Jr. Attending orchestra concerts was something Maria and Frank had done with their two kids ever since the kids were old enough to appreciate it, and the four still loved bonding this way. Friday night Maria, Frank and Anna heard the American Symphony play the Rachmaninov Symphony No. 2 at the Kennedy Center, and they were transported back even though Frank Jr. was absent.

Yesterday they visited the Anthropology Museum at the Smithsonian, Frank's favorite, and had an enjoyable dinner out with Anna and two of her college friends. It was a good break for Frank, but he had not yet told Maria about the professional disaster at Delvono and it had hung over him all weekend. Now he had to do it, end the procrastination and tell her the story as best he could. Like a guy who decides to break up with a girlfriend in a public place to avoid fireworks, he decided to bring it up on the train.

Frank took a sip of his coffee and said, "There's something that's been going on at work, and I have to tell you about it."

Maria looked up from her book. "Can it wait a few minutes? I'm at a good part." Then she put her bookmark in and closed the book. "OK. Doesn't matter. What's up?"

"You know the blogging I've been doing, about the natural medicines and the phony efficacy claims?"

"I've been reading them, and I'll tell you again, I think you're asking for trouble. The latest one was a direct hit on a specific company."

"Yeah, well, there's been a little trouble. I got a call from a lawyer about a month ago asking me to stop. He represents one of the herbal remedy organizations. He said that if I didn't comply, they had ways of interfering in Delvono's ability to do clinical trials. The threat was sort of indirect, but clear."

"And you didn't comply or tone it down why?"

"C'mon, you know me. I'm not gonna back down to threats."

"Alright, so what happened?"

"Well, they got to some influential people who did some complaining I guess. That rat Jimmy and the Board removed me from my position at Delvono." He paused and watched her face as she processed this surprising piece of information. She swallowed then took a deep breath.

"You can't be serious. You're hiding something. They just did this to you without warning. Have they been giving you warnings?"

"No, the bastards just fired me."

"You didn't have any discussions with Jimmy about this? I've been telling you that you were playing with fire. They didn't give you a warning or a chance to stop?"

"Yeah, well, the problems have only been for about a month or two. Jimmy and I discussed it a couple of times."

"And what did he have to say?"

"Basically he just said stop."

"And you didn't stop why?"

"I'm not gonna back down to threats. You know I'm right about these nutraceutical con-men. I have my right to free speech. This doesn't have anything to do with Delvono Inc."

"Apparently it does have something to do with Delvono. You're on the Board. How were they able to do this?"

"It's allowed in the bylaws."

"Who voted against you?"

"Everybody."

He knew that look. Maria was slowly starting to boil. And a betting man would say that this was not anger at Jimmy or the Board, and she was about to let him have it. If they were at home, she'd be speaking quite loudly by now, and with good reason.

"We have a daughter and a son in college, paying full freight because of our combined income. Did you think about that?"

"Don't worry about the money. They're keeping me on as a consultant with a one-year contract at half pay. I'll work this all out."

"And at the end of the year, what? They fired you, right? This wasn't a warning. What about our health insurance?"

"I don't know, I haven't asked. We might have to switch over to your insurance from the hospital. I'll find out right away."

Maria looked straight ahead at the seatback in front of her for about 20 seconds, then opened her book and pretended to read.

After a minute, she said, without looking at him, "The car. That wasn't a stupid prank or some perfect storm of electrical conditions. Somebody blew up my car, didn't they? It was about this blogging garbage."

"I don't know. Maybe."

"You're an idiot, and I guess that makes me the wife of an idiot. You're gonna have to straighten this out."

Chapter 28

One week after the release of Frank Serono's incendiary blog #20, Jimmy was sitting in his Liberty Holdings office in Stamford working the phones. He called Todd Singleton at Phoebus Herbals.

"Hi Todd, how's the weather in Salt Lake?"

"Hi Jimmy, the weather's fine. Any progress?"

"Yeah. I've got it pretty much under control." Jimmy was lying, or at best stretching the truth. He hoped he had it under control as far as protecting Delvono was concerned, and that was where his heart really was. He certainly didn't have Frank under control, although he hoped that Frank had learned his lesson and would now fall in line.

Jimmy continued, "I talked to a few people here at Liberty, in addition to one of our lawyers, and we think it's best to just lay low and not go after the blogger. If we initiate a lawsuit, it could bring press attention to the situation, and he may start to seek publicity about being attacked for his position as savior of the public. So we at Liberty don't support any activity on this from Phoebus."

"But this guy Serono said he has damaging data, and then said, 'FDA take notice'. He said that he gathered the data at that company you personally own. What if he sends data to FDA? They'll be in here looking at our records for everything we sell, maybe tapping phones, who knows?"

"Well we can assume that someone at FDA must be reading his blog, so they already know. I had somebody here contact a regulatory consultant, and she says that the FDA Enforcement Division can't just go off on fishing expeditions. From one perspective, the Drug Division of FDA shouldn't even be involved because you're selling a natural herbal product, and that part of FDA doesn't have authority over such products, thanks to your politicians out there in Utah. It's not clear what would really happen if someone sent real data to FDA, but the government would likely take the position that you're selling an unapproved drug, and only after they've generated their own data. I've been told it would take years to resolve, and you'd probably end up settling with FDA and paying a fine if it comes to that. On the other hand, a more likely scenario is that the FDA Food Division would come after you first. Probably a bigger problem might be lawsuits from people who were endangered by your untested drug product. I'm working on a way to make none of this ever happen."

"How can you make it not happen?"

"I'm working on a way to prevent Dr. Serono's data, if it even exists, from going public or being sent to FDA. But I'm not gonna let you in on how we're doing that."

"That would be great. Hopefully the problem just goes away."

"Alright, so now let's talk about the elephant in the room."

"What do you mean?"

"What do I mean? How did an unapproved drug end up in your natural herbal capsules?"

Singleton gave the answer that he had practiced over and over. "I don't know that there's an unapproved drug in our capsules. We get the formulation from our partners in Malaysia. We used to just buy the herbs from them, but recently we've had them mix in the other materials called excipients, and we review all their manufacturing paperwork. For many products, we just encapsulate the mix then bottle the capsules with our labels. We outsource this to a company here in Utah, which permits us to label the products 'Manufactured in the USA'." Singleton was lying, or at best exaggerating. For products obtained from Malay Botanicals, Phoebus did receive manufacturing records electronically, and they stored them electronically. Nobody looked at them. Ever. "We don't do any chemical analysis of the products here. We rely on Malay's analytical work, which is done to FDA-quality standards."

Singleton did not say anything about the mysterious "special sauce" that the Malay Botanicals CEO Ling Li talks about from time to time. He maintained plausible deniability about that. The European suppliers he had previously dealt with always talked about the "special galenical properties" of their formulations, whatever the hell that meant, and Singleton's planned position was that any "special sauce" talk would be the same kind of thing.

Jimmy said, "At this point, I'd say you shouldn't do an analysis of the stuff on hand. Your position should be that you have no reason to suspect that there's really a problem just because some muckraking nutcase has a blog. Obtain and quickly destroy all the supplies of the product still at your distributors and give them refunds."

"I'm not gonna do that. That's a lot of money. And it's like admitting guilt. Don't worry, I'll figure it out."

"I understand that you're the CEO, but you serve at the behest of the stockholders, and Liberty Holdings owns 100% of the stock. I'm gonna tell you what you're gonna do, and you're gonna do it. You're gonna do this the way the big boys do. Call back the stuff from the distributors, and get a list of who they've already sent product to. Prepare a statement to be sent to all natural food stores who sell the stuff and say that you're recalling the stuff in order to give clients complete faith in their relationship with Phoebus. Say that there have been some unsubstantiated rumors emanating from Big Pharma, and we stand behind our product, and don't want anyone to worry. Maybe even say how your clients know how threatened Big Pharma feels because of your safe effective natural products. Lay it on thick like the radio commercials. Money back or a replacement bottle for everyone who can produce a bottle, whether full or empty. Send a draft to me here and I'll have someone wordsmith it. Don't send it out without me seeing it."

"OK. I guess you're right. I just hate to take the financial hit when we've done nothing wrong."

"Financial hit? Wake up. You've got to get that stuff off the shelves before the FDA buys some and starts analyzing it." Jimmy sighed. "Now the next thing. I don't know what's in or not in those capsules, and I don't want to know if you know. Whatever formal or informal agreement you have with these Malaysian suppliers, call them toot sweet and tell them you don't want some mother's little helper in their herbal formulations. Get some clean stuff made and packaged and out to the distributors. Have it tested by an independent lab before you send anything out."

"Jimmy, if they change the formulation, it may no longer be effective."

Jimmy laughed. "Don't insult my intelligence, Todd. You've never tested the effectiveness of any of your products, and neither has anybody else. If these Malaysian guys are putting unapproved drugs in any of your products, tell them to get it out of there. And tell them fast, before the government starts tapping your phones. We can have a separate conversation about that at some point."

"OK, Jimmy. All doable."

"OK. Get crackin'. Send me that draft announcement for health food stores by tomorrow at the latest. Bye."

Todd Singleton thought *Shit, we were just about to roll out an advertising push about the superior efficacy of our products. Now we're back to selling placebos. I've got to find something else to do for a living.*

Chapter 29

After talking to Singleton, Jimmy called Jan Mullany, the analytical chemist who did the analysis of the Phoebus Herbals product at Delvono. He asked Jan to explain exactly what she did, and Jimmy listened patiently even though he didn't understand all the mumbo-jumbo about mass spectra and NMR spectra and elemental analyses. Mullany convinced the layman Jimmy that the analyses and conclusions were correct.

Because Delvono was a private company and had no government contracts, there was no legal obligation to keep data. Of course, all data related to an ultimate new drug filing at FDA would have to be kept, but Frank's foray into analyzing other peoples' products did not fall into that category. Jimmy also knew that in the corporate world in general, it was important to have a written policy about when to purge business correspondence, emails, etcetera. A typical policy would state that all previously undeleted emails should be deleted after three years. Most employees did not follow such policies for a variety of reasons, the best of which was that people would often ask for information from projects more than three years old and be angry if the information was not available. Delvono had no data or correspondence sunsetting rules.

Jimmy was considering having all records of the forensic work on herbal products purged and destroyed. He asked Jan about these records, and she told him that there were a number of data tables and draft reports stored electronically on her computer and on Frank's computer, and of course these had been backed up onto the company's servers every night. There were also her paper notebooks, which had been witnessed and dated by her lab partner. And the analytical work done by the Spectroscopy Service Group was on their computers. Jimmy realized that it would not be easy to maintain total control over all these records.

"Jan, I want you do a few things to help us limit access to the work you did on the herbal products."

"Sure, whatever you say."

"OK, for starters, please give your bound notebooks for this project to Marge, and I'll have her put them in the safe. Purge your electronic files of any data or reports connected to the project. Also, please gather any paper records, spectra, whatnot, from the Spectroscopy Group and give those to Marge too. I think that'll do it for now."

Mullany was shocked. Like all scientists, she thought of the data she collected as her own, and the idea that she would not have copies or even electronic access seemed bizarre. Sure, she knew that she had signed a contract saying that her work belonged to Delvono Inc., but scientists often wrote up their work, with company approval, to be published in scientific journals or presented at scientific congresses. This is how scientists develop a public professional reputation, which reflects positively on their employers. "Sure, Mr. Delvecchio, I'll do whatever you want, but I want you to know that I'm still working on the newer analyses and we have incredibly interesting and useful information. I'm working up data now on a natural product for anxiety that actually contains an unapproved drug chemically related to oxycodone, and I've got a couple of people here working on some other products that look equally bad. We're gonna blow the doors off these crooks."

Jesus, Jimmy thought, *Serono has a tribe of followers*. He wasn't ready for this.

"Jan, you and your colleagues have been doing a fantastic job on this forensic project, and I appreciate the implications of all the work you've done. But there are potential legal issues related to making this work public, and some have already arisen because Dr. Serono described some of your results in his blog. Let's take a breather while we explore the unintended consequences of this project. I just want to put it on the shelf for a while."

"OK. I have to say that this is disappointing. I assume that I can take a couple of days to finish up the calculations and analyses that I'm working on now."

"No, Jan, I'd like you to wrap up this data protection thing today. And please tell your colleagues who are working on these projects that I've asked them to do the same." To smooth it over a little, he said, "I'll come down there to New Jersey in a few days and I'll sit down with you and your colleagues to give you some more of the rationale." As he said this, Jimmy knew he'd have to be very careful about what he actually told them.

The conversation ended with Mullany saying, "OK, Mr. Delvecchio, you're the boss." However, she wondered how Delvecchio was really the boss when he had left the company two years ago and was working somewhere else up in Connecticut.

Jimmy called Christina Lindbergh and told her that Jan Mullany and her colleagues were now officially off Frank's side project. He asked her to assign them back to drug discovery projects right away, and to let them each choose the project they would like to work on.

Chapter 30

Friday morning, Jimmy left Liberty Holdings in the limo for the ride to New Jersey for afternoon meetings at Delvono and a well-deserved appointment-free weekend at home with Gina. He told Andy the driver to stop at the Acropolis Diner in Lodi for lunch as they had done a couple of times before. As they entered the diner, Nick Kares spotted Jimmy, came over and shook his hand, and said to take a booth in the back and he would eat with him. Andy grabbed a newspaper off the rack by the cashier and sat at the counter.

Nick came over to Jimmy's booth with a waitress and sat down.

"Do you gentlemen know what you'd like?"

Jimmy said, "May I please have a turkey club on whole wheat toast with a half-order of fries and a root beer?"

The waitress responded, "That's very nice asking."

Jimmy said, "I'm a nice guy," and Nick said, "It's true. I can vouch for him."

All three laughed, and Nick said, "And may I please have a black coffee, Bobbie?"

The waitress answered, "Of course, Mr. Kares. I have to say I'm not used to such politeness from customers. Maybe the world has changed." She headed to the kitchen.

Nick opened, "Good to see you, Jimmy. How's Gina?"

"Good. No changes. Still loving the school over in Montclair."

"Have you seen the kids lately?"

"No, we've both been busy, and the kids are busy."

"Jimmy, you don't have all the time in the world, you know. I lost my Sophia, so I speak from experience. You gotta take a vacation. Take Amtrak up to Boston and stay in a hotel, go out to dinner with Anthony. Fly to Houston for a few days and see Linda. She's having a baby, right?"

"Yeah, we're gonna go down to see her when the baby's born."

"No, that's not good enough. I thought you were Italian. Take Gina down to see her now."

"Enough, Nickie, enough."

The food came, and Jimmy dug into his meal while Nick talked about his grown-up kids, the diner, Jersey politics, and what had happened to old high school friends from Lodi. As long time owner of the Acropolis Diner, Nick knew the local news as soon as it happened. Actually, sometimes before it happened. As Jimmy finished, Nick called over Bobbie and asked for a refill and a cup of coffee for Jimmy.

"So how are things at the Connecticut job?"

"Not good, lots of problems with closing and selling old businesses. And I've got problems here in Jersey at Delvono." For 15 minutes, Jimmy proceeded to tell his old friend Nick what was going on at Liberty Holdings, how some of the owners of the old businesses were making unreasonable demands even though they were being given the businesses. How wiseguys were coming out of the woodwork trying to get involved with the legit businesses that Jimmy was overseeing. Then he told Nick all about the Frank Serono nonsense and Jimmy's renewed responsibilities at Delvono. And finally, about the absurd Phoebus Herbals situation, in which Jimmy represented the owners of a company that was being ostensibly attacked by his own company Delvono, via Frank Serono. He even told Nick about the visit with the Senator. Nick was Jimmy's oldest friend, and the only person on earth he felt he could be so open with.

Nick said, "Did you take my advice from last month, and start to position yourself for an exit?"

"No, I've been so fucking busy with crises, I haven't been able to do anything long term."

"Hey, I'm not gonna sound like a broken record and go through all my insightful instructions to you from the last time we talked. But I'll say this. You're 54, maybe 55 years old. I lost track of your birthday. You're wealthy. You don't need to be like these WASP businessmen or Italian mob guys, obsessed with status and accumulating more and more cash you don't have time to spend. I understand that you need something to do, so go back to Delvono and ride herd on that Frank jerk. But you've got family and friends to spend time with. People don't live forever. You've lost your perspective."

"I know. *Campanilismo.*"

"Whatever."

They made small talk for a few more minutes, then Jimmy collected his driver and they got into the limo. Andy said, "To Delvono, right Mr. Delvecchio?"

"No, Andy, screw it. Let's head to my house in Verona."

Chapter 31

The next Tuesday, Jimmy sat on the crowded 8:04 Metro North train out of Stamford, heading to New York for a ten o'clock meeting at a law firm in Manhattan. Two of the industrial laundry companies controlled by *La Famiglia* would be transferred fully to the majority owners. In fact, the majority owners had been owners in name only, and this would be the first of a series of transfers to get the Gentilella family out of these mob-infected businesses. The "owners" were delighted with their pending windfall. Gentilella would be taking a large loss on this transfer that could not be claimed as a capital loss on his taxes, but Jimmy thought *I don't feel sorry for this guy. He made boatloads of cash for years from these laundry businesses, probably also laundered money through them, maybe even snuck a couple of dead bodies out of the city in laundry carts. Who knows? Great country, this America.*

Jimmy got off the train at Grand Central, and slowly moved down the platform with the horde of people exiting the train. A man with sun glasses in a pea coat, black cap, blue jeans, and black sneakers got off the car behind Jimmy's, and also moved with the horde toward the terminal. As he approached the end of the platform, surrounded by a throng of people, the man in the pea coat pulled his scarf up to cover the lower part of his face. Jimmy walked into the terminal, then down the stairs to use the East End Men's Room next to Shake Shack.

The man in the pea coat followed Jimmy down the stairs, turned away from the camera on the ceiling at the bottom of the stairs, turned left and pulled down his scarf as he approached the Men's Room, knowing that this section of the lower level was out of range of surveillance cameras. Jimmy stepped up to the one available urinal, unzipped his pants and started to urinate. He felt a horrible pain in his back, and the last thing he remembered was falling as he lost consciousness.

The man in the pea coat left the knife in Jimmy's back, exited the Men's Room and turned right, covering his face again with his scarf. He took the escalator up and walked through the Grand Central Market and out onto Lexington Avenue where he turned left, briskly walking. After about a block he took off his pea coat and scarf, and dropped them on top of a sleeping homeless man, revealing a black ribbed thinsulate LL Bean jacket underneath. He dropped his cap in a trashcan and pulled a NY Yankees cap out of his pocket and put it on. He walked east one block, turned left onto Third Avenue, walked one block north, ditched the Yankees cap in a trash can, pulled another washed-out grey cap out of his pocket, and put it on. He headed west to Broadway, dropped his sunglasses into a trashcan, got on the 1-Train, and disappeared into the Bronx.

Jimmy opened his eyes, then closed them quickly, blinded by the bright hospital room lights. He felt someone holding his hand and heard Gina say, "Jimmy, it's me. I'm here with you."

He opened his eyes and looked at Gina. He tried to speak, but couldn't. He was confused, in a deep stupor. He closed his eyes and went back to sleep.

Chapter 32

Three days later, Jimmy was sitting in his bed at NYU Bellevue Hospital, finishing off a plastic cup of tapioca pudding when Carmine Casamento came in.

"My little nephew Jimmy, sick in bed."

Jimmy beamed a big smile. "*Zio* Carmine, you're a sight for sore eyes! Good to see you."

"And good to see you. I guess you must have been saying your prayers, the Good Lord kept you with us."

"Yeah, well, maybe that's it, maybe it's because I have some fat on me. Enough of that for now. How's *Zia* Emerlinda?"

"She's good, very good. She's out on the Island, visiting the great-grandchildren. She loves being *Nonna*."

"And why aren't you out there, teaching that little boy to throw and catch?"

"He's got plenty of people to teach him that, a father and two grandfathers. I'm the old great-grandfather. I'd go, but I have work to do. As soon as I heard you were good, I came to talk. I came a few days ago, but you were in pretty bad shape. You were sleeping, so I just sat for a while and talked to Gina."

Jimmy said, "Did she ask you lots of questions?"

"Just a couple. I told her we'd find out who did this and make sure whatever the problem is, we'd get it solved. We left it at that. She knows."

"So did you figure out what the problem is?"

"Jimmy, Funzi contacted me through a messenger, and he thinks it's better that you not be involved. You've got all the clean businesses to run."

"That's nice, he doesn't want me to be involved. You wanna see the hole in my back? How much more involved can I get? You know how much time I've spent talking to the cops over the last two days? They're not stupid."

"Yeah, yeah, I know. But if you just say you have no idea why someone would do this, you just assume it was some homeless crazy nut, there's nothing much the cops can do. There are nuts all over the City, probably one out of three hundred is nuts. I was on the subway last week, and some guy is standing by the door yelling 'Suck my dick' over and over to the poor people sitting in front of him. There are nuts everywhere in New York. Is that what you told the cops?"

"What, 'Suck my dick'?" They both laughed.

"Yeah, that's what we should all say to the cops. But really, what did you tell them?"

"*Zio*, you can tell the boys at the main office that I didn't tell the cops anything. I don't want anybody getting any ideas. Things are bad enough already. Somebody stabbed me in the fucking back. I told the New York cops that I'm the CEO of a company in Stamford called Liberty Holdings. I was going to a meeting at our lawyer's place in Manhattan to sign some papers, and I stopped at Grand Central to take a leak. Some nut put a knife in my back. I didn't see anything. I have no enemies, and if I do, I don't know about it. I haven't been screwing some other guy's wife or girlfriend. I don't buy or sell oxy or heroin. I answered all their stupid questions. They seemed to believe me, but if they start nosing around the laundry businesses, they'll find reasons to be suspicious."

"You have to be ready with good explanations."

"I'm not worried about them digging, but it's a good thing I didn't die, good for Mr. Gentilella and for me of course. If I died, they'd have to go after the murderer more aggressively. If we're lucky, the NYPD will do a limited investigation and come up short. Just hope that the FBI doesn't get involved if the cops get suspicious about the old businesses. But you know, that could have happened any time. I should be squeaky clean, except I'm now helping Mr. Gentilella sell off all the old dirty businesses. I was clean, but now I have a connection to them."

"I think you're right. It'll blow over."

Jimmy said, "Have you personally talked to Mr. Gentilella about this? He sent me those flowers over there."

"No, we haven't talked. But I don't talk to Funzi unless he contacts me. I can't just call him up."

"So who do you think did this, *Zio*?"

"Jimmy, don't worry. We'll figure it out and take care of it."

"How can I not worry about it? When I'm laying here alone, I worry about who's gonna come in here in a hospital worker's uniform and finish the job."

"I understand. Look, here's how I look at it. If you're fooling around with some guy's wife, he might follow you and stab you like that. I'm gonna assume it's nothing personal like that. If the guys in our business want you gone, they use a gun and shoot twice. You don't end up in the hospital. Who stabs with a knife?

It had to be a warning. Have you gotten a warning message from anyone, a threat, a request?"

"No, *Zio*, and if I did I'd tell you. If I have to guess, it's one of our own guys who doesn't like the way the old businesses are being distributed. Somebody wants more. I tell you where I'd look, I'd look for somebody who's pissed about who was getting those two laundry businesses I was gonna sign the papers for. Maybe they stabbed me to stop me from showing up at the lawyer's place. But why hasn't anybody sent me an anonymous message about what they want?"

Uncle Carmine offered, "Maybe it was a message to you-know-who. Maybe it's bigger than you or me."

"Great. A message to Gentilella. *Zio* Carmine, I need a piece. Can you bring me one?"

"What, here in the hospital? You're not that kind of guy. Where you gonna hide it and have it ready when you need it? Don't worry, Jimmy, we're gonna take care of things."

"You're my uncle, forget about the business for a minute. Please bring me a piece with a full clip and a trigger lock so I don't have some kind of stupid accident here. Wipe it good so your prints aren't on it. And put it into some little zippered black bag of some sort, and I can just tell people it's my private stuff."

"No, Jimmy. Sorry. You're a respectable person who runs a respectable business. You get caught with a gun in here, you're reputation is finished."

"I can't ask the cops for protection. I was stabbed by a random nut, that's my story. Who knows, maybe I was."

"You weren't, I'm sure of that. I tell you what, I'll bring you a can of pepper spray if it'll make you feel better. If someone sees it here, you can tell them you're just nervous because of what happened at Grand Central."

"No *Zio*, bring me a piece."

"No can do, Jimmy."

A nurse came in to take Jimmy's vital signs, then Jimmy and his Uncle Carmine made small talk for a little while and Carmine left. Jimmy pressed the button to move the back of the bed almost down flat and put one pillow behind his head and one over his face to block the bright light. He thought *Great, a message to Gentilella. I'm trying to get out and now I'm stabbed to send a message to Gentilella. I'm grooming Harvard and Northwestern MBAs to take over for me and maybe now they're gonna be needed sooner rather than later if I take a dirtnap. I wonder if they're smart enough to realize that the job involves getting stabbed in the back as a message to the owner. They're not stupid. They know the score. I hope I don't start getting resignation letters.*

Chapter 33

NATURAL ENOUGH FOR YA? #22

from the desk of Frank Serono, Ph.D., President, Serono Pharmaceutical Consulting LLC

Kill Your Pain the Natural Way With This Amazing Supernutraceutical!

In my last blogpost, I described how the scientific geniuses at Phoebus Herbals have been putting an unapproved untested synthetic anti-diabetic drug of unknown toxicity in their "all natural" product FenuSeng UltraPlus. The government regulatory term for this illegal activity is "adulteration". All over the US, delighted snookered Type-II Diabetics have been telling their friends about how their sugar is under control with this amazing all-natural herbal product. They don't have to take any of those horrible drugs sold by the big pharmaceutical companies anymore. And their doctors are probably confused and wondering whether there really is something to this supernutraceutical revolution in medicine. And the people at Phoebus Herbals in Utah are laughing all the way to the bank. And the FDA Drug Division is left out of the loop because they are blocked from oversight of "natural" products due to heavy lobbying and the intercession of powerful Utah politicians.

Hold on to your hats, ladies and gentlemen, because we have discovered that the people at Phoebus Herbals are not the only supernutraceutical geniuses out there. The naturopathic people at Sylvan Life bring us "Boscalma", which "smooths pain" (whatever that means). This miracle product contains Boswellia (*Boswellia serrata*) and licorice root (*Glycyrrhiza glabra*). These herbs contain anti-inflammatory, analgesic, and anesthetic chemicals naturally, so there is some logic for their use, however weak the effect may be. We did DNA fingerprinting evaluation of Boscalma, and verified the presence of the two herbs in four bottles of capsules purchased in four different healthfood stores. That's comforting. We also did some analytical chemistry evaluation, and consistently found the presence of approximately 2 mg/capsule of dilaurylmorphine. Morphine is not a natural component of these herbs, and neither is dilaurylmorphine.

Now for a little drug chemistry. The chemical structure of morphine is well known, and this compound is closely chemically related to a variety of sedatives such as hydrocodone, oxycodone, naltrexone, and codeine. If a chemist were analyzing for adulteration of an herbal product with these and related known drugs, it would be straightforward to use High Performance Liquid

Chromatography (HPLC) to search for them, as the chromatographic signatures for these drugs are well known and easy to detect. There would of course be no reason to expect to find these drugs in an herbal pain-relief preparation, unless one were suspicious for some reason, say, because of surprising efficacy. Scientists at the FDA Drug Division would have no reason to do such a forensic analysis because they are not charged with oversight of "natural" products.

Dilaurylmorphine is a synthetic chemical that would be called a "prodrug" in the pharmaceutical chemistry world. This compound has lauric acid groups attached to the two hydroxyl groups on morphine. This is significant for two reasons. First, an analytical chemist looking for the presence of sedatives in an herbal product would not look for dilaurylmorphine because it is not itself a commonly known sedative. Second, when dilaurylmorphine is ingested, the body cleaves off the two lauryl groups, converting the dilaurylmorphine to morphine which will then have the usual expected physiological effects. In fact, the lauryl groups may increase accessibility of the morphine to the brain.

I must say that I am impressed by the disingenuous "naturopathic" scientists at Sylvan Life. These geniuses belong in jail.

FDA take notice.

Chapter 34

Jimmy called Alfonso Gentilella from the hospital and, after an exchange of pleasantries, said that he needed some guidance on a variety of issues related to Liberty Holdings. Gentilella said that he could come to the hospital that afternoon, and Jimmy suggested 1:30 because he almost never had visitors between 1:00 and 4:00.

Gentilella was dressed in his usual "business casual" attire and looked fit, but Jimmy could detect a change. There is a look that a man develops, women too, and it seems like it's almost overnight – from a healthy fit older person to a frail elderly one. Gentilella was on the cusp.

After a brief tete-a-tete about Uncle Carmine and the weather, Jimmy turned on the TV to avoid eavesdroppers and broke the ice. "I have some business things to talk about that I'll get to, but I'd like to get to the main thing right away. To be blunt, somebody put a knife in my back, and I'm trying to avoid a repeat performance."

"Terrible, just terrible. Do the police have any leads?"

"I really have no way of knowing what they're doing, and I'm certainly not gonna pressure them. When I came around after a couple of days, they asked me a million questions, but they were generally personal questions and they didn't bring up anything about business except to ask where I was going that day. They didn't suggest that there was anything suspicious about Liberty Holdings or anything else, but at that point they hadn't done any investigating as far as I know. This wasn't a random attack, right?"

"No, I don't think so."

"Do you know who did it?"

"Jimmy, think about this. If I knew I wouldn't tell you because you shouldn't be involved in any eye-for-an-eye stuff. I have big troubles. Starting to sell off the old businesses has made it very clear to others that this is the end of an era, and they want to control the new era. I've received offers to buy me out from some big guys, but that doesn't really mean changing formal ownership of businesses. It just means that I and my underlings walk away for cash, and they start to use their muscle unopposed to milk the businesses. They own them, even though their names aren't on the papers."

"I don't really understand why this should be a problem once you get your name off any ownership documents. You said you wanted out."

"Well, things are getting complicated. The young turks are rebelling, in our shop and some of the other shops. The chain-of-command isn't being respected, and that's probably because the old personal family relationships aren't like they used to be. Some of the shops have gotten other people in – Croatians, Serbs, Russians, even some Chinese. It made sense, I guess, because that's where the muscle is today. There really are no *famiglie* anymore, at least not like the old days, and the Russians particularly want to be in charge.

"With all due respect, Mr. Gentilella, in my opinion you should just step down."

"Then there'll be a war."

"Just stay out of the line of fire, and tell your son to stay out of the line of fire. Retire, like Joe Kennedy. Your son should retire too, and find something else to do."

"Message received."

"Mr. Gentilella, I want out."

"What's this Mr. Gentilella stuff? With you, I'm Funzi."

"Well, Funzi, I want out. I've done a lot of thinking laying here in this bed. Here's what I'd like to do, and I hope you'll consider it seriously because I've put your interests at the top of the list here next to mine. I want to get out of the business of overseeing the transfer of the old dirty businesses to the people who run them. I shouldn't have been involved in the first place. It just drifted that way. We've already hired a business law firm that does this stuff, so give them power of attorney and let them do it without oversight."

Gentilella broke in, "The problem is that there has to be oversight. This business lawfirm has to have someone they can call with questions. If it's not you, then it's me, and I don't have time for the details."

"No, I think you give detailed instructions to the lawyers and tell them to just use their judgement, and promise that you won't second guess them. As soon as you have someone from *La Famiglia* involved, people think pressure can be applied."

"People will still try to pressure me."

"Make yourself scarce. Just walk away and retire. Have a bodyguard if you think it's necessary. And you have to tell your son he's out, unless he wants to battle with the young turks as you call them. You know, once you're really out, everyone will be so busy fighting over a piece of the action that you'll just be a name in the history books. I guess I'm not asking to be let out of this. I am out. I'm not gonna be stabbed or shot. I didn't sign up for that. The trick to this is to do it fast, as fast as possible."

"We probably should have done it this way from the beginning, but I felt that somebody had to keep an eye on it, and I trust you. I'm OK with this idea. I'm worried though about my son. How do you recommend proceeding?"

"It's pretty straightforward. You and I get our ducks in a row, and then we meet with the lawyers. You just pay them whatever their fee is, which of course has to be negotiated. We give them an inflexible deadline for completion, and the cost will be related to the deadline. Pay more, done quicker. That's what we want."

"OK. I'll seriously consider this, and I'm going to have a long talk with my son. I'll also have to talk to my brothers and sister."

"Keep it simple. Give them a boatload of cash, and don't give them options." Jimmy moved on, "Now on a related subject, would your retirement involve Liberty Holdings in any way?"

"No, that belongs to my personal family as opposed to *La Famiglia*. But I guess you never know what these guys will do. You've been doing a great job with it."

"Thank you, but here's the thing, I want out of that too."

"I don't know, Jimmy."

"Please, hear me out. I stepped up and helped and it was a challenge and the truth is that I enjoyed it. But I'm a Jersey guy and my family is there. I'm even thinking of moving back to Lodi from Verona, which I guess is kind of stupid, but not totally stupid. I want a simpler life, and I love working at my biotech company Delvono. That's what I want to do. And to be honest, I'm a little worried that the other families and the young turks might want to put some pressure on Liberty, and maybe get a piece of it. It's yours, no doubt about it, but these guys don't fight by Marquis of Queensbury rules."

"Jimmy, I think when you got stabbed, it worked. They've got you running."

"I don't agree with that. What it really did was it woke me up and forced me to develop a better plan for both you and me. Or maybe force me to seriously consider what I always knew should be done."

"OK. I'm listening."

"Liberty Holdings is in great shape. I have a guy there, effectively my second in command, named Owen McCarthy, who I've been grooming. He's terrific and has all the right boxes checked off. He was a working class kid from Quincy, Mass, who has street smarts but never got into trouble. Went to Northeastern then worked at Fidelity in Boston, then went to Harvard Business School. One of the smartest and most even-tempered people I've ever met, and somebody who can be firm when necessary. I say put him in charge. And there are people at the next level down almost as good."

"How does this help, other than getting you out?"

"The other necessary piece, you're gonna have to think about it. Convene a new independent Board with no family members. All first-rate successful business people, hopefully a couple from large corporations. And here's the big change. You sell off a piece, so it's not just your family company. I know a couple of clean guys in Stamford who are chomping at the bit to buy in. It's a great stable of businesses. Then you're just one of a few private investors in a company run by excellent people who have zero connection to the Gentilella family or *La Famiglia*. Do this and you're really out. Nobody can put pressure on Liberty Holdings."

"OK. That's a lot to think about. But as usual, you're probably right. When do you get out of the hospital?"

"They say two days."

"OK. Do the planning and start to set things up. We can meet in about a week, after I talk to a few people." Gentilella stood up. "Thank you Jimmy, the day I met you in the park was an important day."

"Thanks, and thanks for taking the trouble to come here to talk."

Jimmy turned off the TV, they shook hands, and Gentilella left.

Jimmy had planned to talk to Gentilella about Frank's blogging and Liberty's herbal supplement companies, but he had already dropped a big load in his lap. And maybe the Frank problem was too down in the weeds to bring up with him.

Jimmy was pleased, very pleased, and felt like a weight was lifting from his shoulders.

Chapter 35

Six weeks after the Grand Central attack, Jimmy was almost back to normal, and could even work out at the gym in Stamford. He was still overweight and had never exercised vigorously, and now had to cut back on the intensity even more. But Jimmy was nothing if not a regular person with regular habits, and one of these was to get to the gym three or four times per week. If someone is out to kill you, though, having regular habits is not a good thing, and he could swear from time to time that he was being watched. Or maybe he wasn't.

Frank had visited Jimmy twice in the hospital, and they agreed not to talk business, only family. It had been uncomfortable, but the reality was that they were friends with a lot of water under the bridge. After Jimmy went home from the hospital, he and Frank had a couple of phone calls about Delvono, and they were warming up to one another again. Frank's ridiculous blogging continued, but Jimmy had managed to convince the Utah lawyer and others that Frank was completely cut off from Delvono, no more than a scientific consultant. Jimmy hoped they realized that he had no real leverage with Frank to get him to stop. Of course, that didn't mean they wouldn't lean on Frank some other way, but Delvono was hopefully out of the line of fire.

It seemed that Jimmy and Frank could get along over the phone, but had problems in person. While Frank was technically only a consultant at Delvono, Jimmy had recently given him free reign to talk to Christina Lindbergh about work issues anytime without a third person on the line, and Frank had visited Delvono a couple of times to talk to scientists there about projects. Frank was not comfortable with Jimmy's pronouncement that Christine calls the shots, and he was starting to understand what he had done to himself. In addition, Frank's marriage was becoming strained for the first time and, without the kids at home to be the center of his and Maria's lives, they were arguing over trivial things. From time to time, Maria would ask Frank what his career plans were, and he didn't have a good answer for her or for himself.

This week, Jimmy decided to work from home in New Jersey, where he had a videoconferencing set-up in his home office to interact with the people in Stamford. Today, Frank and Christina were coming over for an early morning meeting to discuss Delvono projects, and Jimmy had some coffee, bagels, cream cheese, and lox ready. Northeastern New Jersey was probably the only place in the suburban New York area where you could still get good bagels, one more reason for Jimmy to never move permanently to Stamford, Connecticut.

Christina arrived first and sat down with Jimmy at the dining room table to set up her laptop and have some breakfast. They made small talk about Christina's recent visit home to Montana, which fascinated Jimmy, especially her description of a hunting trip with her father, brother, and cousin.

Jimmy said, "Do you miss home?"

"Sure. My parents are great. They still have the ranch, and my brother and his wife live in a new house on the property, so I think it's all gonna be around for a while. I love going back."

"If you don't mind me asking, how did you end up working in New Jersey? Why didn't you go back?"

"Why doesn't anybody go back? One thing leads to another. After Montana State, I wanted an adventure, and MIT was great. So much top-flight science going on. I loved it, I loved the enthusiasm, it was exhilarating really. I made some good friends, went hiking in New Hampshire, just had an all around good time. But nobody talks about going someplace like Montana next. So I spent two years in a tiny studio apartment in New York while I worked at Rockefeller in a Nobel Laureate's lab. Seemed like a good career move but turned into a goat rodeo for me. Basically I just worked for two years. For whatever reason, I just didn't get into New York. I could rattle off clichés about the place, but basically I was a fish out of water."

"Then why New Jersey?"

"Well, Dr. Serono gave a talk at Rockefeller and I was blown away. I wanted to do research on big problems, not teach at this point, and I wanted to make my mark. He did great work without being at a university or a research institute, and I was intrigued. When I visited here and saw what was going on, it seemed so enthusiastic. I figured what the heck. Worst case scenario, I could consider it to be like a second post-doc and then apply for academic positions."

"Have you made friends here?"

"At work? Yeah. A couple of us get together for dinner sometimes and on weekends. It's becoming a little different now that I'm in charge of some people, even temporarily. Research people don't like needing someone else's approval. But things are generally good. And I get together with a couple of my old MIT friends, one in Philly and one at Merck in Kenilworth."

Jimmy was starting to wonder why Frank was late when they heard two loud bangs outside. Jimmy and Christina rushed to the front door and Jimmy opened it. Frank's car door was open down at the street and Frank was laying on the grass. There was a grey minivan next to Frank's car, and a guy got out on the passenger side and calmly walked around the back of the minivan and Frank's car. Jimmy looked at Christina, and was surprised to see her pushing a clip into a gun that she seemed to produce out of thin air. As the guy approached Frank and took aim at him, Christina pushed Jimmy and said, "Get out of the way." She dropped to one knee, raised her gun while supporting her gun hand with the other, took aim, and fired. The gunman fell, then got up on his knees, turned, and aimed at Christina. She got off another shot, this one deadly, and he collapsed.

As Christina and Jimmy ran to Frank, the minivan sped away. The gunman was lying on the grass, not moving. Jimmy kicked his gun away and said, "Frank, are you OK?"

Frank looked up dazed and, holding his shoulder, said, "No, that guy shot me. He signaled me to roll down my window so I did then I saw the gun and tried to jump out of the car. Only my shoulder I think." Jimmy looked at Frank's car and saw that the driver's side front window was shattered. He said, "OK, Frank, you're gonna be OK, just lie there. There's no danger now."

Christina was on her cell, talking to 911, and wondering what she would do if the minivan went around the block and showed up again. She hung up and Jimmy yelled, "Stay low!" and the two of them crouched next to Frank's car in case the other guy came back. Luckily, he didn't, and in a couple of minutes two police cars screeched in to a stop with sirens blaring. Christina realized that she was holding a handgun and immediately put it on the hood of Frank's car. The cops called an ambulance, which arrived in a further 10 minutes. Jimmy and Christina both volunteered to accompany Frank in the ambulance, but the police had other ideas given the dead body on the lawn.

The front yard was cordoned off as a crime scene, and everyone on the block who was not at work or school was out gawking. More police cars came, with enough cops to fight a small army. Two detectives wanted to talk to Jimmy, and especially to Christina, and Jimmy invited them into the house to sit down. After establishing what actually happened, and mostly believing it, one of the detectives started pushing Christina.

"I'm gonna assume for the time being that you're the savior in this situation. But I still have a problem. What are you doing with a handgun?"

"I carry it for protection. I had a violent guy obsessed with me when I lived in New York City, and I have a restraining order against him."

"Do you have a carry permit for the gun?"

"I have a concealed carry permit in Montana, where I'm from. I have a New Jersey permit but not a concealed carry permit."

"If you don't have a permit, why are you carrying?"

"I went down to the local police station in Nutley where I'm living, and they told me that essentially no permit is ever issued to a citizen who's not law enforcement, ex-law enforcement, or has political connections. In principle, you can get a carry permit if you're in some danger, but in practice they're never issued. I'm not gonna leave myself unprotected just because New Jersey has this idiotic position."

The two detectives looked at each other and shook their heads and rolled their eyes because they were thinking the same thing. They have to arrest her and when the news media gets the story she'll be seen as a local hero. Cowgirl from Montana kills assailant. "OK. We're gonna take you into custody. We'll deal with the details down at the stationhouse, and the DA will decide what to charge you with."

Christina said, "You can't be serious. What's this about, hitmen's rights in New Jersey?" She looked at Jimmy for help, but he knew better than to object. He said, "Don't worry, Christina, I'll get a lawyer right down to the police station. We'll take care of this."

She said, "What about Dr. Serono?"

"I'm gonna get in touch with his wife right now and head to the hospital."

The detectives took Christina out to the police car without mirandizing or cuffing her. On the way to the station, one of them said to the other, "I didn't hear any explanation, good or bad, for why that doctor got shot."

Chapter 36

Jimmy called Maria Serono's cellphone.

"Hi Jimmy. I know what happened. They took him here to Montclair General and I was here working today, so I met him just after he came in."

"How's he doin'?"

"He's fine. They did some things to the wound, and the bullet went all the way through so they didn't have to look for it. They say they'll hold him a couple of days to make sure there's no infection. Jimmy, what the hell is going on here?"

Jimmy's mind was racing, trying to figure out what to say and not say. "I don't know. Christina Lindbergh from Delvono and I were at my house waiting for Frank for a meeting when we heard a loud noise. We went to the front door and saw Frank falling out of his parked car. A guy was coming around the back of the car with a gun drawn and Christina pulled out a gun and shot the guy, killed him."

"You got stabbed about two months ago. Then Frank gets shot in front of your house. Then this Dr. Lindbergh pulls a gun and shoots. This is not normal, Jimmy. I know you know what's going on. I can speculate a lot of things, but you know."

"Maria, I don't know. I can speculate too, but I will tell you that I don't think the attacks on me and Frank are related."

"They shot him in front of your house. They thought they were killing you."

"That's possible, but I don't think so. Frank was parked down at the street and I have a driveway and there was an open space in the driveway."

"So you're telling me that someone really wants to kill Frank? That's worse." She was starting to yell into the phone now. "So somebody may come in here and shoot up the hospital? I know you know something, and you better do something about this."

"OK. Maria, please calm down. The important thing is that Frank's OK."

"Don't tell me to calm down. My husband is in a hospital bed, shot, and you say someone really wants to kill him."

"OK. I'm sorry, Maria. I think this may have something to do with Frank's blogging."

"What? Jesus. He told me he had received threats. Oh, God."

"OK. Maria, I'll do something right away. I'll try to get the cops to post a guard at the hospital or I'll pay for a private guard. He's only in the hospital for a day or two. And I'll get a guard for you guys at your house."

"Good. Thank you, Jimmy. I'm glad the kids aren't home. I don't know what to tell them."

"OK. I gotta go and make a bunch of phone calls. I'll be at the hospital soon, hopefully in about an hour."

"I'll see you then. I still need a better explanation from you."

Jimmy sat for a moment and thought *I've got to get my ducks in a row here. We can't be looking over our shoulders for fucking assassins.* He quickly came to a realization. *I'm gonna have to join Frank and blow the doors off all this natural remedies crap and just make everything very public, regardless of consequences to Liberty Holdings' companies in Utah. Make Frank irrelevant to get him out of danger.*

He called his personal lawyer Bill Cassidy and explained what happened, just the facts and nothing about motive, although Cassidy asked. Then he called a detective agency he knew and arranged for 24-hour guard service at the Serono house, starting tomorrow morning. Then he called the Montclair police station and requested a protective guard at the hospital for tonight, although he realized they were unlikely to comply. He called back Maria Serono, gave her the police number, and suggested that she also call and request a guard at the hospital. He also suggested that she talk to the hospital security guys about being vigilant, and maybe putting a guy outside Frank's room. *Ducks in a row.*

Jimmy went to the hospital but Frank was sedated and asleep. He talked with Maria for a few minutes then headed back home. When he got there he covered Frank's smashed car window with plastic sheeting and duct tape, then made himself a gin and tonic and sat in an armchair in the living room staring into space.

Gina brought home some takeout Chinese food and as they ate he told her everything, starting with an explanation for the strange damaged car parked down at the street. Not many things could surprise her. After all, she knew that the Liberty Holdings job was loosely mob-connected, and of course she had already been through the agonizing experience of Jimmy's stabbing. None of those things had surprised her because she had been with Jimmy from back in the truck thievery days when, as a good *famiglia* wife, she just described her husband as being in the transport business. Of course, after Jimmy was stabbed she vigorously pushed the position that he should extricate himself from the Stamford job ASAP. But today she was truly bewildered by the attempt on Frank's life, and by Jimmy's assertion that it might have to do with Frank's blogging. The idea that "clean" businesses would stoop to murder was shocking. She was particularly surprised by the visit with the senator, which Jimmy had not previously told her about. She castigated Jimmy for having been so secretive then said, "Let's go visit Frank in the hospital." So they did.

Christina spent the night in jail.

Chapter 37

The next morning, Christina appeared in court with Bill Cassidy as attorney. He informed the judge that Christina had a New Jersey gun owner's permit, but was unable to obtain a concealed carry permit. Cassidy recounted her home and academic history, and the judge said that she could be released on bond as soon as he received confirmation that she in fact really did have a restraining order out. Cassidy admitted to the large technicality that she had the order out in New York, but did not seek a similar order when she moved to New Jersey. The DA did not raise objections, so the judge let it go. The judge said that he was generally reluctant to approve release on bond for a manslaughter suspect, and that Christina should not leave the state. The DA asked for house arrest, but Cassidy argued that she had a highly responsible critical job overseeing pharmaceutical research and the judge went for it. Christina went back to a holding pen for a few hours and was then released. Jimmy had been in court for her hearing, paid her bond, and later picked her up to drive to his house to get her car.

After they got in Jimmy's car and took off, he said, "That was some shot you took, some two shots really."

"I've never shot a person before, and I feel bad about it in a way."

"You saved Frank's life, and maybe you saved our lives if those guys decided to eliminate witnesses. That was some shooting. You know what you're doing."

"I was on the pistol and skeet teams at Montana State and I was a finalist in the Olympic trials but didn't make it. I joined a gun club in New York City, actually out in Nassau, and now I'm in one up in Mahwah."

"But what made you get your gun out so quick?"

"I've been around guns all my life. When I heard the noise, I knew exactly what it was. I even knew it was small arms. I just opened my bag instinctively, pushed in the clip, and ran to the door. In any other situation, this would have been a stupid overreaction."

"I'm glad you overreacted. What's the story with this violent boyfriend in the City?"

"Not a boyfriend, just a nut. I don't want to talk about it."

"OK."

Christina said, "So who shot Frank? Do you know what this is about? Do you think they were trying to get you?"

"Why me?"

"Look, with all due respect, everybody at Delvono knows that you had a checkered career before you became the wealthy Don of New Jersey Biotech. And there's lots of watercooler talk about your current job in Connecticut. Maybe I've stepped out of line here, sorry, I'll stop."

"No, no, it's OK. It's true. I'm not gonna tell you all my history, but I got lucky when I set up my internet pharmacy company, and got rich when I sold it to some Israelis. But other than meeting my wife, meeting Frank was the best thing that ever happened to me." He smiled. "Alright, I guess I have to say the birth of my children was better, yadda, yadda, yadda, but you get the point. I love Delvono, and want to get back to it full-time."

Christina pushed. "But you were into some questionable stuff when you were younger, right?"

"I'm not gonna get into it, but look, I was born into it. It was the family business, and we knew we were breaking laws, but we didn't think we were really doing anything wrong. It's complicated. I'm faithful to my extended family here in New Jersey and always will be. If you want to talk about my history maybe we can do that some time, but not now."

As they pulled into Jimmy's driveway, Christina said, "But it still seems more likely that they were after you."

Jimmy said, "I don't think so. Are you aware of Frank's blogs?"

"Sure. Everybody at work is. They're wicked. I love them."

They sat in Jimmy's car in his driveway for about 20 minutes, and Jimmy told her all about the nonsense related to Frank's obsession – the lawyer threats, the visit with the senator, about Liberty Holdings and Phoebus Herbals, everything. She was aware that Jan Mullany was doing some analytical work for Frank, but had never seen the data.

Christina said, "I get it. Maybe they were after Frank. What are you gonna do?"

Jimmy said, "I don't know."

Christina thought *I'll ask him about getting stabbed some other time. Enough for today.*

* * *

Jimmy stayed in New Jersey for another day, and visited Frank and Maria when they got home from the hospital. He brought bakery cookies, and the three of them sat in the living room drinking coffee and eating cookies, discussing Frank's situation and what could be done to prevent a repeat. Jimmy decided that at this point he would be open with both Frank and Maria, and that there was nothing significant that should be hidden from either of them. The one exception was Jimmy's meeting with the senator. He figured that was too incendiary to trust to Frank's big mouth.

Maria was still somewhat skeptical that the target was really Frank, and was also very curious about the pistol-packing Ph.D. Christina Lindbergh. Jimmy told them about the Liberty ownership of Phoebus Herbals and the two other Utah herbal remedy companies, which Frank had been unaware of. Frank accused Jimmy of opposing him on the blogging because of the Liberty Holdings companies that Jimmy was responsible for, but Frank was too sedated to get really worked up over it. Jimmy shared with them his conclusion that the best way to protect Frank was to be very forthcoming with the herbal product adulteration data, perhaps going right to the FDA with it. The trick would be to create a situation in which killing Frank would have no effect. Of course, it was very possible, perhaps very probable, that Delvono would suffer for it.

And Frank would have to stop blogging.

That night, Jimmy headed in the limo to his apartment in Stamford. As he sat in the back of the car in the dark, he thought about everything he had to do to get things straightened out. He had this strange feeling like he had been in a fog for years and now he was coming out into the light. His life was in New Jersey, his real work was at Delvono, and Frank was a friend, although a severely flawed one. Status in the old *La Famiglia* was not important, or more accurately, was not important to him anymore. And then there was his old friend Nick at the Acropolis

Diner, who had reminded him that life does not go on forever. He dozed, physically and mentally exhausted.

Chapter 38

The next day, Jimmy went to his Stamford office prepared for a long day of telephone calls. First, he called Christina and told her that he needed some of Jan Mullany's time to do some calculations and report writing. He promised to call back later to talk about her legal problems. Then he called Mullany and asked her to recover her data and to complete whatever data analyses were left hanging. He also asked her to prepare draft formal reports of her completed work to date, addressed to Jimmy as Acting CEO of Delvono, not to be issued until Jimmy and others reviewed them. Mullany wanted to know what was going on, and Jimmy said that they may be sending the data to the FDA. He also told Mullany to summarize what lab experiments were planned when the work was stopped, in anticipation of possibly starting up again.

Jimmy called the Chairman of the Advisory Board for Phoebus Herbals, and told him about the "Natural Enough For Ya?" blogs, and about the data in hand that implicated Phoebus in adulteration of its products with untested unapproved drugs. The Chairman, head of a large Utah pharmacy distribution company specializing in natural remedies, was aware of the blogs. Jimmy offered to send him Jan Mullany's draft report when available, to convince him of the seriousness of the accusations against Phoebus. Jimmy informed him that he would be asking for Todd Singleton's resignation, which as sole owner Liberty Holdings was within its rights to do. Then he called Singleton.

"Hi, Jimmy. How are you feeling? Healing up well?"

"Yeah, I'm almost back to normal. Thanks for asking. I'm calling because there's a change in strategy with the adulteration issue."

"That's fine. But just to update you, we've been getting back supplies from distributors and destroying them. Things seem to be OK at the distributor level and at the store level. It's under control. So what's the new idea?"

"Starting right now, I want Phoebus to quarantine any materials coming back from distributors or customers, and don't destroy any more returns."

"OK, but if the FDA gets their hands on them, we could be in big trouble. And if there are lawsuits, we could also have discovery problems."

"We'll deal with those things if and when they come. I've changed my mind, and would like to opt for total transparency. The bigger issue, and I'm sorry to have to do this, is that I'm asking for your resignation, effective tomorrow. We'll work out a parachute for you, but I want you to step down right away."

"Whoa, Jimmy, please pump the brakes and let's talk about this. I've done nothing wrong, and I've doubled the size of this business. We can get through this bump without doing anything drastic."

"I know you've built the business, and we've paid you handsomely for that. I just think that given the present situation, it's best for you to step down."

"Jimmy, we haven't even analyzed the supposedly adulterated product, and I believe it's a false accusation. And even if it turned out to be true, which it isn't, it would be the fault of the Malaysian suppliers. We certainly didn't adulterate anything. In fact, they sent us the complete formulated mix, so we had no opportunity to spike anything here in Utah."

"I'm sorry, Todd, I can't accept that the buck stops in Malaysia. You're the CEO. This is the nature of being a CEO."

"The fact is that we're blameless here. If in fact anything was adulterated, the adulteration took place without our knowledge."

"And I'm inclined to believe that you knew about it, maybe even asked for it. Even if you didn't, I'm holding you responsible. As far as your public face is concerned, spin it any way you like. My public position will be that the Malaysians sent Phoebus Herbals spiked product without your knowledge, presumably for the purpose of assuring therapeutic efficacy to keep the Phoebus contract. You're taking the hit for running an organization unprepared to detect this adulteration. End of story. I hope there'll be no lawsuits, but time will tell. Tomorrow, Tim Hagen from Liberty Holdings will arrive in Salt Lake to take over as Acting CEO until we can get someone permanent. He'll bring a chemist consultant and an auditor with him to look over your records. I'd like to ask you to be available for one week to help them get started, as a condition of your financial separation package."

"And what are we talking for a separation package?"

"I'm thinking salary and health insurance for four months."

"You can't be serious. I'm the CEO of a $30 million business. That's nowhere near the ballpark of a standard package."

"Well that's the package."

"I'm not accepting it. I'll be getting my lawyer involved."

"Listen, you belong in jail, asshole. You endangered the lives of your customers. From the perspective of the government, you poisoned them. Good for you if you have plausible deniability. I'm not falling for it. Immediately after I hang up, your direct reports will be informed by people from Liberty that you're no longer in the CEO position. In approximately ten minutes, you'll be escorted off the site without your laptop. Your computer access has already been turned off."

"Fuck you."

"Nice." Jimmy hung up.

Singleton quickly attempted to sign on to the company computer system, and was denied access.

*   *   *

Jimmy decided to go for a walk. Liberty Holdings was in a landscaped wooded industrial park with sidewalks that seemed to only be used when people took their daily constitutional during lunchtime. Now in the mid-morning the roads were empty, no cars and no walkers. It was getting a little cool and the leaves were starting to change color. A cloudy day with the dull light filtering through the trees giving a feeling of impending winter. As he walked, he thought through how things might play out, or to be more accurate, what plan would maximize things working out the way he wished.

Goal number one was to prevent another attack on Frank. He had no way of figuring out who was behind the shooting, and it was best to cooperate with the police, although he was skeptical that they would solve it. Sending Frank's and Mullany's data to the FDA, and making it public, would partially remove Frank from the line of fire. Getting the data out had to be done fast. Jimmy debated whether it was really critical that Frank stop his blogging. If he did stop, then the herbal remedy companies might conclude that Frank's contribution to their problem has been contained, and they only need to go through their usual lobbying channels to stop long-term legislative damage. Phoebus Herbals and a couple of other companies might be directly damaged by the data submission to FDA, but that would be the extent of it. If Frank continued to blog, he would be a very public target – killing him would make him a martyr, so they would probably leave him alone. However, if he presents more analytical data on more products, then more companies will be damaged, making eliminating him seem more critically necessary. Frank could probably keep muckraking, but the analytical lab work at Delvono on herbal products had to be history.

As far as Phoebus was concerned, they would just take their public lumps and maybe let the FDA take samples and verify the adulteration. They would have to find a new herb supplier. Should they sue Malay Botanical? A lot of good that would do – a wasted effort. He wondered how many other US natural remedy companies were using Malay Botanical's enhanced formulations. Worst-case scenario – Phoebus suffers multiple large lawsuits and goes out of business. That would be a major hit to Liberty Holdings, and Jimmy would have to prevent it. He would have to use consultants to figure out how to reconfigure the business and have it rise from the ashes with a different name, somehow minimizing losses. Probably bankruptcy. *That fucking asshole Singleton.*

Jimmy changed his train of thought, and realized that from his wife Gina's perspective, goal number one would be to prevent himself from being stabbed or shot. A completely different ballgame on a completely different ballfield. Jimmy felt overwhelmed and thought *how did I get into this mess*, even though he knew quite well.

He went back to the office, got a cup of coffee, and called up Christina at Delvono.

He was feeling more fatherly than professional and said, "How you doin', kiddo?"

"Well, I'm doing well, considering that I could get five years, with parole eligibility after three for the gun possession."

"Whoa. Tell me about this, please, unless you consider it confidential. Do you think Cassidy's the right lawyer?"

"I think he's fine. He's going to hook me up with a lawyer who deals heavily with gun offenses in New Jersey, which seem to be a big thing around here. Concealed carry of a loaded weapon is a 2nd degree felony, and the Graves Act defines the five year minimum sentence. As with everything, there are technicalities that might help. I wasn't technically carrying a loaded weapon until I put the clip in, which I did in your house. You can have a loaded weapon in your home, but in this case I was in your home, not mine. For a first-offender, there's a possibility for what they call a Pre-Trial Intervention, which involves being under court supervision for a year and then the charges are dismissed. Cassidy seems to think it's just a matter of paying this gun lawyer and I have enough technicalities to get off."

"That's good. Whatever it costs, you know I'll take care of it."

"Thanks. But then there's the minor issue that I killed a guy. Cassidy says it's hard to plead self-defense because I was only in danger after I shot the guy once and he aimed at me. He thinks our argument may be that one of your guests was being attacked on your property, and you have a right to intervene, even in a deadly way. Of course, I'm the one who shot the guy, not you."

"But you were a guest on my property when it happened."

"That's what Cassidy says, so maybe this'll work out too. Cassidy had a brief conversation with the DA and says she's not hot about prosecuting me because there'll be a media circus. Did you see the Daily News and the Post yesterday? One said 'Annie Oakley Gets Her Man' and the other said 'Montana Cowgirl Downs New Jersey Hitman'. I don't know where they got that picture of me. I scanned the two front pages and emailed them to my brother and a couple of friends for fun. But it's not fun really. I had a long discussion with my parents back in Montana last night and they're worried."

"So does Cassidy think the murder charge will be dropped?"

"Yeah, he thinks so, but the DA needs some kind of corroboration of our story. There are no other witnesses, so there's no independent proof for who shot who first. The cops repeatedly asked me how well I knew the guy I shot; they kept trying to trip me up. It may help if they identify the guy I killed, and he turns out to be a known criminal. They're looking for some logic for why he would have shot Frank, and don't necessarily buy your story that it might have to do with his blogging. They kept asking me what I know about you getting stabbed. They seemed very curious about that."

"I don't see why they wouldn't buy our story in the end."

"Well to be blunt, Jimmy, your old underworld background has them circumspect. That's what Cassidy thinks. They need to eliminate other explanations for the shootout at Delvecchio's."

"Well don't worry, it'll be fine. I'm presuming they'll know who the dead guy is pretty quickly. They should know by now from his fingerprints. I've never seen the guy before, so I know there's no direct connection to me."

"OK. You want to talk about projects now?"

"No, I'm confident that Delvono is in good hands. I'll arrange a scheduled call to talk about work maybe later in the week, or

I'll do a scheduled drop-in next week. Don't worry about the legal stuff. Focus on your work."

"OK, Mr. Delvecchio."

Jimmy took a sip of cold coffee, turned off his computer, and decided to get some lunch. *I wish I was in New Jersey.*

Chapter 39

After lunch, Jimmy called up Dean Tinney, the external counsel used by Delvono for FDA and foreign regulatory issues.

"Hi, Jimmy, good to hear from you. I read about what happened to Frank. How's he doing?"

"He's home and he's healing. He won't be swinging a golf club for a while."

"Well, I hope he gets back to normal soon. What's up?"

"We have some data at Delvono about some herbal products, and I think the FDA should see it and I don't know how to actually send it to them."

"Is this the thing that Frank called me about before, the unapproved drugs in herbal products?"

"Yeah, I guess it is, but I didn't know Frank talked to you."

"Well, we only had a very brief conversation. As I recall, he wanted to know what government agency would have oversight over such a thing. I told him it seemed like a food issue rather than a drug issue. I said I'd follow up, but I never did."

"Well, we have some data indicating that two herbal products are adulterated with unapproved drugs. I'm calling them drugs, but I don't know what I should be calling them."

"Well, I can think about that, but off the top of my head I'd probably say 'bioactive chemicals of unknown toxicity' or something like that."

"So how do we send this data to the FDA or whoever should get it? We don't just send it to some New Jersey police department, right?"

"There are various ways we can do this, if you want me to help. You should probably send what's called a 'Citizen Petition' to FDA, which is basically just a letter informing the FDA of whatever pertinent information you have, and asking them to do something, maybe in this case to just consider the data and what should be done about it. You can append the data as reports. Because I really don't know what FDA Division is appropriate, I'd probably recommend addressing it to the Commissioner, and let them decide where it belongs."

"OK. Well I want to do this. Who would sign this letter?"

"Frank could sign or you could sign. Anyone from Delvono could sign. Alternatively, we could have it come from our firm and I could sign. Do you have any reports you can send me?"

"I'll have data reports in a couple of days."

"OK. Send me the reports when you have them, and I'll draft the Citizen Petition. After a round of reviews, we can discuss who'll sign."

"Great. Thanks so much, Dean."

Later in the afternoon, Jimmy had a one hour phone call with the business law firm that was handling the transfer of Alfonso Gentilella's ownership of various old businesses to the people running them. The next day he would have to take the train into Manhattan to sign some papers. He laughed and thought *I'll have to decide whether to take a leak in the East End Men's Room at Grand Central again. Get back up on the horse, as they say.*

Jimmy was mentally exhausted. He drove to his Stamford apartment, made himself a baloney sandwich and opened a beer, and watched the evening news.

Chapter 40

Jean Marshak, Assistant District Attorney for the County of Essex, New Jersey, called Bill Cassidy and asked him to come in to her office in Newark with his client Christina Lindbergh. The three now sat in a beat-up conference room in the Essex County Courthouse, along with José Ramos, one of the detectives who interviewed Christina after the shooting.

Marshak began, "Ms. Lindbergh, we've received confirmation on the identity of the man you shot. He was Randall Makepeace of St. Louis, Missouri. José, you want to fill Ms. Lindbergh and Mr. Cassidy in?"

"Sure. This guy Makepeace has a long record in multiple states, and has been in and out of prison. He was tried in California back in '08 for involvement in a murder for hire, but wasn't convicted. The minivan he was in at the time of the Verona incident was stolen and recovered the next day in a garage at Newark airport. We don't know who the other guy was with him, and I suspect we'll never find out. The gun had the serial number filed off, but we verified that the bullet that went through Mr. Serono came from Makepeace's gun. The two bullets in Makepeace were from your gun. No other gun was found at the scene, and it looks like this was an intentional attempt at Mr. Serono's life and not roadrage or something random like that."

Marshak said, "We're reasonably confident that your story, which agrees with Mr. Delvecchio's account, is correct because it also agrees with Dr. Serono's account. We're dropping the manslaughter charge." Marshak knew full well that it was unlikely that she would get a conviction, even on a reduced charge, and it was even doubtful that a Grand Jury would bring charges.

Christina said, "Thank you, that's a relief."

Cassidy said, "And what about the concealed carry charge?"

"Well, there are numerous technicalities here, and it could be argued that Ms. Lindburgh never was publicly concealing a loaded gun because she actually loaded in Mr. Delvecchio's house at the time of the incident. You did have a New Jersey permit to own, and that helped you a lot. We considered a Pre-Trial Intervention, but in the end decided to drop the whole thing. Ms. Lindbergh, I strongly recommend that you familiarize yourself with the firearm regulations for the State of New Jersey and follow them meticulously."

Christina said, "Thank you again, thank you. What a relief. Do you think I might be able to get a concealed carry permit now?"

Marshak said, "I highly doubt it. Your restraining order in New York has expired, and to have it considered to support a concealed carry permit in New Jersey, you probably have to get a restraining order in New Jersey. I'm not telling you not to try, but it's a long road. If you really fear this guy, then try to get the restraining order. If you haven't heard from him for over a year, it'll be difficult."

"OK, thanks, I'll have to think about it."

"Ms. Lindbergh, you're a lucky person on a variety of counts. I don't know what's going on with your colleagues Serono and Delvecchio, but I'd advise you to stay out of it. Despite what you may hear, attempted assassinations are not common in New Jersey. Good luck."

"Thank you. One more thing, can I get my gun back?"

Marshak frowned and Detective Ramos answered, "Sure, I'll have it available at the front desk at the Verona station. You'll need picture ID and your permit to pick it up."

Christina said, "Thanks, thank you both for everything."

After Christina and Cassidy left the room, Marshak sighed and said, "That young lady broke multiple laws but saved a life, and maybe three lives. I can't deny it."

Ramos smiled and said, "A girl from Montana ices a hit man in New Jersey. Ya gotta love it."

When they got out to the lobby, Christina shook Cassidy's hand and thanked him, then sat down on a bench and called her parents.

Chapter 41

Within two days of Jimmy's phone conversation with Jan Mullany, he had draft reports in hand about the adulteration of Phoebus Herbals' "FenuSeng UltraPlus" and Sylvan Life's "Boscalma". In addition, Mullany had prepared a report on the DNA-fingerprinting data that demonstrated the absence of the purported therapeutic herb in a variety of tested products. The report named the products, their manufacturers, the name of the store in which they were purchased, and the date of purchase. To be fair, the reports also included data on the other products that passed muster. Jimmy arranged for a chemistry and a biochemistry professor at Rutgers to look over the data, and they said that it was all fine. Frank also looked over the data, and approved it. He objected to the reports being addressed to Jimmy, and made arguments about how it was his data and he deserved recognition. Jimmy's position was that this was a legal document involving Delvono, not a scientific publication, and he impressed on Frank that a major goal was to keep him out of the line of fire. When Frank continued to object, Jimmy pointed out that he was no longer a Delvono employee, and when Frank persisted, Jimmy told him to go fuck himself.

The regulatory lawyer Dean Tinney drafted a Citizen Petition to the FDA Commissioner, which Tinney agreed to sign. There had been a lot of back-and-forth between him and Jimmy about what to actually petition the FDA to do, and they agreed to request that the FDA Drug Division seek from Congress oversight responsibility over herbal and supplement products targeted at affecting disease. They made no specific request for action against Phoenix Herbals or Sylvan Life or the other herbal remedy companies mentioned in the reports.

Jimmy emailed the letter with appended reports to Tim Hagen, the Liberty Holdings guy he put in as Acting CEO at Phoebus, and scheduled a phonecall for later in the day.

Hagen opened with, "Jimmy, you're not serious about this, are you? Don't you have a conflict of interest situation here?"

"I'm as serious as I've ever been about anything. And there's no technical conflict of interest. Of course this isn't gonna be good for Phoebus in the short term, but I represent the private 100% owner of the company, and if I'm not complaining there's no issue."

"You realize what this is gonna do to Phoebus, right? The FDA Investigative Branch will be in here going through everything with a fine-tooth comb."

"That's OK. I can't predict the future, and I don't know what kind of other crap Singleton was pulling, but I'm presuming that all your in-house data, and the analytical data you received from the Malaysian supplier, will be clean. That means the Malaysian guys are almost certainly at fault, and sent you doctored data. You'll be identifying new herb suppliers, and you'll set up new analytical assays to verify the identity of the herbs and to detect adulteration, and then you're squeaky clean going forward."

"That's all well and good, Jimmy, but we still may be sued by previous purchasers of the adulterated stuff."

"Let's leave that to the lawyers. Phoebus is a victim here, a victim of unscrupulous Malaysian crooks. Let the chips fall where they may. I'm optimistic about this, and you're doing the right things. And now I'm gonna say something I couldn't be more serious about. Don't cover up anything, no matter what it is. Nothing. The plan is transparency, as you business school guys like to say. I'm always available for advice."

"OK, Jimmy, transparency. And please don't leave me out here in Utah forever. I'm a New England guy."

"Well, lean on the recruiter to identify candidates to replace you. But the fact is it's gonna take a few months for the dust to settle, and then finally someone will see it as an opportunity. Fly back as often as you want, I don't care about the money."

Jimmy called Dean Tinney and gave him the go ahead to submit the Citizen Petition to FDA immediately. Then he called his assistant at Delvono and asked her to arrange a press release describing the Citizen Petition and outlining the adulteration data. It was Friday, and the release would be sent out next Tuesday by their PR consultant to the Washington Post, the New York Times, the LA Times, the Salt Lake Tribune, the Newark Star Ledger, the American Medical Association, the Pharmaceutical Manufacturers' Association, John Harbon's Natural Remedies Manufacturers of America, and every member of the House and Senate. Jimmy thought *I'd love to be a fly on the wall Tuesday in Senator Packard's office.*

He turned off his computer, turned out the lights, and walked out to the limo that was waiting to take him home to his beloved New Jersey.

Let the chips fall where they may.

Chapter 42

Jimmy took a long weekend. He and Gina went out to the movies Saturday night, and on Sunday they Skyped with their daughter in Houston and with their son in Boston. They begged off an invitation to Gina's cousin Donna's house for Sunday family dinner, and instead went to the "Isle of Capri", their favorite Italian restaurant in Nutley. Jimmy discussed everything that had gone on last week with Gina, and she approved. "You did the right thing, Jimbo. Now you have to get Frank to come around." On Monday, he turned off his phone and didn't listen to voicemails. While it was hard for him, he didn't look at one email, not even the titles or senders. He read yesterday's Sunday Times, watched Clint Eastwood's "High Plains Drifter" on TV, and at 3:30 when Gina finished work at the school, he met her for a walk in the park. They picked up a pizza and salad for dinner from their favorite pizza parlor in Verona.

Now it was late Tuesday morning, and Jimmy walked into his office at Liberty Holdings in Connecticut after a three hour ride from New Jersey. A paper copy of the draft press release was waiting on his desk, and his assistant Melanie, who was always on top of things, asked, "What's this about? Your Delvono PR person called yesterday and has been calling all morning asking if you've reviewed this yet."

"It's something urgent that I need to do before anything else today."

"Let me know if I can help."

Jimmy read the release, made a couple of changes on his electronic copy, and sent it back to the PR consultant, telling her to release it immediately and to let him know when it goes out. He got a cup of coffee.

About four in the afternoon, he got a call from Dean Tinney.

"My phone is ringing off the hook. You're gonna be getting a monster bill from me."

"I guess we should have anticipated this. I'm glad you signed that thing instead of me. But my name is on those appended reports, so I guess it's only a matter of time. Who's been calling?"

"Newspaper reporters from all over the country, and Congresswoman Beloit's office here in Jersey. What do you want to do?"

"Well, first, keep track of your time. We'll pay." Then Jimmy laughed. "No wait, maybe this is fantastic advertising for you, and you should pay us."

"We'll work something out. I can deal with these people for now if you want. Otherwise, what's your plan?"

"OK. This is basically what we wanted, even though it's a pain. Just tell them we want the Drug Division of FDA to have oversight over herbal remedies. Don't say drugs, because that's the issue, the natural remedy people say they aren't selling drugs. I know this isn't your fight, and I'm sorry about this."

"What if they start asking me about the data?"

"I'd say you're representing a client and you're not a scientist, and you were not involved in the collection or interpretation of the data. Offer to email them a copy of the full letter with the reports."

"And when they ask who my client is?"

"Give them my name. No wait, I don't need that kind of personal litigation exposure. Tell them Delvono Inc. That's where the data was collected, so that seems right. What do you think?"

"That seems right to me. I presume you have business insurance. OK, I'll answer some of their general questions, saying no more than what's in the Petition. I'll keep it superficial. OK?"

"Seems like the right plan for the time being."

Jimmy put down the phone and thought about how quickly things were happening. *Christ, I didn't think this thing through. I'd better get my ducks in a row pronto.*

He emailed a copy of the letter with the reports to Jan Mullany and Christina Lindbergh, then called Jan to tell her that she should not, under any circumstances, talk to anybody who calls about the Citizen Petition. She should give them Jimmy's land line number at Delvono, not his cell number. He called Christina and explained what was going on, and told her the same thing. He asked her to email the entire staff and tell them not to answer any questions about the Citizen Petition or about any work completed or ongoing at Delvono. Then he called his assistant Marge at Delvono, and warned her about the possible onslaught of calls.

Jimmy was hungry, so he headed to the small cafeteria in their building, got a ham and swiss sandwich and a Diet Coke, and sat off in a corner by himself to eat and think. He was too busy with Liberty Holdings to be the person who talks to a horde of reporters about herbal remedy adulteration. It really wasn't even his fight, although he had no theoretical regrets about what he had done. He sure had practical regrets. He knew what he had to do.

When he got back to his office, he emailed Frank a copy of the Citizen Petition and the press release. Then he called Frank at home.

"Hi Frank, I just emailed you the Petition letter and the press release I had sent out."

"So what do you expect to happen now?"

"Well, the main goal has been handled. This will now be so big and so public that harming you would have no effect on any outcome. Somebody may come at Delvono overtly or covertly with a vengeance, but we may even be protected there somewhat by the public nature of what we've done. Time will tell."

"Thanks, Jimmy. I know you did this to protect me. It's not your fight, and you have a lot of cash invested in Delvono."

"Frank, I have more than cash invested in Delvono. It's where I wanna be and what I wanna do. And I think that's the same for you."

"Yep. So what now?"

"Listen, I didn't think enough about the unintended consequences of this Citizen Petition thing, and especially the press release. I guess I'm not really surprised at what's happening, but I am surprised at how fast it's happening." At that moment, Melanie knocked, then opened the door with an urgent look on her face. Jimmy said, "Hold on a second, Frank, OK?" then covered the mouthpiece of the phone with his palm. Melanie said, "Senator Packard from Utah is on line two. Do you want to talk to him?" Jimmy nodded yes, then said into the phone "Frank, can I call you back in about ten minutes? Thanks."

He pushed the button for line two. "Hello, Senator Packard, this is a surprise."

"Hello, Mr. Delvecchio, I guess we're all full of surprises today."

"What can I do for you?"

"This is just a courtesy call. I saw the press release and I managed to get a copy of the Citizen Petition, and I want to express my concern about your company Phoebus Herbals. Apparently you've had some problems there, and I can only hope that this is not a more widespread problem, this adulteration issue. We're very concerned about our natural supplement businesses in Utah, and this is a black mark. I hope you'll be doing something quickly to fix it."

"Yes, Senator, it's an embarrassment, and we've already replaced the CEO at Phoebus. We've tracked the issue to a Malaysian supplier of herbs, and we're working on changing suppliers. We've called back all the potentially adulterated product. As soon as we're back on track, we'll do some publicity to assure our customers that everything is fine."

"Good. Good. I'm very concerned that your company's problem could soil the reputation of all the other high quality herbal remedy companies here in Utah."

"I'm very sorry this happened, Senator."

"Yes, well I'm concerned that your problem could lead some to think that there needs to be more government oversight of this industry. One bad apple doesn't spoil the bunch. That's why I think the request for more FDA oversight in your Citizen Petition is overreach. This industry polices itself very well, and the two cases in your petition are wide outliers. I just want to strongly let you and your New Jersey types know that we have high standards for businesses and for everything else here in Utah. We're not going to stand for criminal shenanigans. Patients deserve better."

Jimmy smiled and shook his head.

"With all due respect, Senator, there were other cases cited, which were quite common, of herbal remedies that didn't contain the claimed therapeutic herb. And some of those products came from Utah companies. And by the way, we're not the only ones who have published such data."

"Yes, well, I thank you for bringing all this to our attention, and I guess it's time for this industry to get a little more self-vigilant. In my opinion, the problem is related to all this importing of materials from Asia. I'll be working to see that our trade groups put pressure on these foreign suppliers. Well, that's it. I just called to express my concern about your company and to encourage you to clean up your act."

"Well, thank you Senator. I assure you that we'll never be an embarrassment to Utah again."

That was weird. I wonder if I should have asked him if he knew who put the hit out on Frank.

He dialed Frank's home phone again. "Hi, Frank, sorry about that. I just had the strangest phone call of my life." He told Frank about his meeting with the Senator in Washington, at which the Senator made unveiled threats, and then about today's phone call in which the Senator basically castigated him for running a dishonest company and referred to Jimmy as "you and your New Jersey types".

Frank said, "That guy's got some balls, huh? It sounds like he's already setting up for the next battle with FDA in the war over government oversight. They have to purge the New Jersey miscreants from this Mother Teresa-inspired industry and all will be well."

"Hey, he's a powerful person in D.C., and he rarely loses. Don't underestimate him."

"Don't worry. I don't underestimate him."

"So, Frank, I called to talk to you about dealing with this Citizen Petition stuff and about Delvono in general. The phones are ringing off the hook, and I'm really not the guy the reporters should be talking to unless we just want to effectively say, 'No comment'. Are you interested in rejoining Delvono in some capacity to be decided, and to be the spokesperson on this adulteration stuff?"

"I don't know, Jimmy. I'm not sure I know what you're exactly suggesting."

"I'm not totally sure either, but here's where I'm leaning. You just got what you've been working for in spades – FDA and the newspapers have damning data on about eight natural remedy companies. It's all public and it's gonna be hard for the Congress to ignore, no matter what Senator Moneybags from Utah says or does. You generated that data. I would've tried to stop you if I'd known, but that's all water under the bridge. You know the data, you know the arguments. Why don't you talk to the reporters? What I'd ask though is that you do it very professionally and scientifically, no exaggerated arguments, no bitterness, just reporting the facts. The voice of reason. I'll back you up."

"Do it professionally, huh? What's that supposed to mean?"

"It means like a scientist, no shouting arguments about or with these garbage herb salesman. Just the facts. You can be the face of the effort, but it's you, not Delvono, even though you'll be working at Delvono."

"Why the change of heart?"

"When they shot you, that changed everything for me. We're friends. And when I realized what that clown Singleton was doing at Phoebus Herbals, I was pissed. Liberty Holdings owns that company, and they were spiking products with potentially toxic stuff. I became a believer. Now that it's all public, nobody gains by shooting you. As a matter of fact, you can make public that you were shot by a known hit man and let people draw their own conclusions. The ship has sailed and it doesn't need you to keep it sailing. But we do need you here to handle this shitstorm of calls from the papers. Do it. You'll enjoy yourself."

"And what about my old job?"

"Well, I'd have to talk to Christina, but my opinion is that she should be back heading a lab program. She's at the age where you make your scientific contributions, not when you should be doing budgets and dealing with personnel problems, at least if you're a scientist."

"I'm pretty sure she'd agree with that."

"OK. How about you come back as Director of Research, your old job? But I have some conditions. We don't do any more analyses of other people's products at Delvono. You made your mark, you got good data on these creeps, and we've made it public. That's it. Just like with any criminal investigation, it's time for the cops to take over. In this case, the cops are in the FDA. Delvono is a drug discovery company, period."

"What about my freedom of speech? Are you gonna demand that I do no blogging?"

"Frank, it's all about whether you hurt Delvono. You have to think about that before you publish incendiary blogs. You wanna blog, go ahead, blog. But keep Delvono's name out of it completely, and my advice is be careful not to libel anyone, maybe even run your blogs by a lawyer before you send them out. Never name an individual, especially our Senator friend. And by the way, what I told you about my interactions with Senator Packard – that's confidential, never to be repeated to anyone."

"If I blog, that's not your business, Jimmy."

"It's my business if it has any effect on Delvono. I'm your friend and I'm giving you what I consider to be good advice."

"So on this Citizen Petition thing, I talk to the press and to the government as much as I want?"

"As long as you come across as the voice of reason, and don't give anyone any basis to doubt the quality and importance of what we do at Delvono."

"But no more labwork on herbal products."

"Frank, the glass is half-full."

"OK. I agree to your terms."

"Good, I'm very happy about this. Come in from the cold. We'll have a welcome back party. I'll tell people at Delvono and the lawyer's office to have inquiries about the Petition forwarded to your number. You want the land-line or your cell given?"

"The land-line for now."

Jimmy laughed. "Marge's nightmare continues."

"Jimmy, thanks. I really mean it. And you don't have to worry. I'm really missing the science and it'll be great to be back."

Jimmy wondered if he had made a mistake but thought *hey, you gotta take chances.* He called Christina to tell her the plan, and she was relieved. *One big problem dealt with. Now, am I ever gonna get out of Liberty Holdings? I'm wearing too many fuckin' hats.*

Chapter 43

Frank moved back into his old office at Delvono the next day
and met for an hour each with the four Therapeutic Area heads to
get back up to speed. It was obvious to him that the place had
suffered a little from lack of direction in his absence, but he
wasn't so naive or conceited to think that it had suffered much.
The big obvious immediate gaps were in the other areas that
were reporting to the part-time CEO Jimmy. These were the
Accounting, Clinical Supply Procurement, Clinical Trials, and
Regulatory Affairs Groups. While things were getting done, little
intermediate-term or long-term planning was occurring. It was
particularly important to maintain good relations with the
academic centers that carry out clinical trials, and Frank figured
that he would have to get out and "press the flesh" sooner rather
than later.

The big surprise was what Jimmy had called the "shitstorm"
of telephone calls from reporters. Frank had no experience with
this sort of thing. After the first phone interview, he decided that
he had to get organized and develop what political people call
"talking points". He sat for an hour and typed out a list of points
he wanted to make and, perhaps just as important, things he did

not want to say. In the things not to say category were things like "do not denigrate particular politicians", "do not insult FDA", "do not mention Delvono", "do not mention attempt on my life unless asked", and such. He decided to refer to himself as a Medical Consumer Activist and to push the reporters to call him that. He dove into this role with gusto, and completed four phone interviews the next day.

When a TV station called about an interview for the national news a couple of days later, Frank called Jimmy about whether and where to do it. Jimmy was absolutely against doing it at Delvono, and Frank agreed. Frank's basement home office piled with athletic equipment and tools wouldn't work, so it would have to be his living room. Frank was starting to appreciate what a time-wasting diversion this was when he had to decide what to wear – he went with the blue jeans, button-down blue shirt, sport jacket, no-tie look. The reporter and camera crew showed up an hour early and rearranged the living room furniture to optimize visuals. They wanted him at a desk, preferably with a bookcase behind, and actually checked out his basement work area and vetoed that quickly.

The interview went reasonably well, at least Frank thought it did, and he stuck to Jimmy's admonition – "just the facts". He was pleasantly surprised how positive the interviewer was about the Citizen Petition. Frank realized that, even though this was about dishonest medical charlatans, from the reporter's perspective it was probably just one more example of big bad Big Business. Frank repeatedly distinguished between FDA-approved medications from biotech companies and the uncontrolled untested natural remedies sold in the spirit of the patent medicine hawkers of old. The reporter did bring up the usual arguments in favor of the natural remedies such as their centuries-old time-tested well-known efficacy. Frank did his best to point out that "time-tested" was just a euphemism for "untested". Frank also emphasized that he was not criticizing the use of dietary approaches to support health. He even pointed out that he mixes flax seeds and berries into his oatmeal most mornings and takes a daily multivitamin.

That night, Frank and Maria watched the CBS Evening News and were surprised that adulterated natural remedies was one of the two major stories covered. In addition to Frank's interview, there was an interview with Senator Packard of Utah, Chair of the US Senate committee that oversees FDA. Frank's interview seemed to come off pretty well; it wasn't butchered by editors and the main points were clear. But the Senator used his brief interview to throw down the gauntlet.

The Senator stood on the veranda of a cavernous hall with marble columns behind him. The scene gave him an air of gravitas that was reinforced by his deep voice echoing in the halls of power. The interviewer began by asking about the Petition.

INTERVIEWER: Senator, thank you for taking the time to talk to us today about natural herbal remedies and oversight of their safety and efficacy. Last week, a Citizen Petition was submitted to FDA that contained data demonstrating that some herbal remedies were spiked with unapproved synthetic drugs of unknown toxicity. And some products did not contain the therapeutic herb that was claimed to be present. The Petition asks for increased FDA oversight of the natural remedy industry. Should there be more oversight by the FDA Drug Division?

SENATOR PACKARD: Jean, it's my pleasure to help clarify this situation. As you know, this has been an area of personal interest to me for most of my career, even back before I became a senator. I've always been a champion of our hardworking citizens, who know a lot more about life than the Washington bureaucratic intelligentsia. If I may go right to my bottom line, this is about the freedom of citizens and their doctors to choose the medicines they want, and not to be constrained because big money interests try to control which medicines can be sold and which cannot.

INTERVIEWER: Who do you mean by "big money interests", Senator?

SENATOR PACKARD: Of course, I'm referring to the Medical-Pharmaceutical establishment, which exerts its influence by having one of the largest lobbying machines of any industry in America. I will always be first in line to applaud the medical advances that have come out of Big Pharma, and my family and I have benefitted from the medicines they've discovered. This isn't about tearing them down, or focusing on the side effects of their synthetic drugs. This is about free choice. Over the last twenty years, there has been a groundswell of interest in so-called alternative therapies, which in fact have just as much scientific basis as the drugs from Big Pharma. Jean, I may have been born at night, but I wasn't born last night. I understand the business world. The big pharmaceutical companies, and their lobbyists, want the FDA bureaucracy involved in oversight of natural remedies in order to inhibit the sales of these time-tested remedies. I respect the FDA and the job it does, but everyone knows it's a slow bureaucracy, and maybe it should be. But there's no need for oversight by the FDA Drug Division of products that are basically foods. It's government overreach.

INTERVIEWER: So what do you say about the adulteration with untested synthetic drugs that was found in some products, and the absence of the claimed therapeutic herb in some other products?

SENATOR PACKARD: Well Jean, of course this is very disturbing. My staff has looked at the data in the Citizen Petition closely, and we have no technical problem with it. Apparently, it was generated under the supervision of Dr. Frank Serono, who is a well-known highly respected scientist. And I thank him for this. However, he has also been a proselytizer for FDA oversight of natural remedies for some time now, and while I believe him to be well-intentioned, I think he may be affected by the fact that he himself works for Big Pharma. He's a good man, but off the mark on this one.

INTERVIEWER: So what do you say to those who want to make sure that the natural remedies they use are safe and unadulterated?

SENATOR PACKARD: I would tell them that we're on the case. The natural food and natural remedy industries do a fantastic job of self-policing, and what has been reported in this Citizen Petition is a rare aberration. We've started looking into this very preliminarily, and it appears that there is underworld involvement in the companies that have adulterated their products. I plan to ask the FBI to get involved. This is an issue for law enforcement, not the FDA.

INTERVIEWER: Thank you for speaking with us, Senator.

SENATOR PACKARD: Thank you, Jean. My pleasure.

Maria said, "Well that was interesting. You came across very well, but that guy Packard is loaded for bear. He's blaming adulteration on the Mafia."

"He's not too far off, but it's not the Mafia of old, it's the Utah Mafia, and I'd say he's a charter member."

"So what's the situation now? What's your continuing involvement?"

"Well. I talk to anyone who'll listen, with Jimmy's constraint that I stick to the facts."

"To state the obvious, I don't want you getting shot again."

"That's not gonna happen. I really have to thank Jimmy for having my back. By making all our data public, and by filing that Citizen Petition, he took me off the critical path for people who want to stop this. No sense shooting me. It won't stop anything."

"To state the obvious again, I hope you're right."

Frank went down to his basement lair. He couldn't let Packard's statements go without comment, so he typed out another blog post. This time he cleared it with Jimmy, who was surprisingly loose about it. They agreed that he should continue to associate himself with his one-man "consulting company", and leave Delvono Inc. out of it.

Chapter 44

NATURAL ENOUGH FOR YA? #25

from the desk of Frank Serono, Ph.D., President, Serono Pharmaceutical Consulting LLC

Citizen Petition to FDA Suggesting Oversight of the Herbal and Supplement Disease Remedy Industry

As some of you may know, a Citizen Petition was filed at FDA two weeks ago titled "Oversight of Natural Remedy Industry". This petition presented data demonstrating, for some products, either (1) the absence of the "therapeutic" herb claimed in the product label, or (2) adulteration with a synthetic chemical of unknown toxicity, said chemical being a chemical analogue of a known drug, or a "prodrug" that converts to a known drug in the body. The forensic data were gathered under my supervision. This Citizen

Petition is a matter of public record, and may be viewed at FDA.gov/documents.

Senator Sam Packard of Utah has long been a strong proponent of keeping the FDA Drug Division out of oversight of the natural remedy business. In doing this, he provides strong support to the business community in Utah, where numerous natural remedy companies are headquartered. Senator Packard generally claims that these products are all-natural, and thus non-toxic by definition, and that government oversight of their efficacy, safety, and purity would be government overreach. He believes that their efficacy has stood the test of time.

My view is different on a number of counts. Unlike the major pharmaceutical companies that test their new drugs in thousands of patients to demonstrate safety and efficacy, the natural remedy companies do none of this. In those cases where someone has tested the natural product efficacy, the results have almost always been negative or inconclusive. To be fair, there are occasional cases in which some level of efficacy has been demonstrated. For example, St. John's Wort (*Hypericum perforatum*) has been shown to be a mild antidepressant, and has also been shown to naturally contain a chemical (hyperforin) that acts similarly to the antidepressant drugs Prozac, Paxil, and Zoloft. Traditional animal toxicity studies of herbs and herbal remedy products are almost unheard of. A recent study funded by the National Institute of Environmental Health Sciences is a step in the right direction.

A long-standing debate has gone on about whether FDA should demand toxicity and efficacy data for natural remedies. Senator Packard and I stand on opposite sides of this debate.

A more pressing issue from my perspective is the purity of products that are currently sold by natural remedy companies. In an interview with CBS News yesterday, Senator Packard said, "The natural food and natural remedy industries do a fantastic job of self-policing, and what has been reported in this Citizen Petition is a rare aberration." I would like to point out that the Citizen Petition contains our data on the herbal content of 30 natural remedy products that we purchased on the open market - in supermarkets, pharmacies and healthfood stores. Only 19 of these products contained the so-called therapeutic herb that was listed on the label. This is not what I would call "a fantastic job of self-policing". In addition, we also found the presence of an intentionally spiked drug-like synthetic chemical of unknown toxicity in two products. This was admittedly more rare. I should hope so.

Now the FDA knows. Please let your congressman and senator know what you think about this.

Finally, I would like to inform my readers that I was shot three weeks ago, and a second lethal shot was stopped by an armed good samaritan who killed the attacker. This assassination attempt was carried out in New Jersey by a man named Ronald Makepeace of St. Louis, MO. Mr. Makepiece had a long criminal record, and was previously indicted for, but not convicted of, murder-for-hire in Los

Angeles. I don't know why Mr. Makepeace shot me, but I bet you can come up with ideas.

In a recent TV interview, Senator Packard implied that the bad apples in the natural remedy industry were somehow connected with organized crime. Well perhaps there is organized crime involved, but not of the sort people usually assume. In this case, perhaps there is collusion between politicians, natural remedy company owners, and lobbyists to undermine the safety of the consumer in order to maximize profit. Perhaps this is organized crime that is not centered in places like New York and New Jersey, but in Utah. And perhaps these criminals would kill someone to shut his mouth.

I am not going to shut my mouth.

Chapter 45

Jimmy got the call from his Uncle Carmine on Sunday night, suggesting they meet Monday morning at the "usual place in Lambertville". Jimmy was happy to have an excuse not to head to Connecticut at 6 AM.

Using what had now become Standard Operating Procedure, Jimmy headed to Washington Park in Lambertville, and parked in the west parking lot. He walked to the lake, and there was Alfonso Gentilella sitting on a bench with his boombox, this time tuned to the talkshow "Curtis and Kuby in the Morning".

"Hello, Mr. Gentilella."

"And so we meet again! Hi, Jimmy."

Of course, Jimmy knew something was up. He could talk with Gentilella on the phone when the subject was strictly about the business of Liberty Holdings, straightforward financial and strategic decisions. Any other discussion that could be misinterpreted, or perhaps interpreted correctly, by law enforcement had to occur outside the range of prying ears, human or electronic.

"How's your family, Jimmy?"

"Very good, thanks. I'm gonna be a grandfather. I'm really looking forward to it, and so is my wife Gina."

"That's fantastic, Jimmy. I have four grandchildren, and there's nothing better. Jimmy, I want to have a discussion about this FDA thing and our companies that make herbal medicines."

"Sure. Whatever you want to talk about."

"Well, I guess I'd like some explanation. As I understand the situation, a guy who works in your biotech company has been making a lot of noise about the purity etcetera of natural medicines. Then he generated data on products from two of our companies in Utah that looked pretty bad, and the data was actually generated in your biotech company. Is that about right?"

"Yes, that's basically correct."

"Then he went public with data on Liberty's two Utah companies in his computer blog."

"Right."

"Then you jumped on the bandwagon and did some kind of notification to the FDA, right or wrong?"

"Right."

"So Jimmy, can you explain this to me?"

"Mr. Gentilella, as you no doubt know, somebody tried to kill Dr. Serono on my front lawn, a hitman from St. Louis. Luckily one of our Delvono employees was there and she was carrying, and she put two in the hit man."

"The Montana cowgirl. I read about it in the papers."

"Well first, I assume without evidence that the attempt on Dr. Serono's life was related to his blogging about natural medicines. I figured the best way to really protect Dr. Serono, who's my business partner and friend, was to make him irrelevant. Somebody tried to permanently shut him up with two to the hat, but if his death would have no effect on his enemy's problems, then there's no reason left to kill him. It won't help.

That's why I jumped on the bandwagon, as you say. I helped to make Dr. Serono's data very public. I realize this was bad for two of our Liberty companies in Utah, but I felt I had to do it. And by the way, the two Liberty companies in Utah were out of control and really were adulterating their herbal medicines with untested synthetic drugs. They were headed for trouble with or without Dr. Serono."

"Do you know who Senator Packard from Utah is?"

"I wish I didn't, but I do. He summoned me to Washington for a ten minute talk about six weeks ago."

"Yes, well I talked to him yesterday, and I want to make sure that anything I tell you about this will remain confidential."

"I swear on my mother's grave."

"Cut the shit Jimmy, don't disrespect your mother. I'm just telling you that this is serious business."

This was the first time that Jimmy ever heard Gentilella curse, and concluded that he must really be upset.

Jimmy said, "Sorry. I've got a pretty good idea what his position is."

"He plans to say that our two Utah companies are mob-run, and unrepresentative of the kind of high quality operations they run in Utah. He wants us to let the FBI in to these two companies, and make us look like shit. Then they can say they've cleaned house and everything's copacetic. No FDA oversight needed for the natural medicines industry. In payment he agrees to call off the dogs from a whole lot of other operations country-wide that *La Famiglia* runs, nothing to do with anything you're doing or even know about."

"Do you realize how ridiculous that is? Phoebus was run by a crooked Mormon from Utah. We wouldn't be in this mess if it wasn't for him. He's the one who was fooling with some

Malaysian guys to manufacture adulterated products. I fired him. His name is Todd Singleton."

"Who's in charge now?"

"I temporarily put in one of our Liberty Holdings guys named Tim Hagen, a good young guy."

"Get him out of there unless you want to ruin his career. Do what you can to wipe him off the records. Can you get this guy Singleton back?"

"I don't know, it would be pretty strange to ask him. Why would I do that?"

"So the bastard can go down with the ship he steered into an iceberg."

Jimmy laughed. "I like your style, Mr. Gentilella."

"I hate this stuff, Jimmy. Once some powerful politician gets involved, everybody becomes vulnerable. They stop at nothing. No loyalty. Just a big fat pile of ego."

"I'll offer Singleton a big salary, and maybe even a small piece of future profits."

"A small piece of future profits, that's rich. And Jimmy, you have to go too."

"What do you mean, I have to go?"

"I've been thinking a lot about our conversation in the hospital when you got stabbed. You said you wanted out, but I wanted you to stay. Your general ideas were right. Put an Irish or WASP guy in charge of Liberty Holdings, and sell a piece to some investors. Then it's not privately owned by just me. It's the right thing to do. And now with Packard breathing down my neck, we throw you to the dogs. You're an old wise guy from New Jersey who couldn't control himself and ran two beautiful Utah natural medicine companies into the ground with your impatient dishonest ways. We kick you out."

"Whoa, wait a minute. I'm not taking the hit for this Utah nonsense. I'm not going to jail."

"Jail? Who said jail? Don't worry about that. We're just firing you from Liberty Holdings. Maybe I went a little too far. Maybe we just say you weren't watching the store. If anyone's going to jail, it'll be this Singleton guy, and maybe whoever is CEO of the other company we own out there, Sylvan whatever."

"You mean I'm a free man?"

"That's right. To make it a clean break, I'm firing you right now. Who would be your favorite for succeeding you?"

"That would be Owen McCarthy. We've talked about him before."

"Would others at Liberty be upset if he was elevated?"

"Very surprised, but not upset."

"OK, then. After we leave the park, please call Owen McCarthy and tell him he's the new Acting CEO of Liberty. We'll keep it "acting" until we're sure he has no skeletons in his closet or leadership deficits. Then please head out to Stamford and clear out your office. But I'd like to ask you to stay in Stamford for two weeks in your apartment there, and tell McCarthy that he can come over to discuss everything that needs to be discussed. I want you to talk with him about selling say 20% of the company to the investors you know. Don't go back to Liberty after you remove your pictures of your wife and kids today."

"There's one big thing that's bothering me. There'll probably be more when I sit and think a while."

"What's the big thing?"

"How do I know that the Senator won't sic the FBI on me because I'm the immoral underworld guy who brought this shitstorm of trouble down on the pristine Utah natural remedy industry?"

"The Senator and I have an agreement. He may be powerful and cagy, but so am I. I've got stuff on him. Jimmy, you've helped me tremendously over the last couple of years. I don't know who could've done the job you've done, with the finesse you used in touchy situations. I'm forever beholden to you. I'd like to give you something, say a big retirement bonus, but I know that money isn't something you need. Is there something I can do?"

"Mr. Gentilella, you're doing it. What I want is to go back to my life in New Jersey and to my biotech company Delvono with my friend Frank Serono. Without anything hanging over my head, and without my reputation ruined. I guess there's one more thing – I want my partner Dr. Serono to be left alone."

"I'll do everything I can."

Gentilella reached down and turned off his boombox then got up from the bench, signaling the end of the meeting, so Jimmy got up too. Gentilella moved over to Jimmy, shook his hand, and then hugged him. Jimmy hugged back and said, "I hope you're not gonna kiss me." Gentilella laughed.

In accordance with standard operating procedure, Alfonso Gentilella headed off to the east parking lot and Jimmy Delvecchio to the west, probably never to see each other again. When he was out of Gentilella's sight, 56-year-old Jimmy Delvecchio pumped his right fist in the air twice and jumped and yelled, "Yes!" He hadn't done that since he was a high school football player a lifetime ago.

Chapter 46

Jimmy ensconced himself in his Stamford apartment Wednesday through Friday, meeting for a few hours each day with Owen McCarthy, and going out for dinner and drinks with him twice. The 34-year-old Harvard MBA was delighted at the opportunity that had fallen in his lap, but the more he talked with Jimmy, the more he realized that he was going to be in over his head for quite a while. He had lots of questions about Alfonso Gentilella and about the "old" businesses that were being dumped. Jimmy assured him that this was now being handled entirely by their outside law advisors and that McCarthy would not need to have anything to do with it. Having observed Jimmy for the last two years, McCarthy was skeptical. When pressed, Jimmy did his best to explain Gentilella's background and current situation without spooking him.

Jimmy also fit in calls to potential investors in Liberty Holdings. It became quickly clear that the best he could do at this point was to just introduce investors to McCarthy, and three lunchtime meetings were scheduled for the following week.

Jimmy was finished by Friday noon, and at the end of the school day Gina took a car service to visit him in Stamford.

Since the day that Jimmy was attacked in Grand Central, she was never at peace, always worried. Now she was delighted by how things were working out, and was looking forward to having him home permanently. On Saturday, they went for a walk on the beach on the Connecticut shore, then out to dinner and a movie. They slept late Sunday, went out to brunch, then spent the afternoon lounging around reading the New York Times. At 4 PM, the car service picked her up for the ride back to New Jersey. She kissed him goodbye, and said "Next Saturday, you're coming home for good. I'm installing one of those electric fences, and getting a zapper collar for you so you never leave home again."

"Don't you think that's a bit extreme?"

"No, it can be turned off if we're going out to dinner or the movies."

Chapter 47

Around 10 AM on Monday morning, the FBI called Jimmy's cell phone. It was Agent Jack Politoski, who Jimmy had met a lifetime ago when a consultant he had worked with in the internet pharmacy days was killed. Politoski wanted to schedule an interview with Jimmy, but was vague about the topic. Jimmy asked if he should have a lawyer present, and Politoski said that he was only seeking information in an investigation but of course it was Jimmy's prerogative to have a lawyer present. Jimmy agreed to meet Politoski at his Stamford apartment at four the next afternoon, then called attorney Bill Cassidy in New Jersey to invite him, or to be more accurate, to contract to pay him to be present.

The next day, Cassidy arrived from New Jersey at 3:45 PM. "So what's this about, Jimmy?"

"I have no idea, but if I have to guess, it's related somehow to one of Liberty Holdings' companies in the natural medicines area. I don't know how much you know about what's been going on."

"Nothing other than that it might be related to Dr. Serono getting shot and Dr. Lindbergh's subsequent problems."

"Well, Liberty owns two herbal medicine companies out in Utah that were adulterating their products with unapproved drugs. It's complicated because I was actually involved in blowing the whistle on them. The guilty parties were so-called upstanding Utah businessmen, and now Senator Packard of Utah is trying to make it look like New Jersey hoods took over the companies and broke various federal laws that the saintly Utah businessmen would never have broken."

"Sounds complicated."

"Very. And I no longer work for Liberty Holdings, so I'm afraid I'm on my own in this and that's why I wanted you here." As Jimmy started to tell Cassidy about the Citizen Petition, the doorbell rang. Jimmy buzzed in the FBI guys.

Agent Jack Politoski had not aged well since Jimmy last saw him about ten years ago – now overweight with graying hair although he was only 41. Collar open, too big for his tight rumpled grey suit. He was accompanied by Agent Bob Shangraw, a bright-looking athletic guy in his mid-20s in a crisp pinstripe suit. The four did handshakes and introductions and moved to the living room. Politoski and Shangraw sat on the couch and Jimmy and Cassidy in armchairs.

Politoski started cordially. "It's been quite a while since we last met. What is it, maybe ten years?"

Jimmy answered, "Jeez, maybe it is, no probably eight, something like that. It was about that guy Michaeli who helped me find pharmaceutical manufacturing partners in Asia. Did you ever catch whoever killed him?"

"No, still an open case. All dead ends. It'll sit until something turns up, and it almost always does."

Jimmy smiled and said, "So what can I do for you fellas?"

Agent Politoski did all the talking for himself and his partner. "We're just running down leads on a case that's gone quiet for a while." He looked at Cassidy and said, "This is just preliminary. Just seeking information about some persons of interest. Mr. Delvecchio is not suspected of anything." Cassidy nodded and thought *bullshit*.

Politoski looked at Jimmy and continued, "Mr. Delvecchio, we've reopened an investigation of a truck hijacking that occurred about two years ago in New Jersey. A very valuable trailer full of prescription drugs went missing. Do you recall it?"

Jimmy hid his surprise. "In New Jersey, two years ago? Oh, of course, it was all over the news, and everybody in the pharmaceutical industry was talking about it. I guess I forgot about it. Haven't seen anything in the news since."

"Were you living in New Jersey then?"

"You probably already know the answer to that. I was CEO of the biotech company Delvono in Clifton. I lived in Verona, still do."

"Why do you have this apartment in Connecticut?"

"For the last couple of years I've been CEO of a company here in Stamford that manages investments for private investors. It's called Liberty Holdings. I spend the week here then go home to Verona on the weekends. I tell you, it's been stressful, all the back-and-forth. Last week I gave up the Liberty Holdings job, and I'm going back to my biotech in Jersey. A real relief."

"I sympathize with you, the drive from Jersey looks easy on paper, but the George Washington is almost always a mess. It took us three hours to get here today." They all laughed. Jimmy said, "Try the Tappan Zee. Longer distance on paper, but almost always less backed up."

Jimmy was getting uncomfortable. *Where is this going?* He offered to get Politoski and Shangraw a water or soda, but they declined. Cassidy got up and said "I'm gonna get myself a glass of water." He brought one back for Jimmy too.

Politoski continued, watching Jimmy closely. "Well, as I said, we're following up on this hijacking from two years ago. A whole trailer of medicine. Then a few months ago some of it turned up in a pharmacy in Kansas City. It got caught in an audit of serial numbers. Do you know anything about this?"

Cassidy broke in. "Is my client a suspect? If he is, I have to advise him to stop this interview immediately."

"No, he's not a suspect and he's not a person of interest. We're just running down leads."

Cassidy again. "Well if that's the case, maybe you can tell us why you're here in his apartment asking about a two-year old truck hijacking. At the time, my client was the owner and CEO of a major biotech drug discovery company and sat on government committees. He was not involved in pharmacies or drug distribution or trucking." He looked at Jimmy and said, "I advise you to stop this interview."

Jimmy looked at Cassidy. "I understand your concern, Bill, but I'm perfectly willing to help these guys out." He looked at Politoski. "Why are you here talking to me?"

"Do you know a Carmine Casamento?"

"Of course I know Carmine Casamento. He's my uncle, my mother's brother."

"What does he do for a living?"

"He's retired. The guy is 77 or 78 years old."

"Did you ever work with your uncle?"

"Sure, when I was in my 20s and 30s. We both worked in a distribution center in western New Jersey. I ended up in charge. That was tough aggravating work – tough to stick to delivery schedules with the weather and unreliable drivers." Jimmy laughed. "Boy, I don't regret leaving that behind. Thanks for reminding me."

"Did any truck hijacking go on?"

Cassidy broke in again. "You're asking my client generic questions about truck hijackings 25 years ago? If you want this to continue, please get to the point. We're not going to sit here and listen and respond to innuendo. My client said that he's willing to help you out, so ask questions about the case you're here to discuss. Unless you're really here to discuss what went on in a distribution center in western New Jersey in 1995. If you are, then ask specific questions about that."

Politoski looked at Cassidy. "OK. Don't get all heated up. Mr. Delvecchio asked why we're here talking to him. We didn't just pick his name out of the phonebook, and you know that."

Politoski looked at Jimmy. "Have you ever heard any scuttlebutt about where that trailer of medicine may have ended up?"

"Not until today when you said it ended up in Kansas City."

"Did you ever discuss that truck hijacking with anyone?"

"Not that I recall, but I can't swear that it didn't come up over lunch at work. It was a big deal at the time because I was in the pharmaceutical industry. People were talking about it at a biotech conference I went to, now that I think about it."

"Did anyone ask your advice on how to get rid of the stolen medicine?"

Cassidy said, "Don't answer that, Jimmy."

Jimmy held the palm of his hand up to Cassidy, then looked at Politoski. "Of course not. If they did, I wouldn't know how anyway. I can't believe you guys never found that stuff until now. With all the regulatory controls on drugs, I would think it would be impossible to get rid of that stuff."

"OK. Just one more question. Did you ever discuss this hijacking with your uncle Carmine Casamento?"

"No."

Cassidy said, "That's enough, Jimmy. You have no information of any use to these guys. Don't let them turn it into a fishing expedition."

Cassidy stood up, followed by the other three. Politoski thanked Jimmy for his cooperation and willingness to help. They all shook hands, and Jimmy let Politoski and Shangraw out.

Cassidy turned to Jimmy and said, "Do you want to tell me anything about this?"

"Nope, I have nothing to tell you because I don't know anything about it. Now I'm tempted to start asking around out of curiosity."

"My very strong advice is that you mention today's visit from the feds to no one. And also ask nobody about that hijacked truck, and especially don't talk to your uncle about it. And don't think that talking in Italian solves your secrecy problem. Cabeesh?"

"Yeah, I got it. I have no interest in knowing what this is about. And by the way, if you're gonna pretend to know some Italian, the second person singular is *capisci*."

"Yeah, like you guys all use the proper endings. You know, on second thought, I'd advise not talking to your uncle at all. Avoid him completely."

"I can't do that. He's my uncle and I'm moving back to Jersey. Wouldn't it look funny if all of a sudden I don't talk to my uncle anymore?"

"I suppose you're right. I'm not going to ask you any questions about this truck thing, but my advice is to make sure you have plausible deniability when you talk to your uncle, or to anybody else for that matter."

"Message received."

"You want to get some dinner? I've heard there are some good Italian restaurants here in Stamford."

"No, thanks. I just want to sit and think, maybe get drunk."

After Cassidy left, Jimmy poured himself a glass of a super tuscan and, after drinking half, thought *It never ends. Marone. It never ends.*

Chapter 48

Frank was back in his element at Delvono. He found that he was enjoying overseeing drug discovery projects much more than dealing with the cyclone he had initiated in the natural remedy industry. Frank loved looking at lab data and discussing experimental conclusions and plans with smart people. He was also delighted to hear that Jimmy was coming back in only one week. Jimmy was superb at running the financial and personnel aspects of the place, and when Frank was honest with himself, he admitted that Jimmy's input on strategic direction was also generally spot-on.

He got a call from Dean Tinney, the lawyer who signed the Citizen Petition. "Hi Frank, you interested in a trip to Washington later this year?"

Frank moaned. He was up to his ears in interview requests and had even been invited to address the Annual Meeting of the Naturopathic Physicians of North America, where he joked he'd probably be wise to wear a bullet-proof vest. For the umpteenth time this week he thought *Be careful what you wish for.*

"I think my dance card is just about full. What's this one about?"

"The Senate HELP Committee has scheduled a meeting to discuss FDA oversight of herbal medicines, and they've asked me to testify because I signed the Citizen Petition."

"What does HELP mean?"

"Health, Education, Labor and Pensions. It's the Senate committee that oversees the FDA. I'm the wrong guy to represent our Petition, and you're the right guy, so I'd like to give them your name."

"I would think that Senator Packard should have been able to stop discussion of that subject."

"Well, the FDA Commissioner requested that this be put on the Agenda, and Packard is Chair of the HELP Committee. There must be some procedural rule that prevents him from stopping it. So can I give them your name?"

"Sure. Do I have a choice?"

"Well, you know you're the best guy associated with our Petition to talk about it. And you're familiar with the other studies that have been published, so this'll be your big chance to push your position. And besides, once I give them your name, you'll probably be subpoenaed and won't have a chance to refuse."

"OK, go ahead. Where do you think this'll all go?"

"Well, I've been observing the government drug regulatory apparatus for about 25 years now, and the word 'glacial' would be too fast to describe the rate at which things proceed. The Senate and its committees are full of lawyers, and they know how to obstruct big-time. If I were Senator Packard, I'd start with a procedural block, saying that herbal products are not drugs. They're plants, and if anyone has a problem with their sale they should approach the Food Safety Division of FDA or maybe the Department of Agriculture."

"The Food Safety Division of the FDA is still the FDA."

"Sure, but he can tie them in knots with semantic confusion and with procedural issues about who can testify and about what."

"You're depressing me. How do you see this all playing out long term?"

"You want the truth? You can't handle the truth." Tinney laughed. "Look, best case scenario, the first HELP Committee meeting on the topic probably occurs in about a year. Then follow-on meetings with rebuttals and rebuttals to rebuttals. And of course something also has to start in the House. And then the big magilla – somebody has to draft legislation to give the FDA Drug Division oversight of something they've never had official oversight of before. This involves need for more FDA employees and increased budget. You may not realize it, but lots of legislation is written by lobbyists, and in this case who's lobbying for this additional oversight? Only the FDA, so they'd pretty much have to draft the bill. Lot's of luck, given their workload."

"And lots of luck, given the financial and lobbying power of the natural remedy industry. So what could possibly move this along more quickly? Who could be our champion?"

Tinney said, "The only thing I can think of that could speed things up is if a few people died from using some natural remedy. But that would probably be more properly treated as a criminal issue, not a regulatory issue. We just go round and round in circles on this – why do we need oversight of natural herbs if they're natural?"

"Because they have physiological effects and are really drugs."

"But I thought your position was that they don't work, and the real problem is that patients are encouraged to use these placebos instead of seeking proper medical help."

Frank said, "I'm getting sick."

"Look, let me try to buck you up here. While you haven't been the first to demonstrate it, you've widely publicized the issue that one-third of natural medicines on the market probably don't contain the medicinal herb described on the label. Now that may be an interstate commerce issue, and hopefully someone will crack down on the specific guilty companies identified by you and others. This is similarly true for the two cases that you found with adulteration with unapproved drugs. I hope that somebody goes after these people, and maybe there's an arm of the government other than the FDA Drug Division that will be interested in pursuing them. But here's the good part. You've probably got these people scared shitless. Most of them will clean up their act, and start selling what they say they're selling."

"Dean, you know that most of these companies are not run by naturopathic believers. They're run by people who used to sell swampland."

"If the feds go after a few of them, most of the rest will fall into line. Of course they'll raise their prices to cover the fact that they now have to provide the right herb even if it's more expensive to source. There's a sucker born every minute – the higher the price the more effective and special the herb must be. Just like cosmetics. Or maybe they'll just move on to some other flim-flam business, which would be good in a way."

Frank sighed. "Like I said, this conversation is making me sick. What about all the bold illegal medical claims made in the radio ads? The label on the manufacturer's bottle says 'helps promote heart health' but the radio salesman says 'lowers your cholesterol' or 'prevents a second heart attack'. That's got to stop."

"Maybe an FCC or FTC or ICC issue. Look, maybe it's an FDA issue of some sort, but who are they gonna go after? The label says 'helps promote heart health'. That's not a drug claim. Are they gonna go after the overenthusiastic radio salesman? Lots of luck."

"So what can I do? Please be blunt. What's our situation here?"

"OK, I'll be blunt. You were naive, correct but naive. I say go to the HELP Committee and give your best arguments about proper labeling and contents, and about print and radio advertising. Also about the undemonstrated efficacy and toxicity, and bring lots of examples. The rebuttal of course will be 'Show me who has been harmed by what toxic product' and you'll probably be stuck. Give it your best shot, but don't expect anything substantive from the government. And of course, you can continue with your blog and be part of the continuing conversation."

"Thanks. To be honest, I feel more disappointed than naive and stupid. I know I'm right."

"In a way you're right, and in a way you're not. If you can identify a group that's been injured, we can encourage them to sue the people that hurt them. But if 'hurting them' means having provided an alternative therapy, again I say lots of luck. And don't forget that in most cases the manufacturer never said that it was selling a therapy for a disease."

"Alright, I've had enough. Give the Senate committee my name, and I'll testify when the time comes. For now, I'll continue to give interviews and make my points. Thanks."

Frank thought *If the natural remedy people had done the same analysis that Tinney just did, they wouldn't have bothered shooting me. They were never in danger of losing this war*. It was two o'clock, four hours before Frank usually headed for home. He turned off his computer, retrieved his swim trunks and towel from his closet, and headed to the Y for a swim.

Chapter 49

Jimmy arranged for a couple of college kids from Verona to drive a Rent-A-Van to Stamford, pack up his non-personal stuff, and drive it back to his home in New Jersey. They piled it all in one of the three bays of his garage, and when Jimmy drove home on Saturday he paid them and gave them a generous tip. Now he sat on the couch with Gina and just basked in the pleasure of his homecoming. They Skyped with the kids in Houston and Boston, and discussed possible vacation plans. He told her that it would probably be a while before he would really readjust to the anticipated simplicity of his life going forward.

Gina said, "I really didn't understand why you wanted that Liberty Holdings job. You already had a job to keep you plenty busy, and we were already wealthy. But I didn't complain because we've been through so much together and you wanted it."

"The job just provided proof of the respect people had for me, people who were important because of my parents and grandparents. But it turned out to be an enormous all-consuming monster. Too many competing interests to consider and too many balls in the air."

"I'll tell you what I think. I think in a way you always wanted to be the Don, the *Capo di Capi*." Gina laughed.

"You're right in a way. When I was young, that seemed like the top. Going to college ultimately ruined that. Even though I worked in *La Famiglia* for about twenty years after school, I knew it was basically the wrong way to lead your life, no matter what my father and grandfather and uncles thought. I saw the other options and I was in denial. But I didn't have the mean gene. I had trouble killing a mouse. How could I rise in the organization?"

"You rose to where you got because you were smart. Look at me, talking about this as if it made sense. I was so glad when you started the internet pharmacy. It was hard to maintain my respect for you when you were in the so-called trucking business. But I loved you and knew you were a good person. And of course I saw you with the Have-A-Heart mousetraps, which by the way I never told anybody about."

"I'm glad you didn't. Thank you. My reputation would have been ruined."

He put his arm around her, and they just sat for about ten minutes. Then she said, "OK. Enough of this. Let's go out to dinner, Jimbo." So they did.

* * *

About one o'clock the next day, Jimmy and Gina drove over to Aunt Emerlinda's and Uncle Carmine's house in Lodi for Sunday dinner. As they walked in the front door, there was a loud chorus of "Surprise!" followed by applause and whooping and yelling. The house was packed with relatives and friends, and across the mirror on the living room wall was a banner that said "Welcome Home Jimmy!". Jimmy was overwhelmed, and wiped tears from his eyes as he worked his way through the room hugging people. A couple of people yelled "Speech! Speech!" and things quieted down a little.

Jimmy smiled and held his hands up in mock disgust and said, "What's wrong with you people? I just had a job in Connecticut and came home most weekends! I didn't go anywhere! Only Italians would think that moving back home from 150 miles away is a big deal."

His cousin Tony yelled, "Hey we needed an excuse for a party!" and everyone cheered.

Jimmy wiped his eyes again and loudly said to everyone, "I love you all. This really is home. I wonder what the party would be like if I really went away!" And again everyone cheered. Jimmy wandered through the crowd, kissing the women and kids on the cheek and shaking hands with the men. He followed his Aunt Emerlinda into the kitchen and said, "Thank you, *Z'Emerline*, this is great. Unnecessary, but great. Now, where's the food?" She pinched his cheek like she did when he was a little kid and kissed him on the other cheek. "*Ti amo*, Jimmy. I'm so happy for Gina. Now she'll have you all the time." He picked a piece of bread out of the basket on the kitchen table, dipped it in the sauce on the stove, and took a bite. He closed his eyes and smiled.

Jimmy had the time of his life and didn't worry about his red wine intake because Gina could drive home. The food was great, the conversation was great, he felt an indescribable warmth that had continuity back to his childhood. No talk of business, just kids, football, baseball, food, and a little politics.

When he got the opportunity, he tore a piece of paper off a pad in the kitchen and brought it into the bathroom and wrote a note:

Can you meet me tomorrow at 10 AM at the vacant lot across from the Milanese in Garfield? Nod yes if you can. If you can't, I'll figure something else out. If yes, go to the lot tomorrow and wait in your car. When I see you, I'll drive out of the lot. Follow me and we'll talk somewhere else I'll pick out. I'll drive slow. Make sure to turn off your cell phone totally, and put your EZPass in the trunk. Destroy this note completely.

Jimmy handed the note to Uncle Carmine, who read it and nodded yes.

After an extended dessert, and after coffee and after-dinner drinks, Jimmy and Gina made their exit. Jimmy dozed in the car as Gina drove back to Verona. When they got in the house, he kissed her and said, "Life is good."

"It certainly is."

Chapter 50

The next morning at about 9:50, Jimmy pulled into the lot in Garfield across from the banquet hall where he had attended three or four weddings over the years. He backed into a spot so he could watch what was going on. About 10:05, Carmine pulled in and gave Jimmy a little wave. Jimmy pulled out with Carmine behind and drove slowly to not lose Carmine. He seemed to drive around in circles, then got on I-78W and got off in Short Hills. He pulled into the Short Hills Mall parking lot and got out and walked into Macy's before Carmine could catch up with him. When Carmine walked in, Jimmy greeted him with a handshake and a hug. They walked through the store to the mall interior, then spoke as they walked around.

"Jimmy, this is strange behavior. Why all the secrecy?"

"I'm not sure, *Zio*, just being careful. I have to ask you are you wearing a wire?"

"What is this, are you crazy? I'll tell you what, you can frisk me. Let's go in the Macy's bathroom."

Jimmy agreed, and they walked together to the men's room, where Jimmy frisked his Uncle Carmine and found nothing. Then Jimmy said, "Now you frisk me. Fair is fair."

"No, I don't need to do that."

"Yes, please do it." So Carmine frisked Jimmy and found nothing. They went back out into the mall and sat in two armchairs that were relatively far from any others.

"OK Jimmy, what's this all about? What are you so afraid of?"

"*Zio* Carmine, last week the FBI visited me. I shouldn't be talking to you about this, but I want to know what's going on. They asked me if I knew anything about that trailer of medicine that got hijacked two years ago."

"They asked you, why you?"

"That's what I want to know. They told me that some of the medicine turned up in Kansas City. How could that have happened if you put the whole container on a boat to Abu Dhabi?"

"Maybe I shouldn't tell you, you'd be better off maybe if you don't know."

"I don't know who I can trust. I hope I can still trust you. I want to know so I can get my ducks in a row if I have to protect myself."

"Don't worry, you're fine. Nothing will happen. I'll tell you. You had the right idea about sending the stuff to Abu Dhabi, but some of the guys they had some ideas of their own. The container got shipped where it was supposed to go, but only after a little tax was removed. Some of the guys thought we should get a little taste for ourselves, a little closer to home. The way the transfer of the trailer to the Arabs was set up, the money was gonna be paid back to *La Famiglia* at a high level. Our local guys figured nobody would notice one pallet of drugs missing from a whole container, and it wasn't like the stuff was gonna arrive in Abu Dhabi with a shipping manifest listing everything."

"Do you know if the Arabs realized they got less than they paid for?"

"I never heard there was a problem. Who's to say what their expectations were?"

Jimmy said, "So you guys grabbed a pallet. Whose genius idea was that? Maybe I don't want to know."

"Look, I had a minor revolution on my hands. One guy had a friend in Kansas City who used to be a pharmacist but lost his license. He made the arrangements, and we each got a little taste. It was a stupid thing to do."

"I explained the issues to you, how it was impossible to not get caught."

"I know, I know, but some of our guys aren't the sharpest pencils in the box. They wouldn't listen."

"When the FBI talked to me they used your name, and asked if I discussed with you how to get rid of the stolen drugs. How did they know your name?"

Carmine said, "They knew my name because I've already been caught. The guys up the line are angry, and it's been agreed that I'm gonna take the fall. I've already been arrested, and I'm out on bond. I'm responsible because I wasn't a strong leader. I let the plan get changed."

"Whoa. I'm sorry *Zio*, this is terrible. Does Z'Emerlinda know?"

"Yeah, she knows, but she doesn't know how bad it is. It'll probably take a couple of years to get convicted, if I do get convicted. *La Famiglia* is providing good lawyers. If I have to go to jail, by that time I may be dead. I'll be 80 and maybe I'll have the cancer and they'll leave me alone."

"What's your story?"

"My story is I don't know what they're talking about. If I have to plead guilty to something, I'll say we found one pallet of drugs in a warehouse in Newark and we took it. I'm pretty sure the other guys will stick to that story if we have to."

"You just found a pallet of medicines in a warehouse in Newark. Give me a break. You think the cops are gonna believe that?"

"We'll say the warehouse in Newark where the cheesecakes from Abbundanzo's are stored and distributed. They've known for years it's really a fencing center, and now they can come in and clean it up. They'll jump at it. I'm all set."

"*Zio*, what about me and my friend's contact in Abu Dhabi? Am I exposed here?"

"No, the other guys involved with the one pallet only knew the container was gonna disappear, so they removed one pallet. I'm the only one who knew where the container was going and who the contact was. And of course a couple of guys up the line knew. I was in charge of the deal, and I thought I'd let my guys have their little taste for good morale, so I didn't stop it. It was my mistake, and I'm taking the fall. Nobody higher than me."

"So what about me? Why were the feds looking at me?"

"They put two and two together. I'm your uncle. You're in the pharmaceutical business, and I'm sure they know you used to be in the trucking business with me. It just makes sense they would think I might go to you. I didn't give them your name. I never will. Don't worry. I'm not gonna mess up your life because I screwed up."

"I appreciate that, *Zio*. But I remember that Mr. Gentilella mentioned that the higher-ups were very pleased with the advice I gave on this problem. He complimented me. So guys further up the line know I gave you the plan and the contacts."

"Jimmy, I can't promise that those guys will never turn you in, but the odds are very low. I'm the highest guy in the club arrested on this. I'm not providing any information to anyone for a reduced sentence if it's offered. Nobody above me is gonna be dragged in. It's one pallet and I'll tell them how it got to Kansas City if I have to. They probably already know. For now, I've pleaded not guilty. I've been a good soldier all my life, and I'm not about to change that now. I'm proud of keeping my mouth shut. You have nothing to worry about."

"How did they get you?"

"I'm not sure, but you say they found some of the stuff in Kansas City, so I've gotta believe they got to my guy's pharmacist friend there and he ratted out my guy who probably ratted out me. My lawyers don't have any information yet."

"Well *Zio*, the fact remains that your crew saw the whole trailer with their own eyes and know it went somewhere, and of course the feds know a whole trailer was stolen. The young guys don't have the commitment to the cause that you do. One or more of them may take a deal, one may have already done so. And they'll say you knew about the whole trailer and where it was going. And some of those guys must know who you report to, and that person may get dragged in. You better watch your back, *Zio*."

"They know I'm not gonna talk."

"I have three concerns here: you, me, and my retired drug company friend with the brother-in-law in Abu Dhabi. What are we gonna do?"

"Jimmy, there's nothing we can do. I'm pleading not guilty and clamming up. If they grab my boss, I can make no guarantees but I can tell you he's old-school. He won't be talking."

"OK, *Zio*, I guess that's enough. Do you think anyone could have recorded the conversations we had back when you first had this truck problem?"

"I don't see how."

Jimmy stood up and said "OK. I'll sit tight and say my novenas. I don't want to talk about this again, so please don't bring it up. I'm not gonna avoid you and Z'Emerlinda. You're my family and I love you both."

"I love you too, Jimmy."

"Why don't you head out to your car and take a roundabout way home. I'll stay here for a little while, maybe get a piece of crappy mall pizza then move on."

Jimmy was vulnerable and he didn't see any way out of it. Multiple guys from Uncle Carmine all the way up to Gentilella knew that he provided the Abu Dhabi contact. He felt like he was playing Whack-A-Mole in an arcade at the Jersey Shore. Every time he beat down a problem, another one raised its ugly head.

Chapter 51

Carmine Casamento pulled into the lot of the Pocono Truck Stop on I-80 at the first exit over the line in Pennsylvania. He parked his Caddy at the edge of the truck parking area, then walked out to the far end of the car parking area, where only one car was parked. He knocked on the window, and Danny D'Addio unlocked the passenger side door. Carmine got in.

"Hi Carmine, how you doin? What's this job you got for me?"

"Hi Danny, you mind if I frisk you for a wire?"

"What's this? Why would I have a wire?"

"Lift up your shirt, let's see."

"OK. OK. Take it easy." D'Addio lifted up his pullover shirt, and Casamento felt around his waist and pockets. He found no electronics.

Carmine said, "Let me see your cellphone."

"Why, what for?"

"Just hand it over."

D'Addio pulled his iphone out of his pocket and handed it to Carmine, who pressed the top button and powered it down then gave it back.

"Carmine, what's this about? Why would I have a wire?"

"You ratted me out on the medicine truck job. Why did you do that?"

"Whaddya mean? They got you on that old job?"

"Yeah, and I figure you're the one who gave them my name. Did they get your Kansas City pharmacy friend first?"

"I don't know what you're talking about."

"The Feds arrested me, and I found out from somebody else that the Feds said that drugs from the missing medicine truck ended up in a pharmacy in Kansas City. The only way the Feds get to me is if they get your pharmacy friend and he gives them you and you give them me."

"Carmine, this must have happened some other way."

"So did the Feds get you?"

"No."

"Look, Danny, we have to work together on this. I have to know what's going on so I can protect myself and protect guys further up in the main office. Are we gonna work on this?"

"I swear to you, I don't know what you're talking about."

"OK. Suit yourself."

Carmine quickly pulled out a revolver and shot D'Addio in the chest, as he assumed he would have to. He took the cellphone out of D'Addio's pocket, opened his door and got out. He wiped off the inside and outside door handles with a Handiwipe from his jacket pocket, then crouched down and shot the slumping D'Addio in the head. He walked back to his car and headed to the Hialeah Trailhead off River Road in Shawnee. He walked into the woods to the edge of the Delaware River, removed the two casings and the unused bullets from his gun and threw them in the water, along with D'Addio's cellphone. Then he heaved the gun as far as he could. He thought to himself *I'm really tired of this shit.*

Carmine got back on I-80 East headed toward New Jersey around noon. When he got to the section high above the Delaware Water Gap he gunned the Caddy to about 90, then turned quickly right toward the guardrail and flew over the edge to the riverbed way below.

*   *   *

Today Jimmy had lunch with a Clinical Research Organization manager in Nutley to hammer out some disagreements on pricing, and returned to the office at about 2:30 PM. Marge told him that his wife had been trying to get him and was upset that he had not answered his cellphone. He had turned it off to avoid being disturbed during lunch, and now turned it back on and called Gina.

"Jimmy, are you alright?"

"Yeah, I'm fine. What's wrong?"

"Oh I'm so glad to hear your voice. I was so worried when you didn't answer."

"I was at a lunch meeting with a vendor and turned it off. I forgot to turn it back on. Something's wrong. What's wrong?"

"I was afraid something happened to you. I called to tell you that something happened to Uncle Carmine."

"What? What happened?"

"He was in a car accident. Jimmy, he's dead."

"Are they sure it was him? What happened?"

"Are they sure it was him? How the hell am I supposed to know? I'm sorry, I'm upset. Your cousin Tony called and said that Uncle Carmine was in a car accident. He was on Route 80 over by the Delaware Water Gap where the road runs along a cliff above the water and it looks like he lost control and went over the edge."

"Were there other cars involved?"

"Look Honey, you're gonna have to talk to Tony if you want more information. I'm so sorry about Uncle Carmine. He was such a nice man. I'm relieved that I got you. I was worried when I couldn't get you."

"I'm fine, I'll be more conscientious about turning my phone on. As soon as we hang up I'll call Aunt Emerlinda. Have you talked to her?"

"No, I haven't. I'll hang up so you can call her. I love you. Bye."

Jimmy was floored. He started to dial his Aunt Emerlinda, but stopped when he started to shudder and have trouble catching his breath. He put the phone down and put his head on the desk and cried. He sat there with his head cradled in his arms for about 20 minutes, during which he dozed off. When he awoke he picked up his cellphone and called his cousin Tony, son of Uncle Carmine and Aunt Emerlinda.

"Hi Tony, I'm so sorry. I just saw your father a few days ago. This is horrible."

"Yeah, Mom is completely out of it, and I'm not doing too well myself. Pop's in the morgue over in a hospital in Stroudsburg, and they want to hold him for an autopsy. Mom said no, but I don't have any problem with it. I have to drive down there later to identify him."

"I don't know what to say. I've been sitting here crying, putting off calling your mother. He was like a father to me. But he was your real father. I'm so sorry. Do you want me to drive out to the hospital with you? That's not something you should have to do by yourself."

"You know Jimmy, that would be great. I'd really appreciate that."

"OK. I'll call Z'Emerlinda right now, and then I'll head over to your parents' place. Is that where you are?"

"Yeah. There are a couple of ladies from the neighborhood here, and my sister's on her way from Baltimore."

"OK, I'll be there in about an hour."

Jimmy called his Aunt Emerlinda and had a relatively incoherent conversation with her. She sobbed constantly and rambled on in Italian and English about some things that didn't make sense. Jimmy assured her that he and Gina would help in any way they could. He called Gina to tell her what was going on and then headed to the house in Lodi.

There was a surprisingly large number of people at his aunt's house. Z'Emerlinda was sitting on the couch with two ladies, and somebody was cooking food in the kitchen. Jimmy quickly made the rounds hugging and kissing people until his cousin Tony said, "Enough, c'mon, I have to get out of here." They took off in Jimmy's car for the one hour ride to Stroudsburg, across the Pennsylvania border.

As they approached the Delaware Water Gap at the state line, they discussed where the accident must have occurred. If Carmine had gone over an embankment, it had to be on the eastbound side, the opposite of the direction they were travelling. Since it was still daylight, they decided to pass over into Pennsylvania, then drive back eastbound to see what they could see. At a point high above the Delaware River, they saw yellow police tape and red barrels by a short stretch of broken guardrail. Jimmy pulled over even though it didn't look very safe. They got out of the car and looked over the edge, and could see a wreck about 100 feet down.

Jimmy said, "Nobody could survive that. He must have been unconscious after only two or three seconds."

"Poor Pop. How the fuck could this happen? This doesn't look like a spot where you go over the side when you lose control. There's not even a curve in the road."

"Maybe a truck forced him."

"The cops told me that witnesses said there was no other vehicle involved, he just drove off the road at high speed."

"Maybe he had a heart attack."

"Maybe. Do you think the autopsy could tell that? Jimmy, do you think he could have done it on purpose?"

"I don't know, Tony, that's kind of far-fetched. If he was having problems, I sure didn't see any. Nah. He must have had a heart attack or something."

They got back in the car, turned around at the next exit, and headed west to Pennsylvania again in the twilight. At the hospital in Stroudsberg, Jimmy volunteered to go in to identify his uncle's body. He said to Tony that he should remember his father as he was, not as he is right now. When Jimmy got back to the car, Tony asked how his father looked. Jimmy lied and said, "He looked like my *Zio* Carmine, not really banged up. What can I say?" They drove back to Lodi in relative silence.

As Jimmy drove home from Lodi to Verona, he thought about the accident scene. Could somebody have screwed with Carmine's car, like fool with the brakes? Unlikely. That only happens in the movies. No guarantee that a fatal accident would occur. If they wanted him to go over that cliff, they would have followed him in a stolen car and forced him over, but witnesses said that didn't occur. Actually, if they wanted him dead, they would have just shot him. Jimmy had to admit the obvious – his Uncle Carmine had gunned the car and driven it over the edge on purpose. He was 78 years old and decided to take one for the team. None of Carmine's superiors would be dragged into the medicine truck mess now because there was no one left to provide solid evidence against them. Or maybe it was like seppuku, a ritual suicide because Carmine had screwed up. Jimmy didn't know who Uncle Carmine's direct boss was, so Jimmy couldn't give the cops his name if for some strange reason Jimmy wanted to incriminate himself. And nobody in Carmine's line of superiors had any reason to toss Jimmy to the cops. Jimmy thought, *Zio Carmine, you saved me. You dragged me into something I didn't want to get involved in, but then you saved me. Grazie, mio Zio amato.*

Chapter 52

Christina's Drug-Resistant Infection Project had grown to involve 26 scientists. Today, she was standing at the front of the large presentation room at Delvono, presenting a midyear progress update on the project, whose name was morphing into the "Biofilm" Project. When Frank and Jimmy renovated the current Delvono building before moving in, they decided that it would be valuable to have a room large enough to hold the entire scientific staff, so they included a large conference room with a sliding wall that could divide it into two rooms for most of the time. With the wall pulled back, the room could seat about 100 people, which seemed logical at the time they moved in, but now with about 200 scientists an all-hands meeting was not possible. This morning Christina would present to the Senior Scientists and more experienced lab scientists, and this afternoon she would repeat her presentation for everyone else.

Christina started with the shocking epidemiology of *Staphylococcus aureus* (*S. aureus*) infections, which have a crude mortality rate of about 25%. These infections range widely: endocarditis, osteomyelitis, chronic wound infection, chronic rhinositis. Very frustrating to physicians, and to patients of course, was the significant incidence of surgical implant infection. She discussed how the Staph bug exists in two states. In the planktonic state, the bacterium is a single-cell free-floating individual that can move through your bloodstream to invade various organs. In more dangerous recalcitrant infections, the bacteria aggregate together in a "slime" or "biofilm" attached to tissue surfaces or to the surface of a surgical implant. Once a biofilm has formed, it is very difficult to totally cure an infection without surgical debridement or removal of a biofilm-coated implant. Of course, acute infections can be treated with antibiotics that generally take care of the free-floating planktonic cells, but the bacterial cells deep within a biofilm are somewhat inaccessible to an antibiotic. This chronic biofilm infection can give way to later acute infections as some of the cells in the biofilm reconvert into planktonic cells and reenter the bloodstream.

Christina pointed out that methicillin resistance just adds insult to injury. *S.aureus* is generally sensitive to drugs of the penicillin class such as methicillin, but bacterial strains have developed that are resistant to these antibiotics. Methicillin-resistant *Staphylococcus aureus*, or MRSA, is generally treated with the so-called quinolone antibiotics and as a last resort, vancomycin. Luckily, resistance to vancomycin is not common, or at least not common yet. Physicians hold back on dosing vancomycin only as a last resort because of fear that more widespread use will result in the development of vancomycin-resistant *S. aureus* strains. "If that happens," Christina said, "the gun cabinet is empty."

Christina then launched into a half-hour highly technical discussion of the components of *S. aureus* biofilms. She speculated on how to interfere with their synthesis or stimulate their degradation to break up a biofilm so the resulting free-floating bacterial cells could be hit with a traditional antibiotic. A particularly interesting aspect was the so-called Polysaccharide Intercellular Adhesins, or PIAs, that form a major portion of the biofilm "goo" in which the bacteria are embedded and protected from attack by the human immune system. She reported that in these PIAs, the chemical bonds connecting sugars into the long polysaccharide polymer chain are different than those in human-generated polysaccharides. This is the hallmark of a target for drug discovery – the opportunity to interfere with the synthesis or degradation of a bacteria-generated molecule in a way that does not also affect something good that human host cells do. The Delvono group had already discovered inhibitors of PIA synthesis that prevented *S. aureus* biofilm formation in animals, and work was ongoing to prepare for toxicology and Phase I human clinical studies. However, she pointed out that they had also observed some low level resistant bacterial strains that were not affected by their experimental biofilm-preventing drug.

Christina then presented information about the myriad other components of *S. aureus* biofilms, and their potential as drug discovery targets. It was incredibly complicated, and an intense discussion about possibilities and caveats ensued.

After Christina's presentation, Frank asked her to join him and Jimmy for lunch at one of the picnic tables outside, and to also invite Avi Thombre, who was the Ph.D cell biologist reporting to Christina on the *S. aureus* biofilm project team.

Frank looked at Avi and said, "Well Avi, what do you think?"

"Well, you heard Christina's presentation. It's complicated. For starters, I think we should look at interfering with the *ica* operon in the bacterial genome to inhibit translation and synthesis of PIA-I and PIA-II. This may be more accessible than attempting to stimulate production of degradative lyases."

Christina jumped in, "But Avi, who knows what other host cell issues will pop up if you intervene at the gene level? I think we should go after small molecule inhibitors of the quorum-sensing system, or..."

Jimmy laughed and held up his hands, "Stop, I give up. Let's speak English."

Avi smiled and said, "Hey, I was only trying to answer Dr. Serono's question."

Christina smiled a broad smile and said, "OK, we get it. I guess you want to talk strategy at a higher level."

Frank said, "Yeah, for now let's keep it at 30,000 feet, but I do want to sit down with you sometime in the next few days to talk through the science. From what I can see, there's lots of public literature about biofilm formation and breakup for various kinds of bacteria, but the specific data on *Staph. aureus* is much more limited. So you have to be careful what you assume about staph."

"Right," said Christina. "And there's lots of conflicting information. For example, there appear to be staph strains that don't make the PIAs but still make biofilms."

"So what are we to do?"

Avi responded. "With the right resources, we could go after, say, six approaches. If two of them work, then great, because that means we could dose both together if we have to in order to cover multiple biofilm-forming strains."

Frank looked at Christina and said, "Christina?"

"Avi's right. Too may ways for the bacterium to get around any one solution, so we need extra firepower. Also there's a logic for the idea of dosing one anti-biofilm drug for say one week, then dosing a different anti-biofilm drug for the next week. This could take care of resistant strains." She looked at

Frank, "We can talk about this in more detail when we meet to talk science in a few days."

Christina then said, "To get back up to the 30,000 ft level, we've already set up most of the necessary *in vitro* and animal models to do all this stuff, but we can't do it all in a reasonable timeframe with the number of people we have now. And we need to set up and do an enormous amount of high-throughput screening."

Frank looked at Jimmy. "We could double the manning if we want, say, give you 25 more people short-term, maybe even more over time. What do you think, Jimmy?"

Jimmy replied, "Hey, this may be the most important project in the building. It's certainly the one with the biggest potential financial payoff. But the big thing is the medical need. I'm all for it. And I'd like to say something more philosophical than scientific. You should worry about the development of bacterial resistance to whatever your first approach does, but don't let it bog you down. If you can save lives for five years then drug-resistance develops, well, we work during those five years to have the next gun ready. You cure the sick person in front of you; you don't let him die for the sake of the wider population. That smacks of eugenics. It reminds me of discussions Frank and I have had about the Tay-Sachs project. If you cure a baby who grows up to pass on the bad gene to his or her baby, so be it. You work proactively to solve the next problem when it develops."

Christina smiled and said, "Job security."

Jimmy responded, "That's one way to look at it."

After a pause in the conversation, Frank looked at Christina and said, "OK, so let it be done. Take a couple of days to put together a relatively detailed list of who you need and we'll try to do at least part of this with quick internal transfers. And one other important thing. Please choose two tough Ph.D.-level people from other project areas to do a "devil's advocate" analysis of your approaches. Talk to Marge and arrange a time, say 1 hour, for a meeting with me and you and Avi and these two designated-skeptics to hatch a plan for how they'll do their analysis. That'll be under my control, not yours, to assure objectivity."

Christina was surprised. "Since when have I not been objective?"

"This has nothing to do with you. This has to do with common sense."

They finished their lunches talking about the Phillies, the Yankees, the Mets, and New Jersey politics.

On the walk back to the lab, Avi said to Christina, "This is incredible. Twenty-five more people, at $250K fully-loaded burn per person, that's over $6 million. When I was in academia, to get one-fifth of that would have taken two years of grant-writing and submission and resubmission, and a lot of luck. This is a great place."

The Montana Cowgirl replied, "It's all jake."

As Frank and Jimmy walked back to their offices, Jimmy said, "Christina's a warrior. We can't let her go."

Chapter 53

NATURAL ENOUGH FOR YA? #27

from the desk of Frank Serono, Ph.D., President, Serono Pharmaceutical Consulting LLC

And the Beat Goes On

The more you look, the more you find. Over the last two days, my casual net-surfing (when I had a few minutes of free time) uncovered the following three items:

I. At the recent Annual Meeting of the American Association of Clinical Endocrinologists, a case was reported on a patient who developed thyroid disease. It turns out that he had been using a supplement called "AA Booster Plus" that he and his friends purchased at their gym. These "all natural" miracle capsules were advertised to "superenergize your work-outs and shred pounds". Turns out that a single capsule of "AA Booster Plus" contains 2,000 micrograms of potassium iodide (not listed on the label), which is greater than 10-fold the recommended daily dose. Two months after discontinuing the supplement, the patient's thyroid function tests were within the normal range.

II. Last week, the FDA ordered the recall of a variety of "dietary supplements" sold by "Florganic Herbals" of Fort Myers, Florida. In this case, the FDA Food Division actually had the authority to do this because these "all-natural" products contained prescription drugs (without mentioning them on the label). For example, the erectile dysfunction drug tadalafil (the generic name of the prescription drug Cialis®) was present in Florganic Herbals' products "Erect", "Crect", "BigStuff", and "Hurricane". (No, reader, I am not making this up.) The female hypoactive sexual desire drug flibanserin (the generic name of the prescription drug Addyi®) was present in Florganic Herbals' products "Tulip" and "Romanza" for women. This is serious business. When tadalafil is taken with nitrate drugs, a precipitous drop in blood pressure may occur. The prescription version of the drug flibanserin carries a warning that it should not be taken with alcohol for the same reason. These "herbal" products can cause dangerous situations because the patient is unaware that he or she has taken a drug.

III. Two days ago, the FDA sent warning letters to 9 U.S. companies that illegally sell 37 botanical products that claim to treat or cure cancer. Of course, a warning letter is not a recall order, but it's a start. I won't get into the outrageous claims made on the labels of some of these products, but will attest that some clearly claim to cure certain cancers. These and similar companies have gotten away with this in the past by including in small print on their labels that the products are "not intended to diagnose, treat, cure, or prevent any disease". I guess their lawyers told them that they could claim to cure cancer with impunity in large print as long as they included this disclaimer in tiny print. I applaud the FDA for no longer letting them get away with this nonsense.

Things are starting to move in the right direction. Please let your Congressman and Senator know that you also applaud the FDA for this activity.

Three Months Later

Chapter 54

Marge buzzed Jimmy's office phone and said, "Mr. Gentilella is on the line."

Jimmy said, "I'll take it."

"Hello, Mr. Gentilella, nice to hear from you. How are you?

"I'm fine, family is good, and how are you?"

"I'm doing fine, my family's good too, and we're doing real good here at Delvono. Lots of irons in the fire."

"That's good to hear, good to hear. Jimmy, I'm calling you because I need your help."

"Sure, Mr. Gentilella, whatever I can do."

"Still won't call me Funzi, huh? I guess that'll never change."

"Respect for my elders, an old habit. So what can I do for you?"

Gentilella said, "Well first, I have some unfortunate news. That nice young man in charge of Liberty, Owen McCarthy, he was shot this morning in Stamford."

"Jeez, is he OK?"

"Yeah, he'll be fine. He's in Stamford Hospital. They didn't shoot to kill."

"Didn't shoot to kill? But you can bleed to death. My God, it's like I signed his death warrant when I recommended him. This is terrible."

"Jimmy, no, don't think like that. We didn't think anything like this would happen. Liberty is a clean business. He's a nice young man, smart, with a real future. I haven't figured out what's going on yet, but you bear no responsibility."

Jimmy felt flushed and like he was losing his breath. "My God, what was I thinking? They stabbed me. What made me think it would stop?"

"Jimmy, I don't know yet how I'm gonna deal with this. I think it's the new people in the City, they just see Liberty as one of the businesses. I've gotta put up walls and a moat to keep them out."

Jimmy got choked up. "I don't think I can talk much right now."

"Jimmy, I need your help. I don't see McCarthy returning after this. I have to ask you to come back and run Liberty. I'm gonna need a strong hand there as I work this out."

"Are you crazy? What, to get killed?"

"No, don't worry, we'll protect you, bodyguards, the whole nine yards. I've learned my lesson. And I think I'd like you to take on some additional responsibilities."

"No, I'm sorry, Mr. Gentilella, I won't do it. I'm out. Jesus, Owen McCarthy. I can't believe it."

"Jimmy, you're right to be upset. Please think about it and get back to me, maybe tomorrow or the next day."

"No, I'm not going back."

"Jimmy, take your time. While you think about it, can you give me a name for someone good at Liberty to take over for McCarthy short-term? Don't worry, we'll put lots of protection around him."

"Are you out of your mind? No." Jimmy hung up. He put his head down on his arms on his desk. *Jesus. It never ends. It just never ends.*

ACKNOWLEDGEMENTS

I am immensely grateful to readers of an early draft, who made many invaluable suggestions: Tim Hagen, John Powers, Wayne Sheridan, Bill Mackey, and Ann Curatolo. I am particularly indebted to Wayne Sheridan and Bill Mackey for extensive insightful editorial reviews. I thank Stephen Rogers for a very helpful discussion about dialogue at New England Crime Bake 2017. I also thank Rod Ray for advice on Western slang, Jeff Chasnow for a helpful discussion of drug regulations, and Karen Brown Markley for her excellent cover design.

ABOUT THE AUTHOR

William O'Neill Curatolo is an Irish-Italian hybrid, born and raised in New York City. A biophysicist by training, he served on the staff at M.I.T. and in the R&D division of the pharmaceutical company Pfizer. He is the author of numerous scientific publications, and holds thirty-five U.S. Patents. His novel *Campanilismo* (2013) chronicled the activities of drug industry physicians, scientists, and businessmen in ethically murky waters. He has written non-fiction pieces on toxins for *Sherlock Holmes Mystery Magazine*, and short stories in the mystery genre. O'Neill Curatolo lives a quiet life on the Connecticut shoreline.

Made in the USA
Middletown, DE
08 July 2018